The Commodore

The Commodore

John D. Lowe

iUniverse, Inc.
New York   Bloomington

The Commodore

iUniverse books may be ordered through booksellers or by contacting:

iUniverse
1663 Liberty Drive
Bloomington, IN 47403
www.iuniverse.com
1-800-Authors (1-800-288-4677)

ISBN: 978-0-595-53237-7 (pbk)
ISBN: 978-0-595-63300-5 (ebk)

Printed in the United States of America

This Book is Dedicated to:

Julia, who I have loved through time;

Inge Wulff Grayson, whose Father died with Paulus's 6th Army at Stalingrad;

Admiral Wilhelm Franz Canaris who tried to save his country and the world from Hitler, as early as 1938;

and

All of those left behind, who will be forever young

Glossary of Allied Code Names

Franklin Delano Roosevelt * * * * * **ADMIRAL Q or VICTOR**

The Russians * * * * * * * * * * * * * * * * **ALI BABA**

The US Army * * * * * * * * * * * * * **DESTINY**

Eisenhower * * * * * * * * * * * * * * * * **DUCKPIN**

Churchill * **FORMER NAVAL PERSON or COLONEL WARDEN**

Stalin * * * * * * * * * * * * * * **GLYPTIC**

Free French * * * * * * * * **GOLLIWOG** (not referenced)

Cordell Hull * * * * * * * * **SINBAD** (not referenced)

Build-Up of American Troops in Britain * * * * * * * * **Bolero**

Across-Channel Invasion in 1943 * * * * * * * * * * * **Round-Up**

Commodore Code Names

Emergency Message ************ **FLASH**

Unquestionable Source *********** **CLASSIFIED-U**

Immediate Emergency *********** **CODE BLACK**

D-Day Carte Blanc Initiating Phrase **

"THREE PENCE BROKEN CANDLESTICK"

D-Day Carte Blanc Counter Recognition Phrase **

"THAT CURRENCY SOUNDS ABOUT RIGHT"

German Military Tactical Predictions ** **CRYSTAL BALL**

Referenced World War II Code Named Conferences

ARCADIA ★★★★   December 22 1941 – January 14, 1942; Washington, D.C.
"Europe First" declaration

SYMBOL ★★★★   January 14 – 24, 1943; Casablanca, Morocco
"Unconditional Surrender" declaration
Italian Campaign plans
Cross Channel Invasion in 1944

TRIDENT ★★★★   May 12 – 27, 1943; Washington, D.C.
Italian Campaign
Increase Air Attacks on Germany
Increase War in Pacific

QUADRANT ★★★★   August 17 – 24, 1943; Quebec, Canada
D-Day set for 1944
Re-organization of South East Asia Command
Secret Agreement on nuclear information

SEXTANT ★★★★ November 23 – 26, 1943; Cairo, Egypt
Declaration for Post War Asia
December 4 – 6, 1943; Cairo, Egypt
Agreement to Complete Air Bases in Turkey

EUREKA ★★★★ November 21- December 1, 1943; Tehran, Iran
First Meeting of The Big Three
Date for Operation Overlord (D-Day) Set

OCTAGON ★★★★ September 12 – 16, 1944; Quebec, Canada
Occupation of Post War Germany
Continued US Financial Aid to the UK
Invasion of Japan

General Glossary

COI **** Coordinator of Information (Forerunner to OSS)

OSS **** Office of Strategic Services (American Wartime Intelligence and Forerunner to CIA)

MI5 **** (British Domestic) Military Intelligence Section 5

MI6 **** (British Foreign) Military Intelligence Section 6

Fleet Train Station, England; 12 noon Tuesday June 26, 2001

Our eyes met and it seemed as though they had met before. It seemed as though it had been a long time in the past but only yesterday. It was the first time that I saw her but I had this strange sense that we both felt that we had only taken a brief absence from each other until we could meet again. It was all rather odd but strangely not unsettling. Actually; an unusual warmth, which I had never experienced before, swept over me and I felt contentedly whole. It was a feeling of wholeness that I had never felt before, at least not in this lifetime.

Her name was Emma and for just an instant I saw her someplace other than in this small train station in Fleet, England; a town I had been drawn to on this day at this hour by powers beyond my understanding. I saw her for an instant, in my mind's eye, dressed in a striking emerald green dress suit from the 1940's with squared shoulders, white trim and holding a matching wide brimmed hat. She had blonde hair flowing in waves to her shoulders with a little shock of hair coming close to her right eye like Veronica Lake, and her lipstick was a beautiful deep red which highlighted her clear white skin and gray-green eyes. I saw this in a flash and in an Art Deco setting. There was also the image of a large clock in the background highlighted with blue light and the word Commodore came to my mind, and then it was all gone in a second, other than this beautiful woman sitting across from me.

She was wearing a simple white summer dress and powder blue blouse with very little make-up, if any, other than a slight touch of lip-gloss; and her hair, parted in the middle and not on the side, was blonde and barely shoulder length. We found ourselves staring

1

at each other and the momentary vision that I had just had, of this same woman in the 1940's, left me both startled and enraptured.

I had stood and, without taking my eyes off of her during that first encounter, walked the 10 yards to her without a second thought.

"Hi, I'm Jack", I stated simply with my hand extended.

She took my hand softly, staying seated, and looked at me with warm curiosity as she slowly questioned, in an American accent which I could not place, "Where have we met before?.............. I'm Emma."

"I don't know", I said as I pondered the possibilities, "but I know that we've met someplace .... sometime."

"That's curious," she nervously laughed, "you say that as though it were another lifetime."

"Strangely enough, that's what it feels like," I muttered just above a mumble without truly thinking about it.

"Strangely enough, I .... feel the same," she stammered nervously.

"Where are you from in the States?," I stated, changing the subject.

"I'm not from the States."

"You're kidding."

"No, I'm German."

"It's amazing, you also sound so familiar, besides sounding like an American."

"I get the '..sound like an American' quite a bit but never the '...familiar', I've just always been good with languages and even though I grew up in Germany American English always felt familiar; maybe it was American movies," She said averting her eyes and then looking back at me with confused emotion now visibly showing in them.

"What brings you to Fleet of all places?" I questioned, suddenly feeling as though I should know.

"Oddly enough, I can't say", she said as I took a seat next to her while her eyes followed mine, "I'm a doctor and I had this compelling need to work in the Cambridge Military Hospital this summer. That's in the next town over from this one. And stranger still, I had a compelling need, for some reason, to be by the last door of the fourth car back on the first 'slammer' to London leaving at noon, or just after, on this day but instead I decided to stay in this waiting room. You may find all of that odd and I don't know why I just told you all of this. It's strange but I just had this need to be here ……………… as though my happiness depended on it".

"'Slammer', I've not heard that term in a long time if ever but just as you said it I knew it referred to the trains with the access doors along its sides which slam behind the last person to board or get off."

Laughing intuitively, Emma said, "Very deductive of you having traveled on them, I would assume many times."

Smiling with embarrassment I had to admit, "I've never actually been on one, I flew into Farnborough right down the way; I just knew it strangely enough. I too felt compelled to be here."

At this we both just looked at each other in brief silence. Then this ridiculous rhyme came out of my mouth without forethought: 'Slammers are old and certainly cold and when one hears that old familiar door it reminds one of home.'

Startled, Emma commanded, "Why did you say that? Where did you hear that?"

"I don't even know what it means", I said with confused concern.

"The scary thing is that I do. The door of the 'slammer' sounds like the walk-in freezer door of an ice cream shop someplace in New York where I have dreams, strangely enough, of being home, even though New York is far from my home."

I felt chills as I knew what she was talking about but I couldn't quite put it together. I knew at that moment that I loved this woman deep inside of myself beyond all reason. I started to feel comfortable with the idea that I had always loved her even before this life and that I would protect her with my own life. I found myself at peace in a strange and frightening way. I could see the same feeling in her eyes as I heard the 12:10 train for London pull out of the station. What was going on?

On The Train to Fleet, England December 12, 1942

The Allied landings in North Africa had just taken place in November and there was now a damp bone-numbing chill in England as Sam looked across the short distance between seats at Madison. They smiled knowingly at each other and did not speak loudly as it would be odd to hear a young American couple talking intimately on a train in England in December 1942, unless they were in uniform and then it was still not yet all that common.

Madison the military/political analyst and person, at the end of the first full year of WWII for the United States, was taking on the weight of every Allied setback in North Africa and Sam was worried about her. Seeing her eyes wonder off into a daydream, as he knew she thought of home, Sam leaned over and, moving Madison's wavy blonde hair aside, whispered in her ear, "Slammers are old and certainly cold and when one hears that old familiar door it reminds one of home." Then he kissed her lightly.

"You're so ridiculous and definitely not a poet," she whispered back with a smile. Then she squeezed his hand across the short distance of the seats and continued, "but you always know what to do to make me feel safe, 3 letters" '3 letters' was their own oral cryptogram for 'I love you' as they were lovers in the middle of a clandestine affair which started as a young romance back in 1938 while they were finishing their undergraduate work in Boston.

◆　　　◆　　　◆

Both Sam Harbour, she called him her safe harbor on rare occasion, and Madison Bell had obtained their Phd's in their early

4

twenties. Sam had gained his in statistics from MIT with a good dose of history in undergraduate studies at Boston University. Madison had gone to Radcliff undergraduate where they had met and the source of her doctorate in history was a well kept secret as it was arranged as a low profile audit of classes in predominately all male courses. She already had a US government security clearance while in graduate school due to a paper she had written in her last year at Radcliff in concert with a Sam Harbour. The paper was written in 1938 and was prophetic of events to come in 1939 with Hitler's move into Poland and the new concept of Blitzkrieg.

Madison was ahead of her time in her thinking and this left her in a state of suspended animation at times. By 1942 she had a fairly sound idea of what was coming in the future of the war. She would confirm this through Sam's statistical work and submit the analyses to the Allied High Command, and spin the wheel hoping it would land on the proper reaction to their, by this time, joint work. But inter-Allie politics were not pragmatic and much of their analyses contradicted the British strategic mapping of the war, which they found themselves combating in 1942.

Just before U.S. entry into the war, and through the early years of U.S. involvement, President Roosevelt seemed to react to Prime Minister Churchill as the older brother to look up to, unlike his true older half brother James Roosevelt Roosevelt, who had little if any contact with his younger half brother Franklin. This reaction by the President helped to give more weight to the British war strategy. But Madison and Sam were not politicians nor where they psychologists. Massive numbers of lives were on the line and they, and in particular Madison, felt responsible for them. But on too many occasions, recently, they had been left helpless with regard to positively affecting this responsibility. They wanted to use their abilities and influence to end the war as soon as possible in order to save lives, and to save themselves and live life. Madison felt driven to create a better world to live in, a better world to live in before she and Sam could possibly have a family.

Sam and Madison had fallen in love while working on that 1938 paper. Actually, they knew they were in love the first time that their eyes had met. Madison had always joked about the proverbial 'eyes meeting across a smoke filled room' but in this case it became reality. She was sitting in the Boston Gardens in early spring of that year 1938 and in deep thought over a political research paper on Otto von Bismarck, which she was reading, when the voice of a research colleague snapped her back in time to the present. As she looked up she noticed another man standing next to him. As soon as her eyes met Sam's the sounds around her faded and she did not even hear the introduction other than the name Sam. As she stood Sam extended his hand and simply said, "I've heard so much about you but.............but I didn't expect you to be so beautiful."

Madison just blushed and said, "And I'm a historian too", 'how ridiculous' she thought just as she said it, as they still held hands in an unfinished handshake. She didn't know what else to say, nor did he.

Their mutual friend John was caught standing in the middle of the two watching their awkwardness and he just laughed, "For two of the brightest people I have ever known you both sound like bumbling school children."

They laughed as well and released each others hands but they both knew that day that they had traveled far in their lives just to meet each other and a happy warmth enveloped them both. They were able to collaborate on the paper that had so impressed the government that Madison was moved into a graduate program set up by the Department of State as a result of conversations with the War Department's Military Intelligence Division, better known as G-2.

Both Madison and Sam were later given security clearances as they started contributing to US intelligence analysis of European activities. By the summer of 1941, even while finishing their graduate work, and doing it in record time, they would be working for the newly formed Coordinator of Information (COI), who was a man by the name of 'Wild Bill' Donovan. And near the end of the summer of 1941 they submitted their first report to the President of the United States on Europe, through what was then called the Research and Analysis Branch of the COI.

Madison was from an old Englewood, **New Jersey** family. She had grown up in this Victorian town just **down** the hill from the Palisades, which overlook the Hudson, and not too far from the new bridge into Manhattan named after the first President of The United States. Sam was from Newburgh, New York and he was only an hour and a half from Englewood by car or an hour by train, which was easier. Sam lived in the large stone Victorian home, overlooking the Hudson, which he had inherited from his parents who had been killed in a small plane piloted by his father in 1933. They both had a love of the Hudson River and sailing. They would spend their summers together on the Hudson as they completed their graduate studies.

Just as their second summer started they had found themselves once again sailing on the Hudson. It was May 31, 1939 and it had just hit 96 degrees Fahrenheit as they sailed past West Point and headed to the bend in the river near Noah Point. They waved to the cadets way up on what is known, at the Academy, as Trophy Point. As they waved a tear came down Madison's cheek and she quickly wiped it away that day, but Sam had noticed.

"I saw that," remarked Sam, "what's wrong baby?"

"War's going to start and you know it just as well as I do and those young men up there are going to be in the middle of it."

"They know that."

"But they're so young and bright and happy,……..I can't stand the thought."

"They're also capable. They're the best and the brightest and I couldn't feel safer knowing that. One way or the other they will be alright because of their capabilities and they know this."

As calm as it was they were still making headway with Sam tacking the 26' Wianno Senior with the name "Whisper" painted in white script, like a whisper, on the transom of the boat; but just as he finished speaking he looked at Madison with concern on his face, steadied the boat, got up and brought the sails down. Then sitting down again he reached over and brought Madison to him and held her tightly as she cried, her head cradled warmly by Sam between his neck and shoulder. Madison knew history too well and no matter what Sam said to try to make her feel better she knew that many of those bright young faces waving from the Point, way up above them, would not make it past their twenties.

That was the day that they sailed back instead of continuing further and around the point, partly because it was the hottest day on record for that day and partly because now they could not get those young men out of their thoughts, thoughts characterized by the secret knowledge that they both had with regard to what was going on in Europe and in the War Department.

They tied up in Newburgh at 12:59 in the afternoon and Sam told Madison that he wanted to take her to a special place on Broadway that he had never taken her to before.

"So where is this special place and why have you never taken me there before?", she queried with a curious grin and her head tilted slightly sideways in the special way that she did it that would usually get Sam to reveal that which he hadn't intended to reveal.

"I can only tell you that it is 26 minutes away and I needed an appropriately hot day to make it truly special ", said Sam with a cryptic smile on his face as he checked his watch, which showed exactly 1 PM. He would never tell her how she tilted her head with a completely captivating, quizzically naive look when she wanted him to reveal something; he never wanted her to change it, it would always offer him an incredible degree of warmth and she could have anything from him that she wanted at those times.

Exactly 26 minutes later they were at the front door of the Commodore.

"What's this?" stated Madison with a surprised smile, seeing the display in the window advertising Breyer's Ice Cream and malted milks with a little art deco man in an apron holding his hand open to a milkshake glass standing almost as tall as he.

As Sam opened the door they both looked at the blue neon light lined clock on the far wall, up above the door, way to the back of the building, at the same instant, and the minute hand was on 26. She turned before entering and seeing Sam's smile said, "Statisticians. 26, you're very proud of yourself aren't you?," and she laughed.

As she turned and they entered he just said, " No, pure luck. 26 is my lucky number".

"Who has a lucky number over 10 and besides, that's my birthday?"

"A statistician; I like the 26th cycle of repetitive events and the fact that it's your birth date in the sixth month is an added bonus."

And he smiled as she looked back at him again and said, "You're crazy;" and she started to feel better again. This man had a way of wrapping her in his arms even when he wasn't touching her. He made her feel safe, especially during these times, and she briefly thought how she wanted to make love to him at that moment.

"Why is it called the Commodore Sam, that's a strange name for an ice cream shop?"

"You're the one with the graduate degree in history, I've just dabbled in it as a poor undergraduate," laughed Sam.

After no more than a couple of seconds of thought Madison blurted out, "Vanderbilt".

"Bingo."

"But why name an ice cream parlor after Cornelius Vanderbilt?"

"Ah, I'm glad you ask. The 'Commodore', along with a fellow named Drew, finally connected northern New Jersey and Hudson Valley New York by train in 1852, before that it was two separate lines. The man facilitated the romance between a New York boy and a Jersey girl way into the future and what could be more appropriate than to name an ice cream parlor after him. The great Erie railroad, it'll hold its own through the rest of this Depression if only to keep us easily connected."

"That's what I love about you, among other things", whispered Madison as she wrapped her arms around Sam and buried her head into that special place between his neck and shoulder for a brief moment before they took a booth. She loved his romance and his optimism as one who, as a pure historian, tended to see the downside of most things.

The Commodore stood on the right side of Broadway coming up from the water and was quite a way up the hill and into town. It had a cool recessed door with the Art Deco letters spelling Commodore just above it. The doors were a dark wood with half moon glass forming two opposing eclipses occupying the top third of the two doors with long brass handles almost traveling the length of the glass on the inside of each door. When they walked in the soda fountain was to their left surrounded by art deco fixed swivel stools with a low art deco metal back to them and chocolate brown cushions. Over the back of the fountain was decorative laminated wood with different layers of brown moving up towards a peak, which formed an art deco square. Booths lined each side of the shop. You had to step up and into them to sit and each decorative wood table was lit by an elongated art deco sconce set against the wall in middle of the booth. The light itself was softened by the elongated and decorative smoked glass shade with art deco lines in it. The woodwork for the whole shop was lined laminated board of soft and dark browns which terminated in the back of the parlor at a short corridor to the bathrooms crowned by a large clock highlighted by a soft blue neon light running around the inside of its circumference. To the right of the door, coming in from the outside, was a floor to chest level display case filled with chocolates. The interior was lit by three art deco glass chandeliers hanging low off the ceiling and running up the middle of the shop. The whole scene was cooled by three dark colored ceiling fans, one hanging between each of these small chandeliers.

That hot day in 1939 became a special day as they had ice cream in the Commodore and laughed about things that had nothing to do with the world outside of that little world in Newburgh, N.Y. that day. They would go to the Commodore many more times and even on cold fall days they would go there to discuss theory and just to be with each other. It became their secret, their safe haven from the reality now growing around them which was highlighted by Hitler's execution of what, they know knew, was called Case WHITE in September of that year when he invaded Poland. The time when Madison was proven correct in her assumptions, about this invasion, backed up by Sam's statistical data.

They had worked for the Research and Analysis Branch of the COI while finishing their graduate work in the summer of 1941 and then at the end of that summer, shortly after submitting their first report to the President through the COI, Madison found herself sitting alone in the Commodore waiting for Sam. He was to have met her at exactly 1:26 that day, a time that was part of their joking with each other and part of Sam's preoccupation with time and punctuality. They had made the date two days earlier. It was past 2 o'clock and still Sam had not arrived.

She went to the telephone booth in the back beside the clock and called Sam's number with no answer in return. Then she called her parents in Englewood to see if Sam had called there.

Her mother told her it would be better if she came home that there had been an accident.

On the train back to Englewood that day Madison just stared out the window at the beauty of the Hudson Valley in late summer and the only thing she could hear was Sam's laugh and feel his love of the art of The Hudson River School, which she herself learned to love. She could feel him inside her as though he were part of her and his voice was part of her voice and she could feel his face as part of her face. They were so intertwined and she was now sick with fear. She hadn't even asked her mother what it was about, she knew in her heart that Sam was gone and her introspective demeanor, interrupted only by short periods of quiet tears which punctuated her memories, attested to this.

When she arrived home late that day she found a Colonel from the US Army Signals Corp waiting for her in her parents' front room. He informed her that Sam was being flown back to New York from a meeting in Washington, D.C. in a small military plane when it went down in the Chesapeake without a trace. He was so sorry but the government would keep her informed as Sam had named her his next of kin. All she could think of was the loneliness that Sam must have experienced as that plane was going down knowing that she was his only next of kin and that he would lose her too; then she truly realized that she had lost him and then she lost her footing to fall into a heap on her parents couch in a blur of uncontrollable tears.

◆   ◆   ◆

A month later in September of 1941; with impending war and FDR's secret 'Germany First' or Europe First policy, as it would later be termed by some analysts, in place with Churchill, Madison was offered a position heading a small American analysis group attached to British Military intelligence in Aldershot, England. Madison took the assignment wanting to get away from her memories along with the need to wrap herself in her work.

She started her work in late September of 1941 with two Americans and they had a small office in the great dome of the Cambridge Military Hospital. They were posing as research doctors with a temporary British military intelligence liaison officer assigned to them by the name of Colonel Clive Mumfreys.

The code name for the group was *Commodore*.

Colonel Clive Mumfreys was a British career officer with excellent social connections, having come from the upper class, which gave him a quick boost to his current rank. He is basically a good man and an intelligent man and he temporarily starts to fill the void left by Sam. Madison is not in love with him but she quickly starts to love him for the strength that he seems to have and the protection that he offers her. They would marry at the end of October of that year after she becomes resigned to the fact that she will never be completely happy but that she will be safe once again.

Madison found herself almost overwhelmed with the analyses that she was running and at the same time she was impressed with the data coming into her from many different sources. This was now November 1941 and U.S. intelligence in Europe was up to full steam before The United States was even in it.

Many of her analyses were going to Cambridge, unbeknownst to her, and coming back with additional statistical data attached to be re-evaluated for any changes that would be created by the statistics. Much of the statistics was beginning to seem oddly familiar to Madison in the way that they synchronized with her group's analysis, which was then compiled and summarized by her. She found herself strangely drifting back to the Commodore in Newburgh and those wonderful days of discussing basic theories with Sam. Through these discussions she had learned to develop historical theories for modern warring Europe based on statistics representing repetition of patterns created through human nature and old unchanging political lineage. This political lineage in Europe came from the hierarchical Europe of old and had not really changed in hundreds of years, unlike the new political character of the young democracy America. Sam taught her to understand and appreciate, and then to rely on the statistical data that would support her theories. As he taught her more she learned to better interpret her own theories so that they would be set up for support by the appropriate statistics in the manner that Sam used them.

These new statistics that she was receiving in England by November of 1941, and their use in support of her reports, reminded her of Sam. She thought of that day when they had sailed under West Point and how he had comforted her about the future loss of all those young men, and now he himself was dead. She was on the verge of tears this early December day as she came to the end of the paper she was re-reading, with the new statistical data incorporated. It made no sense now as she lost her concentration in the blur of just words. Nothing made sense until she came to the end of the paper and read for the first time, *'This precedent will always take place statistically on the 26th cycle of repetitive events'.* She stumbled in her thoughts; she must be delirious she thought. How innocently cruel the imagination can be with such great loss. But it was there and she read it again, and then again slowly as if to keep it from disappearing in front of her eyes. She just started to cry slowly and as her tears dripped like soft rain on the paper one tear dropped to perfectly highlight 26, enlarging it by moistening the black typewriter ink. The 26 grew in her blurred vision as more tears came.

"Sam" she cried softly and more tears came down her face and further blurred those final words, "Oh Sam, it can't be; are you alive?"

As she put her hands up to her face and let the tears flow she finally realized what a nightmare she had been living. She hadn't given herself one minute to truly contemplate the reality of Sam's death after she had collapsed at her parents' home in Englewood that day.

"Oh why did they do this to us?" she muttered to herself as pain, joy and relief flooded her emotions all at once. Could this truly be real or just a cruel game she was playing with herself? It was true, and no truth had ever been so pure and her tears warmed her as though she once again had her head cradled up against his shoulder with his hands holding her safe from everything that she had been battling.

◆   ◆   ◆

Sam Harbour was alive and working at Cambridge University as a guest professor of statistics while he interpolated, using statistics, different analyses coming in from British intelligence. The data was not labeled as coming from any particular group but several reports seemed familiar and reminded him of those days on the Hudson at the Commodore with Madison. When he was told that Madison was killed in an auto accident and burned beyond any recognition he could not bear to remain home. He was told a day before they were to meet at the Commodore, where he was going to tell Madison that they needed him in England and that he would not be away for long. They had him on a Pan Am Clipper within a day and told him that he couldn't even contact Madison's family; they would do that for him.

They sent him on the large Boeing 314 flying boat named the Yankee Clipper so that he would be safe from U-boats in the north Atlantic and also so that he would be noticed by Admiral Wilhelm Canaris's men of the German intelligence force the Abwehr. The Abwehr was known to closely watch the Pan Am Clippers in Lisbon, Marseilles and in Southampton since their inaugural trans-Atlantic flight on the 20th of May 1939 from Port Washington, N.Y. to Marseilles via Lisbon. They were watched so closely that on the evening of October 11, 1940 the Yankee Clipper NC-18603 was forced to land in Manhasset Bay accomplishing the first night landing by a commercial flying boat. Before the clipper could dock at its Port Washington facility a small launch took two mechanics out to the flying boat and returned with a flight engineer who was actually the 34th passenger although the passenger manifest showed only 33. Captain A.L. McCullough had determined, in route to the US, that maintenance was required on the rudders of the big plane and he had deviated to Bermuda where he covertly took on board a Polish spy working for the British by the name, simply, of Oscar. These large flying boats were being used by American and British intelligence; sometimes covertly and sometimes right out in the open, as in this particular case, where it was its own type of camouflage.

The big flying boat left Port Washington with Sam on board while Madison, unknowing, grieved at the home of her parents but 26 miles away. Upon landing in Southampton Sam was noticed by the Abwehr and it was confirmed that he was a visiting professor from The United States; this was 'out in the open camouflage'. This high visibility arrival reduced the suspicion that a low-keyed arrival by sea might cause, if discovered, even though the airfare was an exorbitant $375 that Cambridge University had openly covered. "Wild Bill" Donovan also wanted to have Sam in the files of Canaris so that he might be used later with established authority; how, Donovan wasn't quite sure but he had more than a sixth sense about his soon to be adversary. Shortly after the invasion of Poland in September of 1939 Canaris; horrified at the mass murder of Polish nobility, clergy and civilians; sent one of his colleagues, Pastor Dietrich Bonhoeffer, on a flight to Sweden to meet secretly with Bishop Bell of Chichester, England. Following Admiral Canaris's instructions Bonhoeffer told Bell of the horrors that were occurring and assured him of the growing resistance in Germany with regard to these acts.

The British and Donovan knew that the enigma Canaris was somehow working behind the scenes to bring Hitler down. Donovan felt that such a sly, and known to be well-read, man would take personal note of the arrival of an American professor, even though his agents might not as the arrival was of such high visibility as to be discounted in its importance.

◆   ◆   ◆

Madison went directly to her current paper, rushed it to completion and at the end she put the words, "Commodore theories in statistical data may be applicable if one works off the theory of the 26th cycle of repetitive events," against all the rules put in place to prevent the identification of specific sources of intelligence; as well, the team name Commodore had never been added to a document before. She added this and sealed the paper into the courier's envelope and then ordered up a courier.

Due to secrecy Madison did not know where her reports were going for their statistical enhancements, or additions, in the same manner that Sam did not know where the reports that were coming to him, at Cambridge, originated.

Sam received the new report from '*Commodore*' the following day and when he read the last line a rush of shock ran up his neck to his head and he felt light headed as he whispered ,"Madison, my Madison, oh God.......". He knew they had been deceived in the most horrible way in the name of national security. He was elated and filled with pain in the same instant. "What have they done!?" he whispered to himself.

Sam quickly started to complete his statistical analysis and added, "Setting up this statistical repetition would, without considering any unpredicted obstacles, be as simple as saying, ' let us meet at 1:26 PM every Saturday in front of the clock tower at King's Cross station in London.' King's Cross was Sam's station when he took the train from Cambridge to London.

He finished his report and sealed it in the courier's envelope with an excitement he hadn't felt since the first time he had met with Madison after that day when he was introduced to her in the Boston Gardens.

Saturday was in two days and he would not even wait for a reply, he would simply be there.

◆   ◆   ◆

Saturday; December 6, 1941 King's Cross

Sam was standing in front of the clock tower, in front of the station, at 1:26 when he saw a familiar figure coming across the street from his left. As soon as he recognized Madison he could only see her, as everyone else around them seemed to disappear in the background. He thought he was seeing a ghost but knowing it was actually her he could feel his whole body truly come back to life and the world gain color again after months of a type of darkness that he'd rather soon forget. Just then she saw him too as she tried to hold back tears and walk calmly to him.

They could not make a scene but as Madison came to him beautifully dressed; in the emerald green suit with squared shoulders and white trim, which Sam had last seen earlier that summer at the Commodore, and a matching green wide brimmed hat with white trim and carrying a valise; she had tears running down her cheeks. She dropped her small overnight bag and fell into his arms in front of that landmark clock tower crying softly and just buried her face into that familiar spot between his neck and shoulder, "Oh Sam."

She could feel once again the safety and love of that familiar hold that only he had when he wrapped his arms around her encompassing her completely. He held her snugly enough to prevent anyone from taking her away again.

"Oh Sam, why; ….. why did they do this to us?"

"It's just the time we live in, it has gobbled us up but we're alright now, we're alright now", he said as he stroked her soft blonde hair.

Madison hesitated and held him tighter and whispered onto his shoulder, "Sam, I'm married; they told me you had died in a plane crash." She then pulled back from him and looked into his eyes. "He's basically a good man and, ... and I felt weak and alone; oh God, what do we do?"

Sam hesitated briefly with concern on his face. Then, trying to hide his shock from Madison said, "We'll just have to straighten it out." She was being taken away from him again but at least she was safe.

"He's my military liaison with the British; God, it's a mess. His name is Clive and I can't just leave him. He rescued me."

"And I thank him for that Madison but.........."

"I can't just end this, not only because I owe Clive and, to a degree, love him but it could blow my group apart. Oh God Sam I want to end this horrible war before it really starts for us and destroys us piece by piece."

"What group, Commodore?"

"Let's head inside and down an empty platform,............... please," she said as she grabbed his right hand with her left and almost imperceptibly reached down and grabbed her valise with her right hand in one fluid motion.

As they walked arm-in-arm down one of the platforms; just vacated by a departing train, and not noticing that each was carrying a small overnight bag, Madison told Sam about the Commodore Group and also about Clive's sensitivities. Clive had admitted to her, after their marriage, that he truly could not live without her and that if she left because of the American War Department or for that matter just left him, war or no war, he would raise hell with everyone involved and he was not above using his Webley service revolver. At the time she was not worried about this acute kink in Clive's armor as she herself was at the weak-end of her rope, and she felt that he was basically a good man. But as time moved on this conversation had worried her almost to the point of making her report it to her primary contact in the U.S. War Department. She had told Sam everything with the exception of Clive's mention of his service revolver. She knew that if Sam had heard this, war or no war, he would intercede for her safety. She decided to worry about that later.

◆   ◆   ◆

Their affair started this day as they found themselves at the Savoy Hotel, on The Strand along the Thames, checking in as Dr. and Mrs. Harbour. Thank God they didn't ask her for her passport after seeing Sam's Cambridge identity card. They would have to figure out how to handle this but for now, once in their room, they fell into each other's arms with a beautiful view of the Thames in the background. They had both packed a small overnight bag and when they had finally realized this they just started to laugh the way they had many months before and any tension over their present situation was gone.

The next evening, the 7th, they attended Noel Coward's comedy 'Blithe Spirit' at the Art Deco Savoy Theatre adjacent to the Savoy Hotel. The play was intended to be a comedy but it touched too many raw nerves for Madison and Sam. It took death lightly in this tumultuous time and it seemed to belittle women, and it had a love triangle; albeit one piece to the triangle was a ghost by the name Elvira. Instead of two men and a woman as the triangle it was two women and a man. Its light hearted humor towards death and love and life just served to bring the tempered reality of their lives home to them in shocking clarity.

Right in the middle of a laughing spell by the ghost character Elvira the house lights came up. Madison was briefly thankful for the interruption as it brought the audience to a cacophony of confused whispers and then a rather short and frumpy man came on stage to the further confused chuckles of the audience who assumed that it might be part of the play. He promptly stepped center stage and in a theatrically trained voice, which reached everyone in the theatre, he announced, "Earlier this evening The United States Navy was attacked by Japanese naval aircraft at Pearl Harbor in the U.S. territorial islands of Hawaii and it is anticipated that a state of war will shortly exist between The United States and Japan to also include Germany."

There was a brief hesitation of quiet disbelief then a cheer went up from the audience. Madison and Sam could only look at each other; the night had become surreal. Then clutching Madison's right hand in both of his large hands Sam acknowledged, looking closely and reassuringly into Madison's eyes, "Well it's finally happened as we knew it would. We both have to head back."

They left the theater immediately and instead of staying an extra night in London they were both able to catch their last trains out, one to Cambridge from King's Cross and one to Aldershot from Waterloo Station. They had taken a cab to the Embankment station of the Underground and they had both taken the Northern Line but in opposite directions with Sam heading north to King's Cross and Madison south across the Thames to Waterloo Station. They would now be in the thick of things with America mobilizing.

Over a year later, on this train to Fleet, they found themselves living an affair; the last thing that in 1938 they would have thought that they would be doing. Their concern for the positive effect of their work and the quick end to the war prevented them from causing a scene involving Clive, and possibly their units and work.

They were on this familiar train to Fleet and the cottage Sam leased for his work, and for them. It was legitimate for this American research doctor to visit with the American statistician, from an academic viewpoint. It might even make sense if word got back to the British military if they didn't look too hard into Sam's background, which would cause a little bit of political turmoil with the U.S. State Department to do so. The British did not know the extent of Sam's involvement with the American COI, they looked at him purely as a statistician with minimal security clearance in order to add statistical interpretation to incomplete military theory. And they were not aware that it was COI that had supplied Cambridge University with the funds to fly Sam over to 'The United Kingdom', as Great Britain and Northern Ireland together were being termed as of the 1930's. Sam's open travel had managed to reduce his seeming importance to the U.S. intelligence service and remove him from the spotlight, which is exactly what the COI and the U.S. State Department wanted. It was always better to "… hold your cards close to the vest and out in the open...." as 'Wild Bill' Donovan would say on occasion. That vest also had hidden pockets to change cards covertly if need be.

Not only were they worried about their future but they became worried about the state of alliance with their British 'cousins'. The term 'cousin', which to both Madison and Sam was a misnomer, seemed to hide the true character of the alliance. It was more like détente.

The President's relationship with Churchill worried them and it was a worry that Madison could not get out of her mind. The invasion of North Africa, or Operation TORCH, launched in November, was against the joint analysis that she and Sam had developed. They believed simply, that Hitler's commitment of the German Sixth Army in Stalingrad, and his war with Russia, would help keep the German army occupied and actually suck in more troops as the ensuing winter took its toll. This in turn would allow for an alternative strategy to the invasion of North Africa and then to follow, Italy; an alternative strategy that they had believed in earlier that spring. They believed this British tactic of securing the Mediterranean from North Africa up through Sicily and the boot of Italy would kill more troops on all sides and prolong the war. The agreement to move on Sicily and then Italy had not yet taken place but they knew that it was coming and they knew that it would kill any hope for an early cross-channel operation. This reality did not sit well with Madison.

They did not like seeing The United States once more making suggestions but allowing the 'allies' to have their way and in this case that was the British. The last time that the U.S. did this was at the Treaty of Versailles, which in effect had given them this new war.

Since Hitler's opening of a second front with his invasion of Russia on June 22, 1941 and now his suicidal commitment to Stalingrad, as far as they could discern from the little communication intelligence they had been given, both Madison and Sam held strongly to their strategic beliefs. Their analysis, which was completed months before Hitler's initiating attack on Stalingrad on August 21, 1942, strongly supported an American proposal which was two part and which had been authored the previous spring. The first part was code-named BOLERO. BOLERO would allow the United States to build up massive forces in the U.K. and by the following spring, or April of 1943, they would launch Operation ROUNDUP or the invasion across the English Channel.

With the build up of air power in England and on the Continent to comprise an estimated 6,000 Allied aircraft, after secondary landings in France, they felt that all lines of communication, or railroads and roads on the Continent, could be controlled to slow and deter enemy reinforcements to the beachheads on the French coast. As one American general said "It would chew them up on the way to the party." This would take place while 48 American and British divisions moved forward through France systematically drawing in the German Wehrmacht while the Russians kept pressure at the backdoor. The flat terrain was perfect for this type of drive along with a direct supply line across the channel. The terrain historically allowed for Sam's statistics to work unencumbered unlike the mountainous belts and rough terrain in Italy with an indirect supply line. A non-stop charge right across France into the heartland of Germany, like a lance, had been the focus and thrust of their analysis. If they could encircle an army or two along the way it would serve to speed the end of the war.

The fact that the German Sixth Army was fully engaged in Stalingrad confirmed their earlier analysis. The fact that they were not getting relief or more German troop commitment was the reality of the Allied invasion of North Africa. Now Hitler was simply sending the German Sixth Army to its death, which was abhorrent to Madison as well. Madison was fluent in many languages and the plain text version of Hitler's field communications coming out of intelligence before being translated, which she was able to get in its original German on occasion, told her a great deal and set off the small hairs on the back of her neck with a slight shiver. He was going to let these tens of thousands of men of the 6th Army just die in brutal cold and combat or in equally brutal Russian prison camps. She was horrified by this savage death sentence of so many young men that she found herself conflicted as an analyst, they were not just numbers. Hitler was unpredictably predictable through his brutality and lack of any compassion unless it was self-serving. She found herself falling back on her rudimentary knowledge of psychology more than she deemed wise. She wondered what else she could see if she were to receive every field order issued by Hitler instead of just those deemed important by the British.

They had drawn the lion out before they had the sword drawn and prepared, now the sword of Damocles hung over Madison's head. She was taking the loss of life in North Africa hard. When American forces were fired upon by French Vichy troops she knew the true story as she read the intelligence and unlike the general public she knew that the French had machine-gunned Americans helpless in the water due to two ill-conceived British plans for landing smaller groups of American troops in separate operations to take out smaller objectives. The British tactics had lacked planning and basic tactical understanding. She was inconsolable as she took these events as her failure and she knew that there was a good possibility that among the American officers killed in those operations there may have been one who was standing on Trophy Point that day that she and Sam sailed by and waved. She also knew that such an officer would have known that the British plan was ill-conceived tactically but would have followed orders to follow the command of foreigners. She ultimately felt that this war in Europe was not America's war but American youth would once again pay the price.

Sam knew that Madison was a brilliant analyst and with his statistics she was frighteningly accurate to a point. He also knew that a mind like this lived with guilt when their dire predictions were born out after the alternative move was bypassed.

"Do you remember our discussions at the Commodore when all of this was pure theory and our days of sailing the Hudson? That was a time of wonder which we'll see again", he whispered as the train screeched to a halt and the doors of the 'slammer' opened as passengers from London exited at Farnborough Station.

"Yes but now theory becoming reality feels as though it's rolling over me."

"We can only do our best, and then hope for the best; we have no control over this thing and if you think you do you will kill yourself and then selfishly where am I, I ask you."

Her flat expressionless gaze faded and her eyes lit up with a smile, "Hum, it's always about you", and then she reached over and pulled his head forward towards her and gave him a long passionate kiss on a very British train. Pulling away and laughing she whispered, "What do you say now?" , while matronly British women glanced over in horror and the British men just smiled. They both knew how dangerous this one act could be for them. No doubt they would be noticed. These crazy Americans would stand out on such a train as they were somewhat small communities serviced by this rail. Their covert '3 letters' just flew out the window of the 'slammer' but Madison had a smile on her face once again.

Sam, with very red lipstick covering his lips could only smile and shake his head at this beautiful blonde with gray-green eyes. As he did so he could see her in the Commodore that early summer day in 1941when she was wearing that emerald green dress suit with squared shoulders and white trim along with that beautiful matching hat with the wide brim that might be worn to Saratoga on race day. And he also thought how beautiful she was in that dress when he saw her 'ghost' coming towards him in front of the clock tower at King's Cross. He could not get the thought of her in that dress out of his mind and he was happy about that. She was an absolute wonder to him and to her he was what protected her and kept her safe and warm and above all deeply loved no matter what she may have thought she had done to wrong him.

The train came to a halt. They were at the Fleet Station once again. They exited the 'slammer' through the door right next to their seats and let it slam behind them with the sound of a freezer door as they headed for the exit gate and The Links pub. The pub was just over the rise from the station on the corner where Elvetham Road makes a sharp right turn toward Fleet Road and the village stores. They would sit off to the side in The Links and Sam would have a pint of ale while Madison nursed her martini, a drink she had to teach the bartender to make having also supplied the bottle of vodka. They had a source for vodka so Madison had reinvented the martini using vodka instead of gin. Sam with a devious smile had suggested she patent the new martini and call it a 'Madison'. She had told him that he was 'such a child' and he had smiled even larger.

At the Links they would talk about anything but work, as it was a public place. It was public and she was supposed to be a medical doctor doing medical research at the Cambridge Military Hospital up the road in Aldershot, and he was assumed to be a visiting professor from Cambridge University adding his expertise to the research. Madison's secret office remained in the dome of the clock tower of that old Victorian hospital whose design was influenced by Florence Nightingale and her experiences coming from the Crimean War. Madison's knowledge of history even told her that the larger of three clock bells in the tower was one of the two Sebastopol bells taken from the Russians during the Crimean War, its twin was at Windsor Castle. The bell hadn't rung officially since 1914. It was one of those bits of history that Madison found fun to keep to herself as a bit of 'secret' history in close proximity.

At the Links they would talk about home and art and their mutual love of architecture before heading the half mile up Elvetham Road to the 350-year-old cottage that Sam had rented and now called home. It was the old 'chimney sweep cottage' tucked snugly into the middle of two other identical cottages built at the same time. The town's official chimney sweep lived there for a couple of centuries and Sam and Madison loved this type of simple history and the romance of it all. The cottage was drafty and cold unless one sat in front of the fireplace but they loved its quaintness and, of course, its history.

On their walk home, to the cottage, Madison took Sam the long circular route, first going up Fleet Road towards the village and then taking the first road on their right. She took Sam into the graveyard of the church they came to on their right and Madison walked Sam to the one military grave to the right of the church and near the center of the graveyard, and stopped. Before them was the grave she had stumbled upon one day in her wonderings. It was the grave of J.C. Morgan, a Canadian, who had died 15 months into the first World War in 1915, and no doubt at the Cambridge Military Hospital; he had been just 18 years old.

"This is what I keep in mind as the war gains momentum and I try to get ahead of it. I haven't told you, but I visit this grave once

a week and I promise him that I'll help make this one end faster."
Said Madison looking intently at the gravestone.

Sam looking down at the grave just nodded and said, "And
I'll help you."

Ten days earlier the first nuclear chain reaction (fission of
uranium isotope U-235f) was achieved at an abandoned football
stadium on the campus of the University of Chicago under partial
direction of Enrico Fermi who had fled fascist Italy. Eight days
earlier the British had been forced to evacuate Tebourba in Tunisia
after suffering heavy casualties. Seven days earlier the German
hospital ship Graz was torpedoed and sunk off the Libyan coast.
Two days earlier the Fourth Panzer Army, with the aid of seven
German divisions drawn from the Caucasus and Orel fronts began
an offensive to relieve the Germans trapped around Stalingrad.
Only the previous day U.S. forces were moving into Iran and Iraq
to help protect Russia's soft underbelly and use the region for
embarkation. The pieces were fitting into Madison's analysis puzzle
but the wrong puzzle and with the first nuclear chain reaction taking
place both Sam and Madison knew the clock was ticking. Operation
ROUNDUP, or a cross channel invasion in the spring of 1943, was
all but history as they were starting to see it.

Letting Madison into the cottage before him Sam ducked
through the low doorway as he entered and closed the door behind
him. Madison threw her leather brief case on the overstuffed chair
next to the sofa and sat down and removed her short heels, and then
stared up at Sam as if to say, 'What can I do?'

"Baby you can't control this," Sam said reading her thoughts.

"I know what's going to happen and I can't stop it," she muttered
with a deeply saddened expression on her face.

"This is the game that we're in since that day we sailed by West
Point and realized the reality of this war; we can only hope that we
have some positive effect. Would you want to sit on the sidelines
and let others try to do our work and have no chance at making
things better?"

"No, but.............., every day seems to be painful. Hitler is
sending troops to break through to his troops in Stalingrad just as
we had predicted but not the troops we had looked at because we

invaded North Africa. General Kurt Zeitzler, now Chief of the Army General Staff, it appears has put up an argument to try to withdraw the encircled Sixth Army in a breakout because the General Staff has started to switch to the Mediterranean threat, even if Hitler has not fully done so, and before we make any attempt on Sicily or Italy. And along with this realization by the German High Command the potential of a nuclear explosive exists and we know that they're working on it. Our timetable to end this war has been shortened and FDR has chosen the long, slow bloody British approach to the goal. He's lengthened the war and given them the time to get that weapon before us. Zeitzler is a logistics genius and from what we can determine, from some of the communiques we're intercepting, he's starving himself on the same rations that the men of von Paulus's Sixth are getting so he can better conceptualize the problems and Hitler has ordered him to go back on a normal diet. This man is definitely not a politician and his eyes are on the Mediterranean long term with us now in North Africa. We found the Hitler order communiqué to Zeitzler alone very strange until we put it together.

I have to hand it to the man and I'm horrified what's happening to those German troops in the pocket even though it takes some pressure off of our troops. Hitler is proving to be the criminal that he is, he has written the death warrant for 240,000 of his own troops besides the 10's of thousands of Russian troops and civilians that will be killed by the end." Madison finished as though she just drained herself of one batch of worries she had been contemplating.

" Slow down Baby, slow down. Why else do I know the name Kurt Zeitzler?"

"He led German troops against the landings in Dieppe in August where too many Canadians were killed, I know that you have the numbers. What you may not know is that we had a team of U.S. Rangers go in with the operation and it was another British disaster tactically. It seems that the British are quick to put Americans or Commonwealth troops such as the Canadians, Aussies or New Zealanders into the meat grinder before they do it to their own. You know Gallipoli from history, even though the English took heavy casualties themselves they were quick to put the ANZAC's into the meat grinder. Sam, I feel like we're running out of time and another

English lead Gallipoli, especially with American troops, is my worst nightmare."

"The statistics are in our favor to reach the finish line before the Germans; do you trust me?"

She smiled as he touched her check to remove the sadness and then sat next to her holding her against him with his hand cradling her head, again, warmly between his neck and shoulder, just as he did that day on the Hudson in what seemed a lifetime ago now. She had almost answered his question 'but at what cost?' and instead just said. "I love you Sam, I love you."

"I know Baby and I love you beyond all reason," He said and then whispering to both of them as he rocked her slightly, " beyond all reason."

"Sam, you can never leave me."

"I'll never leave you..........., never."

"You can't die............, please."

"I'm not going to die, I can't leave you; I'll always be with you even beyond all of this."

"We can't control anything."

"Yes we can. There is a power in us that is greater than all of this. It is that same power which gives you such fear in losing it. You can't lose it once you have it, never. In all of this grand world we have, even in its present state, we were able to find each other. That was not a miracle, it was meant to be. Both fate and statistics played their part but it was something else. There is something greater than us that transcends the numbers, the research and chance and makes things happen for a reason. There is a reason for us beyond what we can do to influence the final end to this war."

"I believe you and because of this I am afraid of losing you just the same."

Sam slowly moved her from the crook of his neck and shoulder until her eyes were looking up at him with helplessness softly residing in them. He leaned forward and kissed her on the forehead and then each eyelid before kissing her on the lips and with this last kiss she could no longer hold the tears, as subtle as they were, and he held her again tightly and rocked her, "We'll get through this and see the sun again from that boat on the Hudson. We'll look up at those new cadets once again in a world without war and then death will have no place with us. Please trust me, we'll be there again and I will never leave you so help me God……., I will never leave you."

Sam just held her on the sofa in front of an empty fireplace until he could feel her calming, he then lay her down on the sofa covering her with a blanket and headed out the back door to get some firewood, a rare treat from coal, and open a bottle of Madison's favorite wine.

DECEMBER 1942

In December of 1942 Hitler's armies controlled Europe from Norway south to Crete and from the Spanish border with France east to a pocket around Stalingrad where his 6ᵗʰ Army was trying to hold on. German forces were fighting the Allies in Tunisia to keep a foothold in North Africa.

Christmas day 1942 found Sam in the cottage in Fleet alone. Madison was with the Colonel attending a Christmas party at the home of a general officer in Fleet. Fleet was a village of larger than normal homes and properties just a stone's throw from Aldershot, the home of the British Army, and many general officers had homes in the town. Madison was at one of these homes not more than a half mile from the cottage and she intended to sneak away to see Sam.

The Red Army's winter offensive was well underway this Christmas. Just three days earlier Soviet forces had made new attacks in the Caucasus striking southeast of Nalchik as the Germans started to pull back. Again, Sam couldn't help but feel that if it were not for the Allied invasion of North Africa with Operation TORCH the German High Command, under Hitler's direction, would be pumping more troops towards Russia just as their intelligence analysis had outlined. It was a thought that would not leave either of them alone but Sam would not let Madison experience his frustration with that poor strategic choice. It was starting to seem to be too late for a smart execution of the war; Churchill had the President of The United States wrapped around his pinky and they just had to do their best to prevent British disasters from occurring.

Sam had plenty of time to sit quietly beside his small Christmas tree in the cottage with a martini in his hand and a coal fire in the very small fireplace. They now had a whole case of Russian vodka from their source, a Russian liaison officer who took a liking to Madison. It was actually a miracle to get such a thing. They even had a whole bottle of vermouth to scent the martinis as they didn't put much in the mix. Actually, Sam would put a little in the glass stirring pitcher, swish it around and pour it back in the vermouth bottle before adding the vodka to the pitcher. The only items he was missing were olives; a dog and, of course, Madison; and then he found himself laughed alone about it all on this Christmas day.

He had time to think both about he and Madison and their work as it was all becoming one. They could now not separate their personal lives from their work and what was going on around them, and in this world at war.

For a brief moment Sam glanced over to the right wall next the small dining room table, in this small darkly lit cottage, and he smiled at the thumb and child hand sized gifts that he had re-hung after opening them. They were hanging in numbered order on a long colored string running part of the length of the twenty-foot long wall. Madison had wrapped a small gift for Sam to open every day of December. It was her wonderful version of an Advent Calendar for Sam and meant to keep him company. With all that was going on in the world, with her being right in the middle of it, and she still had the time and the sensitivity to do this. He just smiled, took a sip of his martini and glanced down at his imaginary dog. The fact that he had re-hung the gifts would bother her and she'd say that they were meant to be used, and he knew he would have to tell her that they gave him more joy hanging where she had first hung them and he knew that she would then smile warmly and fall into his arms.

Even though he could smile briefly, and for that one instant escape all of this with the woman he loved beyond words, Sam was becoming worried about Madison as she was now taking every little mis-movement of the Allies personally as though, somehow, it was her fault. Madison was good and she was good because she was intense with regard to her subject. In college she would not drop an issue when she knew that the data clearly supported her by more than

90%. She was not stubborn but, rather, had this strange character of being the standard bearer for the truth that would benefit all, and she was a pragmatist. She was responsible because she was given this great gift to see well into the future with regard to current history.

Sam started to think about a new concern that was beginning to occupy much of Madison's thoughts and this was the recent elevation of General Bernard Law Montgomery, as a result of the battle of El Alamein, to the status of a great Mythical Greek warrior. Madison knew that he was anything but and that this elevation to hero of a lesser and deficient player could cause problems down the road; he was simply a poor tactician as well as probably being a poor strategist, too unsure of himself and hesitant even though bombastic. He was still hesitant as he continued to pursue Rommel into December allowing the Afrika Korp to escape time and again as he delayed. Ultimately he was carelessly putting men's lives at risk and he lost opportunities by waiting until the time was right to attack, and it always seemed that the time was never right with this man. He was also a commander who was overly demanding of attention and involved himself too much in higher strategy for a 'field commander'. His strutting pomposity reminded her of an American general, who she had once met, by the name of MacArthur; the thought of this made Sam smile. Sam knew that after meeting MacArthur Madison made a note to pay special attention to him if he became part of her area of intelligence as she felt that he would react out of personal bravado for personal elevation and not out of sound tactical reason, she could see this general defying the Supreme Commander if a situation came to push vs. shove. Now Sam knew she had 'Monty' as he was starting to be called along with his fame.

The British had made a big deal out of this little rail station El Alamein, which had been almost at the center of a medicine ball of attrition moving back and forth between the British 8th Army and what was left of Rommel's Deutsches Afrika Korps. They were making Montgomery out to be a god after the battle for this piece of real estate. When after all was said and done, Rommel had at one point been beaten down to only 26 tanks by superior numbers of Commonwealth forces under General Claude Auchinleck, well before Montgomery was on the scene. Rommel had been denied two additional divisions due to Hitler's pre-occupation with the Caucasus in Russia, which Madison had predicted in an analysis before the request even went to Hitler, and he was only getting one fourth of the fuel being sent as the Allies were sinking three out of four tankers sent to North Africa. The Australians and New Zealanders, or the Anzac Commonwealth troops, had already shut down the Italians who were with Rommel.

The British needed a success and unfortunately Montgomery was in the light when it needed to be played.

Rommel's army was a mere shadow of its former self by the end of July 1942 when the first battle of El Alamein had come to a standstill. General Auchinleck had done his job but he was to be relieved and replaced by Lieutenant-General W.H.E. Gott. Churchill wanted to get new blood at the head of the British 8th Army. Before Gott could take over he was killed when his plane was shot down while flying back to Cairo from the battle area. Montgomery was next called on, by default, and Rommel attacked this new general on August 30, 1942 to throw him off balance, but low on fuel he called off his attack three days later.

Montgomery was privy to secret communiqués to Rommel and those between Rommel and Hitler so he knew Rommel's state with regard to equipment, fuel and ammunition. More than this, he knew Rommel's moves before he made them. This is something of which Madison was fully aware. Montgomery also knew that the Allied invasion, or Operation TORCH, was to launch into North Africa in November while his supplies continued to pour in. The strategic character of Bernard Montgomery was to appear for the first time: wait, wait and wait until you have superior forces and supplies and then wait some more. This was unsettling to Madison who was more familiar with military history than most generals.

Montgomery had kept Rommel's attention until he had 2:1 advantage in manpower and 3:1 in tanks along with complete air supremacy. Churchill had demanded that Montgomery attack and Montgomery had refused and waited. In the meantime Rommel was removed to a hospital in Germany for multiple ailments including fatigue, while General Georg von Stumme took over.

Montgomery had finally attacked on the night of October 23, 1942. He opened his attack with a 900 gun artillery barrage at the end of October knowing that once TORCH started on November 8 the Axis forces would have to retreat to save Tripoli. Once again the excellent Anzac troops of New Zealanders and Australians were thrown into the breach.

General von Stumme died of a heart attack caused by an exploding mine and on October 25 Rommel returned to the field from Germany.

On October 26 Montgomery had ordered a pause to adjust 'the plan' after his operation stalled. On October 27th, as some progress was being made by Montgomery's troops, Rommel counter-attacked and Montgomery's forward progress stopped again. Montgomery then changed his plan, again.

Montgomery's new assault had begun on the morning of November 2 and Rommel was out of fuel. Rommel was told by Hitler to 'stand and die' but he broke off with no other choice and retreated to save his troops. Madison remembered reading the 'stand and die' communiqué in German shortly after it was deciphered from code. She knew Rommel and she knew that he would save his troops. She also knew that if he had obeyed Hitler it would have probably caused Montgomery to halt again.

The use of tenacious Anzac troops for a frontal assault on Rommel, with no room to maneuver and outflank, worried Madison. It reminded her of Gallipoli again and Dieppe and of the British disregard for troops other than their own and sometimes she wondered about that as well, as they never seemed to be in a rush even if British troops were in need of relief. Sam thought how much this all weighed on her as he sipped his martini and pondered the future with Montgomery.

The 8th Army had suffered over 13,000 killed, wounded or missing. Just under half of Rommels 100,000 force were either killed, wounded or captured.

Once again a British general officer had pushed Anzac troops, some of the best troops in the world, along with other Commonwealth troops into the meat grinder just like at Gallipoli because they were Commonwealth troops and not British. Now they were making this man a hero, which would only allow the potential for disasters into the future. Sam knew that Madison's fear was that with this broader battlefield, encompassing the Mediterranean region, with an eye towards the continent 'eventually', there would be too many command opportunities for a man like this and surely American troops would be adversely affected. In those ranks would no doubt be some of those young men who had waved to she and Sam on that hot day on the Hudson a century ago now, and he knew that she could never stop herself from thinking about that.

In the end Montgomery had been, to a degree, suckered in by Rommel who's intent was to maul British troops and then make an orderly withdrawal. Rommel had set his Corp up, with limited resources, in El Alamein because the only approach was a frontal approach. He could not be flanked and he thought he could draw Montgomery into a kill zone which, in the end, he did. The Anzac troops were pushed into the lead and paid for it. The Australian troops of the 9th Division were tenacious and kept moving forward into fire. Rommel had achieved the bloody nose he wanted to achieve while in retreat.

Madison had discussed, at length, her concern about the hesitation displayed by General Bernard Law Montgomery along with his bombastic personality and self-righteous approach to tactics and strategy. Madison was well placed enough to know that not even Churchill could stand the man but it kept coming down to the simple and uncompromising fact that the British desperately needed a hero at this point in the war. This would give the man unwarranted influence in operations to come, a man who Madison felt was almost like a schoolyard braggart trying to overcompensate for his subdued inferiority complex. Madison was not a psychiatrist and tended to shy away from bringing up her basic psychology studies but it did serve her at times in marking an historical figure for special attention, attention that would force her to read the individual not based on historical data but on personal history in the current historical context. She would be dealing with a growing problem as this man grew in hero status. She did not want to see more troops used as cannon fodder, especially not American troops.

Sam knew this worry could drive her past breaking; she was like a brilliant scientist driving herself faster and harder to single-handedly keep ahead of the rest of the world's scientific community. Something would have to give along the way as the British seemed to be in the political driver's seat.

The British had too much influence over American troops and the ill-conceived prosecution of the war as illustrated so far in Operation TORCH. Americans were great tacticians with uncomplicated strategies, which allowed for direct and quick approaches to winning. This American quality was being adversely affected by this British influence as Madison put more and more pressure on herself to counter its effect through her reports and presentations, as well as through her influence, as it were. But Sam knew that it was all not quite enough.

At the same moment Sam was thinking about all of this Madison was reflecting on the Christmas party she was attending with general officers representing a government and a military that was still, to a degree, back in the Edwardian Age of Rudyard Kipling and H.G. Wells; didn't these fools remember the horror of the trenches in the last war, which ended that Age of high society.

◆   ◆   ◆

It was early evening and as Sam sipped from another martini a slight smile shown momentarily across his lips as his mind's eye saw Madison rebuffing one of those old stodgy generals, some still of the old trench warfare mentality. Madison did not suffer fools well even though she would try due to her position and a need to keep her job security tight.

The remnants of the smile were just fading as the front door to the cottage opened slowly and there stood Madison in a red dress draped with an ankle length black mohair coat backlit by the waning moon which had been beautifully full just a few days earlier. Her hair was that beautiful blonde with a very slight hint of light brown and brushed over to the right like Veronica Lake and her dress was one to show her great legs and not a long gown as material was scarce these days. She was stunning there, frozen safely in the moonlight. For a moment there was peace in the world and it was

Christmas and then he noticed a sudden sadness and vulnerability invade the simple beauty of her face as she moved inside towards him closing the door as she came. With only the orange light of the coal fire to highlight her she looked even more stunning as she came into Sam's arms.

"They're mad, they're all mad," she angrily whispered.

"Need I ask who that might be?"

"You bloody well know, to use one of their damned words. Why do they have to relish it so much?"

"What?"

"This war. They talk about it as though it were a grand crusade. They talk about obsolete maneuvers and theory as though it's a new invention. They simply don't get it."

"And what did you say to all of this grand talk?"

"Nothing of course; all I could see were those young cadets at the Point and know that some of them are under direct or indirect command of some of these people. I can't stand it." And the sadness in her face grew more distant as Sam held her for moments before speaking again.

"You can't take the entire weight of the Allied war strategy on your shoulders or you will adversely effect your analytical effectiveness."

"It's difficult not to cross that line for me," she whispered sadly.

"I know but the only thing that we can do is to give the best joint analysis that we can possibly give and maybe jump months into the future through a trend we can pick up. With specific statistical models in mind we can look for German communications that may help us to put together a predictable long-term scenario or strategy. We may be able to pull out a multi-layered strategy and discover the pieces that comprise it. If we can predict the pieces we may have an audience for the overall theory. German military tactics are characteristic and serve a specific purpose unlike this Mediterranean campaign starting with North Africa, which we more than assume will be pushed even further into the Mediterranean. Statistics are more reliable as a predictor with the German military model. We may even be able to predict what they are going to do before they know what they are going to do, it's all possible. The only adverse variable is Hitler and we would probably have to model for him as well and the two models would most likely have to sync to predict. This is where it gets complicated, how do we model or read one individual who is unpredictable and irrational? But it has to be doable."

"Can you put together a simplified shopping list of what to look for, for the military model? I have the manpower............of three very good analysts," she added with a sly smile.

" I'm happy to hear that you've included yourself. I've already been working on it and can get it to you within the week."

"You've had this up your sleeve all along?"

"I had to figure out some way to give you the edge you needed to break through the politics."

"I love you Sam.................I can't lose you."

"You'll never lose me and you know that."

"We're in a war."

"I've told you that it won't happen."

"Make me a promise Sam."

"Anything, what do you want?"

"If anything happens to us let's make sure we meet again.

I've always felt that I've always known you and I don't want to take the chance that maybe there is another life after this one and I won't know how to find you."

"I know that I've known you before; I've been well trained to listen to you."

"I'm serious and I've been thinking about it. I have fears and my plan is the only thing that has kept me sane."

"And what is that?"

"That we meet in the seat by the last door of the fourth car back of the 'slammer' of the first train, depending on future schedules, leaving at either 12:00 or just after for London from Fleet station on my birthday in exactly 58 years........., or better yet just in the waiting room of Fleet station at noon on that day."

"My God, you've really been thinking about this. Why 58 years?"

"That is 2001 or the next year after the first full year of the new century; this one has been too devastating in too many ways other than what we had at the Commodore and those sunny days on the Hudson."

Smiling warmly, with his head slightly tilted as he looked Madison in the eye, he just said, "sure" with all sincerity and Madison knew that he had meant it and that that date would become as important to him as it had become to her while she ran the intellectual maze of trying to figure out how to save them. The other method was to end this war faster, which is what Sam was trying to help her to do with his modeling.

Looking back at the wall as she sat on the sofa Madison said to the wall, with Sam listening, "Why did you re-hang the gifts, they are meant to be used like that shaving brush I know that you always wanted but wouldn't buy for yourself." Turning back she looked at him waiting for the answer almost reminding Sam of his 8th grade teacher waiting for his answer to the question she had posed on Beowulf.

"I will use that wonderful brush of brushes in due time but for now I want to enjoy the gift as a whole. It gives me incredible warmth and joy just to look at that against the wall. You give me the greatest of gifts", he said with a smile touched with a slight bit of humor.

"I love you," she whispered as she once again fell into his arms.

They spent an hour in front of the coal fire that Christmas night before Madison had to run back to the party. She had left to check on something that was classified that she could not speak with Clive about, at least that was her excuse. The following day would be Boxing Day and the officers were getting fairly intoxicated so she wouldn't be missed that much. For that hour they discussed the politics of the Allied cause that they were trying to steer and it seemed, steer against those politics.

Some months earlier Madison had discussed, with Sam, a letter from Churchill to FDR dated December 7th 1940 and the irony of that letter. She was amazed that the 20 page war dictate from the Prime Minister to the President of the neutral United States had actually suggested that The United States extend their right through the reassertion of, as stated by Churchill, "....the doctrine of the freedom of the seas from illegal and barbarous warfare in accordance with the decisions reached after the late Great War and freely accepted and defined by Germany in 1935." He had suggested that the U.S. project power out into the Atlantic to protect her shipping to a non-neutral trade partner such as the U.K.. It stated that this would not provoke Hitler as he was still busy with Britain and that he would not go against his maxim "one at a time". The Prime Minister went on to say, "Further, could not United States naval forces extend their sea control over the American side of the Atlantic, so as to prevent molestation by enemy vessels of the approaches to the new line of naval and air bases which the United States is establishing in British islands in the Western Hemisphere." He went on to say that such assistance in the Atlantic would not jeopardize U.S. control in the Pacific. A Year before Pearl Harbor he was manipulating U.S. entry into the European war. The first indications of the Prime Minister's fixation on Africa and the Mediterranean were briefly revealed in the letter as well when he discussed prevention of the spread of German 'domination' of Europe into Africa and into South Asia. He went on to say that this domination, if left unchecked in Africa, would eventually spread to South America. By-passing Africa and attacking directly at the heart of the Third Reich was not in his vocabulary.

The letter was a blueprint of things to come in the U.S./U.K. relationship. Churchill talked about applying superior air power to the German homeland and the importance of the Mediterranean as "..the attitude of Turkey and indeed the whole of the eastern basin depends upon our having a fleet there."

Early on Churchill was pre-occupied with Turkey and the Mediterranean as though he wanted to still win WWI's Gallipoli and this had sent chills up Madison's spine when she had read it. His implication that the Axis powers, lead by Germany, might move on to South America after their domination of Africa touched on the Monroe Doctrine and its responsibilities to the region, which as a student of history Churchill well knew. It had a desired effect on the President of The United States.

The Prime Minister even went further in this letter when he stated that the Irish in the United States might want to use their influence to get the Government of Eire to do the right thing by, "…pointing out the dangers which its present policy is creating for The United States itself." His suggestion was to use U.S. influence with Ireland.

He went on to conclude that Britain would be the one giving its blood and that it would then not be fair of the U.S. not to financially back them once they had stripped themselves of all "saleable assets". He reaffirmed Germany First more than a year before the ARCADIA Conference held from December 22, 1941 to January 14,1942 where "Europe First" was affirmed by the British-American Combined Chiefs of Staff.

Churchill suggested that all convoys of materials leaving America for Great Britain be accompanied by U.S. battleships, cruisers, destroyers and air flotillas and that the use of this protection would be more immediate and effective if the US obtained bases in Ireland. He stated, "I think it is improbable that such protection would provoke a declaration of war by Germany upon The United States though probably sea incidents of a dangerous character would from time to time occur." Not only was he trying to set the U.S. up for entry into the war but at the same time he was trying to quell a potentially disruptive Ireland.

The letter was filled with suggested moves that would cause enough of a provocation as to garnish The Unites States a proclamation of war from the Third Reich. Further to this it outlined the war production that the United Kingdom needed the U.S. to undertake in order to fuel England's war needs.

What subtlety Madison found interesting was that Churchill said it would take The United States two to three years to gear up its industry for war production once war was declared. In reality it started to produce within six months. Madison always noticed the subtleties as they were overlooked by most and in some of these subtleties there was a wealth in intelligence to be found. Churchill in this case was showing that he underestimated the ability of The United States to shift gears, to procure quickly and get the job done within specified timetables. After all, the U.S. was successful before the Depression and coming out of it because of the 'can do' mentality, which was required when starting a country from scratch. But Churchill did not understand this or if he did, he denied it, which was worse. This also implied that Churchill viewed the U.S. military in the same light. He either could not see, or did not want to see, the can do and do it quickly, and be direct mentality of the U.S. military. This in turn would not allow him to appreciate, let alone accept, American war strategy.

It was a fairly well crafted letter and quite transparent, at least to Madison, in its manipulation of FDR to do exactly what Churchill and the British planners needed the U.S. to do. It ironically ended with the statement that "…you will regard this letter not as an appeal for aid, but as a statement of the action necessary to the achievement of our common purpose, I remain, yours very Sincerely, Winston S. Churchill."

Madison rehashed this document over and over in her subconscious and Sam knew it.

Before she left, Madison had a martini with Sam and just contemplated his face as she sipped it. There were many times when they did not need to say a thing as they already knew what each other was thinking. She had curled up briefly into a fetal position next to Sam just before getting up and putting her shoes back on to return to the military party.

Boxing Day 1942

Boxing Day December 26, 1942 came and went with a whimper. It seemed that the only people busy at work were Madison and her two-man 'Commodore' team, and Sam. Sam was busy in the Fleet cottage finishing up his checklist for Madison's team to use against incoming intelligence. The research model for the German military would identify patterns in statistics; the patterns would provide pieces to the puzzle to form the end model. The checklists were accurate enough that if a communiqué satisfied 70% of the checklist it would contribute pertinent information to insert into Sam's model. The statistics concerned numbers and types of equipment and the state of equipment. What had to be taken into account was that German troops, unlike American troops, would leave equipment, which had broken down, instead of repairing it. Americans would repair equipment, especially anything automotive, with whatever was available. This was an important statistical variable, different from the German thinking, that Sam attributed to American 'backyard' mechanics, which he experienced while growing-up. Shipments of ammunition and food, and types of ammunition shipped and amounts of specific types were of course another important statistical factor to be worked together with the equipment factor. The list also consisted of types of troop movement and times. A great deal of this information was easy to get. Sam did not know where it was coming from but he did not ask, he felt as though he were the proverbial kid in a candy store.

The criteria that Sam set forth to determine the value of the data did not follow the guidelines that determined the priority of the data that contributed to the typical military analysis of the same information. Much of this data would be considered superfluous to standard military analysis but Sam and Madison were trying to put together a long-term prediction of things to come with small to medium 'military operations' being revealed in the process, which in turn would help their case. They also, of course, applied historical data going back as far as the Franco Prussian War and Otto von Bismarck's plan to create a unified German Empire. This would be Madison's contribution once she understood what it was Sam's model was uncovering.

Thinking of Otto von Bismarck and his importance in this new approach fueled by Sam's statistics had reminded Madison of the Boston Gardens and reading that paper on Bismarck when Sam first appeared in her life. Destiny ran on a short track once it got started she had thought to herself, then she had laughed as that was something Sam would have said; they knew each other so well that they had fragments of each other imbedded in their souls.

Sam had the final criteria checklist in Madison's hands that night as she came to the cottage once again from her team location in the 'Dome', as they now 'officially' called the bulbous porthole encompassed lower section of the Cambridge Military Hospital's clock tower.

She stepped through the cottage door wearing jeans, an old cowboy shirt and a New York Yankees ball cap.

"My God, don't you think you may stand out in a get-up like that?." Sam said in laughing amazement.

"It's past 9 in the evening, no one will see me and if they do they'll just think it's that crazy American research doctor at the Cambridge. What spy or secret analyst would be so stupid as to be so obvious."

"You've got a point" he said still laughing,........................ "My God."

"What now?", she demanded.

"You look unbelievably sexy, a cowgirl in a Yankee cap; now that is provocative and dangerous."

With that she pounced on him and they wound-up upstairs in the bedroom leaving the Yankee cap where it had fallen in front of the fireplace.

She had to leave once more at 11PM and she would leave with a brown packet under her arm.

Referring to the packet Sam said, "It's pretty well self explanatory once you read my overview notes. Your job is the history stuff and man will you have to go back a bit. I think it's important to interpret the final data we come up with applying historical military context going back to the Franco/Prussian War as I know you are already doing," and then he winked at her.

"Is this what I get for leaving you alone once more," she said joking, but it wasn't a joke.

"It hurts when you leave but I'll take us any way I can; start doing your homework and maybe we can help make this thing end sooner...."

On her way home, in her husband's MG, that night Sam's words, "...make this thing end sooner..." resonated in her thoughts. She actually felt excited in a positive sense for the first time in awhile feeling that she could finally do something that would have more of an impact. She let the wind toss her hair as she accelerated the small car with a small smile of joy on her face, which she allowed herself this night.

January 25, 1943

A new year had snuck in and the war was still raging, and ready to escalate. On January 14; Roosevelt, Churchill and the Combined Chiefs of Staff of the Allies met at Casablanca to plan future Allied Strategy. Stalin was tied up with the German Army in Russia and did not make it to the conference.

The meeting ran through the 23rd and had just wound up two days earlier to this 25th day of January 1943. The American Chiefs of Staff pushed for a 1943 cross-Channel attack or Operation ROUNDUP, but Churchill argued for a more limited operation against Sicily, which Madison and Sam knew was coming, and which was agreed upon in the end. Churchill had summed up American involvement in the Mediterranean as "in for a penny, in for a pound" in reference to US involvement in North Africa. The Americans had been blind sided as they were informed that this was a planning meeting and they came to work on plans, Commodore had not been consulted. The President had failed to inform the Chiefs of the armed services of the true nature of the meetings, which they soon discovered. The British already had their plans in hand and were well briefed to prevent the discussion that the Americans had prepared for. It was a done deal and no doubt talked about between FDR and Churchill well beforehand.

This is what Madison had feared, American strategy undermined. The buildup for the invasion of France was to continue but it was now secondary to the invasion of Sicily and then, most likely, Italy against the advice of the American Joint Chiefs headed by General

George C. Marshall. A great deal of what had transpired at the Conference harkened back to Churchill's December 7, 1940 letter to FDR and the early warning of things to come as Madison had initially interpreted it in early 1941, and interpreted it correctly.

At the nine day meeting Roosevelt called for an 'unconditional surrender' to which the British stated that they were completely surprised and that such a declaration would make the war more difficult and extend it; but they, in reality, were fully aware of it well before FDR introduced it. Madison was part of a team of analysts who had war gamed war with Germany and in their analyses had firmly recommended 'unconditional surrender' as a requirement for German surrender.

There were many reasons for this requirement of 'unconditional surrender', of which Madison was a driving force. The starting baseline was comprised of the lessons learned at the Treaty of Versailles in 1919 where the American delegation had been duped by European manipulation, which finally lead to another war. This was simply where the argument for 'unconditional surrender' started. It was later applied to the war with Japan as well. But of equal importance was the argument that 'unconditional surrender' would not give any room for negotiations or compromise between Hitler and his generals. The German General Staff and the entire Prussian hierarchy of the German Army were not in agreement with Hitler, starting with Case WHITE, or the invasion of Poland. They did not feel that they could invade Poland until after March of 1945 if not much later. In essence they did not agree with Hitler's timetable for this war if even the war itself.

The analysts that Madison worked with, before the war, had intelligence coming out of Germany from the old German Officer Corp. It was being obtained through private correspondence which had been compromised, to a degree, by the British actually hand searching mail moving back and forth between the U.S. and Europe on the Pan Am Clippers. This was all done with US sanction. The German Officer Corp had a tradition of staying out of politics and serving the Fatherland but Hitler was slowly altering this Germanic commitment to duty without challenge. This was transparent in many private pieces of correspondence and evident through early rumblings heard by U.S. diplomats in their semi-private, as well as private, interchanges with their German counterparts and highly placed acquaintances. Once this tradition was changed Madison's pre-war group of analysts knew that the Officer Corp would go to extremes to remove Hitler. It was thought that this traditional hierarchy of officers might be pushed over the edge if Hitler were to break the Non-Aggression Treaty signed with the Russians on August 23, 1939, which had happened in the interim. Operation BARBAROSSA launched on June 21, 1941 ended the treaty and started a second front with the German invasion of Russia, something that the English had said Hitler would never do but the Americans felt sure would occur. With BARBAROSSA Madison knew the 'unconditional surrender' ball had been put in play.

At present Madison and Sam had predicted that a select core of Hitler's officers would take extreme measures to assassinate him. The probability of this was over 90%, which put it above the realm of pure possibility or theory where it had surfaced during Madison's pre-US entry analysis. In the ensuing years, from the first war gaming of war with Germany, reactions within the German Officer Corp to Hitler's actions and commands had strongly pointed towards assassination as a means of removal. They as well had the knowledge, through 'Wild Bill' Donovan, of Admiral Canaris's potential involvement and the fact that it was now felt that the Admiral was supplying Hitler with misinformation in order to try to steer the war to an end. Sam had unknowingly helped with the statistics used to support this theory of the 'Admiral's misinformation'.

Madison and Sam predicted two assassination attempts triggered by the invasion of Russia and more importantly the mishandling of Stalingrad. The second attempt would be a back up to a failed first attempt. An 'unconditional surrender' put forth by the Allies would force elements of the Officer Corp to expedite the assassination of Hitler. A conditional surrender, which Hitler would never negotiate for any reason, would only take the pressure off of the Officer Corp to take matters into their own hands. This sounded contrary to rational thinking at first but it was felt that the revelation of an 'unconditional surrender' would send Hitler into a prolonged tirade once it reached his ears and that this tirade, over months, would make him carry out even more irrational actions which would force the Old Officer Corp into action on their own sooner rather than later.

Madison was not only disturbed by the Allied agreement to invade Sicily, which implied that the mainland would be next with a move up the boot of Italy, which would turn the war into a slugfest and cost American lives, but more so she was disturbed by the British reaction to the 'unconditional surrender' requirement. She had known Sicily was coming, as indicated in Churchill's preoccupation with the Mediterranean as outlined in his December 7, 1940 letter to FDR, and that it would be agreed upon as they were already in North Africa. But this British reaction to 'unconditional surrender' was disturbing as Madison saw it. She saw it as a set-up by the British to enable them to force more decisions on the Americans in the future, if they agreed to this one with protest, by stating strongly that they were not happy about it and it would, in their opinion, prolong the war. Madison once again knew that she had her job cut out for her and the ball was now in England's court which, however she looked at it, would allow them to get their way in future operations with a deadly outcome for American troops.

She knew that the US Army could ill-afford British strategy and British manipulation. Her work would have to be as solid as it could be. She would push her reports through to joint U.S./British intelligence emphasizing the two assassination attempt theory on Hitler as soon as they were complete and both she and Sam were satisfied that their were no holes in it. The probability of this theory becoming reality, of course, was increased by Hitler's invasion of Russia and the 'unconditional surrender' dictate, about which the Germans now knew. But she could and would keep the effect of the 'unconditional surrender' out of her work to the British so that she could use it as an ace in the whole later on down the road. No doubt the 'unconditional surrender' decree would have set Hitler off into a tirade and, in theory, prompted him to put forth a scorched earth policy. Such a policy would further embolden any plan by the German Officer Corp to attempt his assassination and sue for peace, allowing themselves to be fully demobilized and become occupied rather sooner than later. A policy of even implied scorched earth would move those in positions of power and responsibility to the Fatherland to act along the lines of what the Allies wanted. A true scorched earth policy would require that the German Army burn everything as they withdrew, including their homeland, this would cause the irreparable break in the chain of command from Hitler on down. They would want to save their country from being burned to the ground by a madman. After all, their duty was to the Fatherland and not to Adolf Hitler.

Madison and her pre-war group felt that a conditional surrender could, eventually, force the German High Command to violently remove Hitler but without such great expediency. They also felt that once this did occur it would possibly allow the High Command to get more aggressive without him in the way knowing they could sue for conditions of peace at some point. If they gained the tactical upper hand, by keeping Hitler from interfering, they could possibly negotiate for terms from strength. This was a fear that American planners maintained after entry into the war. America's military wanted to end it quickly and sharply, no holds barred as Civil War generals William Tecumseh Sherman and Phil Sheridan believed except they were more concerned than their Civil War forefathers about the civilian population.

Another event that occurred at the Casablanca Conference (Codenamed SYMBOL) that disturbed Madison was a report from Brigadier General Carl A. Spaatz. Spaatz, who had been Commander of U.S. Army Air Forces in Europe and was currently overseeing Allied Northwest African Air Forces as Commander of the Twelfth Air Force after reorganizing these Allied air forces, was reporting after a meeting he had had with Churchill. This report further informed her that she would be fighting an uphill battle with the British in trying to get the job of ending this war quickly accomplished.

The General had been sent to Casablanca by the commanding general of the American Army Air Force Lt. Gen. Henry H. "Hap" Arnold. He had been sent on January 17th, the day before a planned meeting between Churchill and commander of the American Eight Air Force based in England Maj. Gen. Ira C. Eaker. He was sent to loosen up the Prime Minister for the formal meeting with Eaker set for the next day when Eaker would give a presentation on 'Daylight Bombing' by the American Eight Air Force. Eaker was still furious that the Prime Minister was trying to, and it appeared successfully, persuade FDR to convert American daylight bombers to a nighttime force. He had simply stated to Arnold when he heard this, "That is absurd. It represents complete disaster. It will permit the Luftwaffe to escape. The cross-channel operation will then fail. Our planes are not equipped for night bombing; our crews are not trained for it…If our leaders are that stupid, count me out. I don't want any part of such nonsense." It was also felt, by the Americans, that mass and precision daylight bombing of strategic targets, and not civilians, would help attain 'unconditional surrender' in the briefest period of time.

In his report General Spaatz had described his discussions with the Prime Minister while the Prime Minister was taking his bath and chomping on a cigar. Spaatz was put in the absurd situation of pleading with the Prime Minister to allow American bombers to bomb Europe in the daylight. The Prime Minister kept preaching that the loss rate would be high as British Bomber Command had tried this briefly, he also wanted to area bomb the "Hun" at night and "….bomb them into oblivion and create more refugees in Germany." Spaatz felt that the Prime Minister did not want the Americans to achieve something the British could not so he did not mention the need of daylight to effectively use the Norden bombsight. The Norden sight would allow American bombers to hit strategic targets with precision, which was how the crews were trained, instead of forcing them to area bomb everything at night, including civilians. Spaatz put forth the "24-hour" theory that bombing the 'Kraut' 24-hours a day around the clock would hammer them into the ground without relief and drive down moral. The Prime Minister fell for this and "allowed us to undertake the higher-risk higher-value daylight bombing," as Spaatz put it.

In his meeting with Eaker the next day the same approach was made to the Prime Minister in a thirty-minute presentation. This meeting was a formal meeting and the Prime Minster was dressed in his air commodore's uniform. While reading this Madison visualized the Prime minister behind the counter of the Commodore in a white

Commodore's suit for one brief instant and smiled to herself. This was Sam's humor, which she had so nicely picked up. He would throw out visuals like this when they had serious conversations in the Commodore and he needed to lighten her up a bit. She was thankful for this.

The Prime Minister had also stated that up until then the US Eight Air Force had not been able to hit Germany. Eaker had curtly informed the 'Air Commodore' that this was due to the fact that most of his equipment had been diverted to North Africa and Operation TORCH. The discussion ended and daylight bombing was officially 'permitted'.

Madison heard that "Hap" Arnold had calmly noted several days later that, "Whether they were fearful we would use our airplanes ineffectively in the daylight mission: whether they were afraid we would waste airplanes: or whether they feared we would do something they could not and had not been able to, I do not know." But he knew, as did most Americans involved in the issue, that the whole affair did not inspire confidence in the great alliance between the two nations.

◆   ◆   ◆

General Friedrich Paulus and the German 6th Army were still hanging on in Stalingrad, barely. Madison was amazed and ever horrified. She was reading the same communiqués that the German High Command was reading, again thanks to a source unknown to her.

She was still horrified that Hitler was going to leave these men to die but she wasn't surprised, it fell into a pattern that they were starting to slowly put together on Hitler. She was amazed at how this force was holding on in the dead of a brutal Russian winter on what amounted to starvation rations and dwindling ammunition. She was also horrified at what was happening to these young men as a result of this madman's delusions. They were slowly freezing to death and she was in a place of intelligence to know exactly what was happening to them. They weren't just the enemy but young men much like those on Trophy Point from that warm summer day long ago. What had added to this horror was one small communiqué that said that they did not need field dressings with any re-supply as the cold was freezing the blood of bleeding wounds allowing the men to last a little bit longer in the frigid cold. She sensed some dark irony in the wording of the communiqué as she read it in German but she kept that to herself and she cried inside for them all but did not show a tear. She cried deeply in her soul because she knew what was happening to these men and what might come for others in a winter yet to come.

Hitler had committed a full army to its doom. He had pumped more men into the fray and Madison now realized that if it were not for the Mediterranean campaign of the Allies the Germans would be fully occupied, with Russia eating up all of their resources in a concentrated fight. It would have been a fight, also, where an entire army, such as Paulus's 6th, would not have been left on its own for no military purpose. A scenario such as this concentrated fight with the Russians, without any diversion of German troops, would have been a perfect prescription for Operation BELERO to be followed by Operation ROUNDUP. It would have allowed the Allies the time that they needed to accomplish both of these operations. ROUNDUP might have forced the German Officer Corp to take quick and immediate action against Hitler. It would have saved many untold American and other Allied lives and this realization just made Madison drive her team harder for the data she was trying to glean from some of the most innocuous of military communiqués. Some of these communiqués were so innocuous that it was to the point that her two team members questioned the validity of their concentration.

On January 15 Hitler had ordered the Luftwaffe to airlift 300 tons of supplies daily to the Sixth Army at Stalingrad. The impossible requirement was not being attained, although German efforts were sped up under the most adverse of conditions. Luftwaffe airlift deliveries averaged only 94 tons daily.

On January 22 the Red Army forces launched an offensive to retake Voronezah. Paulus radioed Hitler from Stalingrad: "Rations exhausted. Over 12,000 wounded unattended in the pocket." Hitler responded: "Surrender is out of the question.". Madison had the transcript from the Paulus/Hitler communiqué and she had no idea where it had come from, as usual. Knowing the source would help her analyses but she understood the limits to "need to know". In her business everything helps, much like a forensic detective can use the minutest, or most trivial, of information to help the whole puzzle to come together.

She had had the team go back on old data starting 6 months prior to September 1, 1939 with the launch of Case WHITE and the invasion of Poland. Much of this old information was sketchy as it came in before the British had their current intelligence assets in place. It was enough, though, to give Sam what he needed. The team also questioned the need for the old data, but not as much as they had questioned the 'innocuous'. They knew how good Madison was and how she could integrate statistics with historical data and current intelligence to come up with great analyses. So they re-trained themselves to look for the basics with regard to logistical communications.

On this day, January 25, 1943, she thought she had the data Sam needed. Now she would have to work late hours with him to put the history and the numbers together properly to come up with the bits of the puzzle which they would then have to piece together as more events started to take place. As the actual events moved the puzzle pieces together they would start to form models which, in turn, would predict current events and when that happened it would start to confirm their long-term scenario. Especially now with Stalingrad all but lost the German effort would switch with a concentration on confronting the Allies in the Mediterranean. Madison and Sam had lost their first battle with politics along with ROUNDUP in the upcoming spring so they would have to work even faster.

Sam did not have to return but once a week to Cambridge where he would run statistics for other analysts. He would also run a great deal of this work out of the Fleet cottage then take it to Cambridge and have it couriered to wherever it had to go. This was way outside of the security regulations to have this data outside of what was considered a secure zone but Sam had no choice if he and Madison were to work evenings putting the 'puzzle pieces' together; and besides, he and Madison were now together most nights until midnight. Clive was away from Aldershot a great deal of the time in places unknown. The only item Madison could get out of him, even with her security clearance, was that he was working on "schemes" for future operations. The use of the word 'scheme' with regard to a military operation that dealt with life and death on a large scale unsettled Madison, especially after the staged response by the British delegation at Casablanca to FDR's 'unconditional surrender'. Scheme to her meant 'scam' which is exactly what the British reaction to 'unconditional surrender' turned out to be.

It was January 25th 1943 and the Stalingrad pocket that held the remainder of Paulus's 6th Army was starting to close down and collapse in on itself even though they were still hanging on. It wouldn't be long now before that winter nightmare was over. The Russians would come full bore at Germany but it still would not take any pressure off of the Mediterranean. The modeling she and Sam were working on had to work and give them a chain of successes that would back their final analysis or predictions of a major focal event or series of events bringing the Allies and the Axis to the 'pinnacle' as Madison and Sam called it. The 'pinnacle' would be the high water mark of the war or the last great gasp of the Axis at a point where they could look over everything and know that it marked the beginning of the end.

They were going to determine the next chess moves by the German High Command and this would all be influenced by Hitler and the state of the German lines of communication. Key to properly interpreting the effect of the lines of communication, or logistical support, was the state of overall equipment from transport trucks to heavy armor. The only unpredictable element was Hitler himself, and determining his influence was crucial. If their final analysis on the assassination attempts on Hitler were proven correct it would add even more credence to their future predictions in the eyes of their own intelligence group and, hopefully, in the eyes of British intelligence.

To Madison and Sam they were not predictions so much as they were part of a roadmap formed by statistics and historical events, which formed a pattern which all together formed this roadmap of major events. In order to be more than just predictions they prayed for the aid of the "Hitler attempts" as they called them. If the first attempt worked they would have to re-write all their data, but they would prepare for this and write two sets of analyses. One set would assume the attempt or attempts had failed and those would be issued as soon as possible before any attempt occurred. The second set of analyses would be held back and account for two possibilities. One: that Hitler was killed on the first attempt. Second: that he was killed on the second attempt, which would allow some disturbance in the Officer Corp, if not straight out execution of some major players, depending on the time between attempts. They determined this time to be a matter of days or a week at the most in order for the plotters to take advantage of the chaos created by the first attempt. The work involved in this would be intense and stimulating, and it would certainly take its toll on their well-being.

They would also be together a great deal under these conditions which only served to stimulated them even more to do everything that they could to help put an earlier end to the war so that they could sail the Hudson again under sunny skies empty of war clouds. They looked forward to those sunny days when they could run up the hill to the Commodore and just become engrossed in each other's knowledge, or would they. Would the war take all joy out of this and their love for history. At the least they would finally meet at the appointed hour which had been taken away from them with concocted stories of sudden and unexpected death and which had let them realize what life would be without each other. Madison was also married as an after effect of one of these stories; the brutal telling of the loss of a plane with the man she loved aboard it. She remembered the pain of feeling him die in the same manner that his parents had died, a childhood trauma which had been so devastating that he had just revealed it to her in its detail only a month before. She was now, in retrospect, even more horrified at the tale told to her so officiously in her parent's front room. She was terrified of the memory of the fog that she had lived in until she discovered Sam alive again through his work; that had been a day.

January 31, 1943   Stalingrad, Russia

On January 31; Paulus, promoted to field marshal the day before, surrendered at Stalingrad. With the loss of his only airfield on January 22, and his army split into two pockets, the general surrendered his pocket. When told of the surrender, Hitler said, "Paulus did an about-face on the threshold of immortality."

On February 2, the second pocket of Paulus's men surrendered. Madison then felt the sand run out of the hourglass. Hitler would defend against the Russian advances and focus on the Americans and the British in Italy. The stage was being set for the slugfest on the Italian Peninsula. More pieces would start to be added to their puzzle.

On February 2, all resistance at Stalingrad ended. Approximately 147,200 Germans were killed in the extended and abortive campaign for the city, and another 91,000 surrendered, including 24 generals; most of whom Madison and Sam knew would never be seen again. Only 34,000 men ever made it out on the airlift. A thousand Luftwaffe crewmen and 488 transports planes were projected to have been lost in the re-supply and evacuation effort.

On February 3, Berlin acknowledged the end of the fighting at Stalingrad, saying that "the sacrifices of the Army, bulwark of a historical European mission, were not in vain." Germany began a three-day period of national mourning. Soviet forces advanced on all fronts.

On February 14, German forces launched a powerful counteroffensive from the Faid Pass in Tunisia and broke through to the Kasserine Pass in North Africa. Allied Forces began pulling back west toward Sbeitla.

On February 20, Axis forces cleared the Kasserine Pass. The U.S. II Corps fell back to avoid being totally routed. The Germans and Italians swung out and started driving northward toward Thala and westward to Tebessa.

American troops in their first major encounter with Rommel's Afrika Korp were under British control, with a weak American Corps commander and in a two mile wide pass occupying the low ground where they could only move backwards without maneuver. It was a blow to U.S. moral and another lesson against allowing British oversight and/or direct control of U.S. troops. Things would only escalate from here and Madison and Sam could only hope that U.S. forces under Patton would be able to rally and gain some respected capital with the other Allies, which would give them more leverage with their analyses. They now needed American audacity to show and be successful in the way that Americans had always been successful when they went for broke, because their analyses would have similar character.

February 21, found Madison and Sam together in the Fleet cottage at their small dining room table just off of the kitchen and in front of a small window looking onto the back parking area put in, in the 20th century, just for one small car. Madison had borrowed Clive's red MG TA as she had done many times while he was away and it was now parked in that spot. The train tracks were just beyond that and sunken down ten feet, and beyond the tracks was the North Hants Golf Course. There was just a slight dusting of white on the stones that made up the parking area. It was 7AM and they had decided to make an early start of it.

Just as the 7AM train out of Fleet station rumbled by outside and gently shook the glass of the back window Madison looked up from a paper to Sam's eyes. "Here is the last of the data you wanted up through yesterday, there will be additional communiqués tonight and over the next week on Kasserine Pass, it's a mess to say the least. The Brits at Aldershot and elsewhere are already painting it as an American failure to give them more ammunition for more control."

"How do they cover up their involvement?"

"The same way they did in the initial invasion of TORCH, they just avoid all mention of their command involvement and talk about American casualties as though they are at fault for making themselves casualties. It amazes me, but at the same time that they do this they discount American dead and imply that our casualties are nothing compared to what they have lost, they even refer back to the last war for God's sake. It's actually rather dreadful to listen to and it clouds proper analysis on the part of the Brits. A great deal of our data is coming from the Brits and it gets reviewed and edited before we see it, and painted to make them look better, but we've learned how to read between the lines using US generated field intelligence. This is not an easy task to get you the pure numbers that you need Sam."

"I never said that it would be."

"Are all statisticians such reticent enigmas when it comes to their numbers?"

"No, only when I want to surprise you."

"Such as the time it takes to walk from the Hudson to the Commodore."

Sam smiled, "And other surprises. What if I tell you that I have the empirical truth that Hitler would be steaming if we invade Sicily."

"A statement with 'empirical truth', now that's not purely scientific but I'd say that you're right. How does that play out on paper?"

"Actually very easily for a good numbers guy" smiled Sam briefly, "Come here and take a look."

As Madison came around the table and closer to him her eyes gained a devious look and Sam just smiled again, and said, as she put her arms around him, "I ask you to view something of great importance and you can't keep your hands off of my scholarliness." With that she just laughed and kissed him and their work was interrupted for the first time in weeks as Madison headed up the narrow stairs to the small upstairs bedroom with Sam scrambling up behind her. Hitler could wait.

They both knew Hitler would not let the Allies walk up the boot of Italy but Sam's 'puzzle pieces' were starting to come together as he worked towards a model of the German High Command, now to a degree with Hitler in the back of his mind as well as in some of his numbers. This model could help to see into the future as well as back up their theories.

The upstairs had two small rooms. The master bedroom in the front of the cottage and, across a very narrow walkway, to the right of the stairs coming from this room, was a small sunroom facing the rear of the house and the green of the links behind it when it wasn't winter. Outside of the occasional rumbling of a passing train this was the coziest room in the cottage. This was the room where they would escape to together.

◆   ◆   ◆

The early morning sun was just starting to warm the window panes and spill its soft light onto the small bed in the room that now held the two of them in its warm embrace. Madison had managed to find some fresh freesia at a mysterious place in Fleet that supplied her as well with an occasional pound of good Columbian coffee. It was her secret and the yellow and red freesia were now catching the early light as they reposed in their water filled Mason Jar, a childhood flower-filled gift from her grandmother which Madison had brought over from the States. Being with each other on this small island in the sea of turmoil, now surrounding both of them and the world, was more than just loving each other tenderly; it swept them off to a place together that they both had never imagined that they could ever experience.

As they lay side-by-side Sam softly whispered, "You bring out the magnificence in this life and world even as mad as it is right now."

"What do you think you do?"

"Go off to another place which is beyond anything I could have ever imagined."

"You do the same thing to me and more," Madison whispered back as though someone else might overhear her then she gave Sam this wonderful smile which made everything right with the world. He was always so amazed that this wonderfully intelligent woman, who was an absolute genius at her work and who he admired greatly, was such a tender lover and attentive confidant that he, as a man, was living something that he thought he could never have. She knew everything about him and he was comfortable with that. More than comfortable, he was made richer by it and he knew that his work excelled as a result of it.

Sam just handed her a small scrap of paper saying, "I jotted this down quickly the other day and was going to throw it out but you might like to read it."

As she slowly unfolded the partially crumpled up paper her gray-green eyes put their full attention on the words:

> *Hair of silk God's breath doth tickle*
> *Such beauty to make the emotions stop*
> *Save for one, which sings to such*
> *Fine strings a harp falsely interprets*
> *With joyous song it hopes to honor.*
> *Such hair is gold*
> *Richer than any sweet melody it doth behold*
> *Such hair is yours*
> *Heart and soul to flag*
> *No nation great such banner, same or more, to have*
> *Such silken flag the sun to behold*
> *Such beauty as God doth play for me*
> *Such gift be mine to touch*

With tears in her eyes she looked up at him with slightly tilted head and said, "Why are you so wonderful?" Then she added as she wiped away the tears and started to smile, "Even if you forgot the 14th line."

Clearing his throat Sam said, "So, are you going to tell me where you were able to get the freesia?"

"I can't, I've made an oath of secrecy to the shop-owner. You'll simply have to use your powers of insight into my soul and a well rounded understanding of basic statistics to figure it out."

"Funny girl. So I take it that the American Mason Jar came from the same location. Unless that is the same one your grandmother gave you filled with get well daisies, which would confuse the equation, and me, with possibly two different locations in the mix," he stated with a humorously sarcastic grin on his face.

"Ah, so now it's a 'location', are we now turning into a pure statistician?"

"Come here, I don't think I have enough data to properly answer that question."

Madison smiled and just sighed, "You damned analysts are all the same." And they retreated once again that morning to that island, and everything was good with the world.

◆   ◆   ◆

Later that morning they had some of that precious Columbian coffee from the secret shop along with scones from the local bakery in Fleet, and their discussion had changed.

"I want you to take a look at these compiled statistics on equipment in specific theaters, destroyed equipment and anticipated movement of replacement equipment," said Sam referring to the paper on the dining room table in front of them both now. "This is all the data that your team supplied me with but as you'll note, I've rearranged it in columns of numbers with cross references. An important variable is the repair rate. American forces tend to repair and reuse damaged equipment, or broken equipment, even to the point of repairing and using German equipment if necessary, whereas the Germans tend to leave it. Leaving repairable equipment goes against American thinking and needs to be kept in mind. Another variable inside this variable is: what degree of repairable equipment does actually get repaired by German soldiers in the field?, " queried Sam.

"That was somewhat long winded. What are the boxes highlighted in red, they seem to be anomalies with regard to the rest of the numbers?"

"Smart girl, they are way out of whack with the rest of the numbers. The rest of the numbers represent normal movement and replacement of equipment as best we can tell if we look at the rest of the data. Then if I take into account your historical data on previous conflicts and battles involving German forces I see a notable pattern in the anomaly."

"Only a statistician could find a pattern in a break in the pattern."

"The breaks are notable because we are dealing with German troops and the German High Command made up of officers from the Old Prussian Officer Corp. The troops follow certain operational procedures and don't deviate from the norm much, as you find with American troops going back to the Revolution and up through WWI. This reliability in procedure helps to create patterns even in anomalies after they occur. Then you work into the equation the style of the different German generals, which I culled off of the profile data that you supplied, and you get somewhat predictable patterns."

"Style, that's some choice of word for tactical and strategic methodology of particular members of the German Wehrmacht's High Command."

"I thought you might appreciate that."

"The anomalies themselves don't seem to have a pattern at first glance."

"Ah, but they do if you take into account activity in the entire theater of German European operations. What is going on in the weeks leading up to the appearance of an anomaly? If you look at this data, or your area of expertise, you'll see someone's thumb print."

Madison started checking the timelines on the anomalies, events she knew intimately, and in a matter of minutes her eyes lit up with a sparkle Sam hadn't seen in months as she looked up at him and smiled, "Hitler."

Sam just smiled back.

"Don't tell me that you've put predictability on Adolf other than his madness like Stalingrad!"

Sam just smiled. "Now it's up to you to figure out how to use it. This Hitler anomaly and predicting its occurrence may wind up being a determining variable in the equation of event prediction once we find some usable pattern. It also may be influenced by the German Military model and as the Hitler model may in reverse effect the military model, they may form a type of synergy just before effecting an event."

"It'll be an uphill battle to make it useful, they're putting all their faith in this special team of psychiatrists to predict him. Statistical predictability may be too reliable. They seem to be caught up in the human side of this analysis and then they demonize the character which further corrupts any usable analysis."

"If we had direct or even indirect access to the source of those operational Hitler communiqués that you seem to get every so often it would help in our argument with some additional data that we're probably not seeing. If the same source had access to Hitler's personal communiqués as well, we could prove our point but that might be a stretch to think they do. You also seem to get more out of the few that you get still in the original German before the Brits tamper with it," Sam added.

"I'll have to go to Clive on this one as a wife with high-end security clearance.

"Well, that'll be 'peachy' won't it."

"I've sure complicated things; I'm sorry."

"We live in complicated times, there's nothing to be sorry about. I guess if we weren't so good at what we do, because we learned from each other during our Commodore sessions, they wouldn't have killed us off earlier."

"Well, we're alive now and I'll have to deal with Clive when this thing is over."

"You mean the war, by 'this thing'; well we can certainly help with that and I don't mean to snip at Clive, he actually seems like a nice guy, at least on the one occasion I met him."

"That must have startled you when he appeared at Cambridge."

"I thought it was about you."

"That's the difference between the two of you, he is all business and you are the best at what you do and you know how to love me. His existence centers around engraving his name permanently into the history of his regiment."

"Well, I was there first and I only have a simple regimen that I follow like any good statistician."

"What we have was not made on this earth, I've always felt that and your regimen has always been thoughtful even with a full workload. When the war is over I'll be able to explain to Clive who we are. Nothing could ever separate us and he's an intelligent enough man to understand and appreciate everything that went before." She still didn't mention Clive's threat to use his service revolver and the fact that she was actually quite worried about his reaction. She knew that Sam mustn't know or else Sam might be put in jeopardy.

"If he sees just a small part of what I see when I see you he will not be happy to see you go, although I would let you go without a second thought if I knew it would make you happier," added Sam.

"You make me happy and I love you even more because I feel what you just generously put into words."

"Do you think you can get access to those communiqués?"

"I don't know what I'll run into when I broach the subject but Clive prides himself on the authority that he does have so his pride may aid us in gaining some degree of access. Until that happens I'll just have to piece together a workaround."

"And what's your workaround?"

"Goebbels."

"What?"

"Head of Third Reich propaganda; Propaganda Minister Josef Goebbels."

"I got that part."

"Propaganda is just that. It's information released to the general public, which includes us by the way, to create a desired impact either negative or positive. The man emulates the Fuhrer to the point where he even pounds the dais on occasion. The man has such an inferiority complex, along with the fact that he is a cripple under Arian rules and such cripples are not desirable, that he has his hand on the pulse of Hitler. I can pretty well read the private side of Hitler, to the degree that it exists, or what he's truly like, behaviorally, through Goebbels. It's just a matter of connecting the dots when presenting the analyses."

"Well, now we've added another layer to this whole procession. We need to read Hitler during specific timelines and I mean read him in reading his operational communiqués, without the benefit of personal communiqués. Short of this we are going to use Goebbels public propaganda output to determine his thinking behind those communiques and we will need to establish this connection as a direct gauge, not a partial gauge, of Der Fuhrer. That is a handful and, by-the-way, are you becoming one of those head doctors?"

"I hope not but I know them fairly well and I think I may be able to incorporate their psychiatric menagerie and let them legitimize it which may be key in my getting the high command to accept the anomaly timeline as Hitler speaking."

"Good plan, I'm glad you're dealing with those fellows."

"Are you pleading lack of an id and running to the safety of the realm of pure numbers."

"They're not all pure, but yes; and with my ego intact."

"I may need you to back me up with some numbers, sort of how many times the mouse responded to the food light, they like that kind of thing."

"Ah, now you're being unkind but if you need me to dance for them I will."

"You're so theatrical."

"I'm glad you finally noticed. By the way, speaking of theatrical prelude can you get some footage of Herr Goebbels, that might help the cause a little bit?"

"I thought you were the numbers guy."

"I have hidden talents as you've pointed out."

"The psychs have a good deal of it, much of it was captured in North Africa. I guess they needed to entertain the Afrika Korp but the Corp never seemed to have the time as the seal on the cans was still whole when captured. I've seen enough of it to see characteristics that I can draw on. I think it's probably the same characteristics that the psychs are seeing so my job may be easy."

"I've only seen some of the pre-war footage released to the news services."

"It hasn't changed much."

"Good, I'll keep that in mind."

"I won't see Clive for probably another week, according to him, but I'll start on the team of psychiatrists later this afternoon." But she actually had a strange feeling that he would return that night; she didn't tell Sam.

"Sounds good, where's Clive if I can ask?"

"He's in London, most likely spending some time at Eisenhower's headquarters trying to sell one of his 'schemes'."

"Schemes?"

"That's his word for Operations."

"No wonder the British moves are faulty, scheme makes it sound like a con-game."

"Don't get me going on that. I know I'm going to have a run in with him at some point as much of my analyses contradicts current British tactics besides their overall strategy, which our joint work hammers a bit."

"A bit? It runs head on into the British war plan; you're not getting weak on me now are you?"

"No, I'm more the zealot than you; I'm just putting off the confrontation with Clive in my own mind knowing full well it's going to be messy and I may be in the unenviable position of trying to take him down in front of the General Staff."

"He has that much weight in British planning?"

"Yes, and then some. Family connections have helped along with regimental ties but he is fairly good at what he does. My concern is that his talent may get blinded by the need to preserve British tradition no matter what the cost in human life and this is where we are going to lock horns in public."

"I think in front of the General Staff is a bit more than in public."

"I'll need your support on this."

"You know you have it and more."

"I know," whispered Madison dropping her serious tone for one moment.

"We're just going to do what we set out to do and that's ending this war as soon as we can and that's going to take a lot of confrontation especially the way the politics are heading. The Brits are going to use FDR's 'unconditional surrender' decree as a tool against our proposals and the U.S. war plan until it sounds as though the President of The United States is on the side of the Third Reich."

"We have one benefit there, I'm in the British camp. I can engage Clive in discussions with regard to 'unconditional surrender'", that is, when I finally see him. He's not aware that I was part of the team that developed the policy."

"That's an understatement Madison."

"Well, he doesn't know and I can try to act ignorant as to the effects of such a decree on a European mind, especially a German one. I'll let him know that I need to fully understand the ramifications of such a decree, which is very American, and then he should feed me the British plan hoping that I'll make it part of my official analyses."

"Clever Madison, it sounds like you've already spent a great amount of time with the head doctors just as I thought", Sam complimented with a conspiratorial smile, "I'll allow you to have a malted milk when we finally get back to the Commodore."

"Oh you will; it won't ruin that figure you keep talking about?"

"Nothing could ruin your figure, the sight of you walking down a street is enough to wake even the dullest of men............"

"Oh, thanks."

"............along with the wittiest of us."

"You're playing up that theatrical comment. I just gave you a little too much to play with."

"I'll take whatever I can get."

"And I am so glad you're here to do so. I never want to go through losing you again, I won't survive next time," she said taking on a more serious and softer tone.

"There won't be a next time, I'm too ornery to go anyplace, other than here, before you."

"You remember your promise if anything should happen to us!"

"6/26/2001, always the numbers guy."

"Now, for that, guess what you get!"

It was early afternoon and they slept with the scent of freesia romancing them once more.

◆   ◆   ◆

Later that day Madison had a visit with the psychiatrists, who she had met on more than several occasions to the point of developing a working friendship with them. The team was made up of three Americans and three Englishmen and to further cause dissention among the ranks half were Jungians and half were Freudians. Madison just smiled at this thought as she entered their office to the rear of the Cambridge Military Hospital in a private section near the Leishman Laboratory.

Milton Lennox was the lead of the American team and her contact. Actually Milton was the strongest force on the team although Sterling Grafton-Barkley, of the British side, gave him a run for the money. They were all older academics in their late 50's and early 60's.

"Madison Bell to what do we owe this honor? The last time we saw you was two weeks ago. Do we make you nervous?"

"Two weeks ago? Why Milton you are counting the days! Does that constitute acute paranoia with regard to a strong female with high security clearance? I am not the female version of an alpha male and I don't bite."

"Ah, clever Madison; I do enjoy your little stop-bys, as erratic as they may be."

"Are you saying that I need to be more predictable Milton?"

"Never Madison, never; what fun would that be, then one would never trust your work."

"So, you trust me as an independent thinker."

"You are the only one in this room, currently, who I hold in that regard."

"I heard everything Milton," muttered Sterling through his walrus mustache.

"I said that just to get you to speak up Sterling; I always like to know that you're thinking."

"Ah, you are funny old chap."

"I know that you appreciate me Sterling. How would you do without my Yankee know-how?"

"You Yanks are really taken with yourselves."

"No Sterling; we're just usually right and when we're wrong we admit it."

"And what does all of that rubbish mean?"

"Why, my dear Sterling, old boy, I do believe that you just cussed."

"Boys, boys." Interrupted Madison, "I need your expertise, your joint expertise on a little fellow by the name of Josef Goebbels; you know, the one married to Magda."

With this the chatter stopped and they looked at each other.

"Goebbels." , Milton just stated not really a question or an exclamation, then they looked at each other again like they were kids caught in a prank.

"I seem to have struck a cord Milton, why the familiar reaction to Geobbels? Don't tell me that you've been actively profiling the man."

"Well, in a round-about way we have been."

"What do you mean in a round-about way?" stated Madison now a bit more serious and talking to them like an adult trying to get the truth out of a couple of rambunctious children.

"Well you see, we've actually been using Mr. Goebbels as what you might say is a model," volunteered Sterling.

"Might that be a model of Adolf Hitler you are creating?," queried Madison like an adult who knew all along what the kids were up to and just revealed it to surprise them into the truth.

"Well………", said Norman, one of the younger Americans looking over at Milton and Sterling as though he had been caught doing something he shouldn't have been doing.

"Yes, my dear Madison we have been that." Said Sterling as Milton just smiled at her.

"Why do you appear so smug Milton?"

"Ah clever Madison, don't tell me that you are tripping down the same rocky path. I thought analysts scoffed of anything that dealt with anything other than hard facts, especially our science of the mind."

"We can't always deal with hard facts when trying to deal with this one. Without revealing too much I need your help."

"And you shall have it dear Madison," Piped in Sterling. Milton just turned and glared briefly at Sterling's comment.

"Well, I guess you've won over Sterling," commented Milton, "and that brings me along too. Where do you want to start?"

Madison spent the next three hours going over a brief workup of the types of events that they were concerned about with regard to eliciting a particular reaction from a particular individual with a question about what those particular reactions might be and then she answered the questions of the doctors. Between them they put together a refined list of types of reactions, actions and counteractions of a personality type by the name of Adolf Hitler using Joseph Goebbels as the primary model or 'reflective model'; or, in the end, as his doppelganger. The doctors had done a great deal of work on this over the past month so the refining process went along smoothly.

Madison walked out of the Leishman section of the Cambridge Military Hospital that day with a smile on her face and a new found respect for her 'head doctors', as Sam called them. She was actually excited that this all might work and she was more than gratified that the doctors had come to the same conclusion that she had: use the man who is publicly mirroring Adolf Hitler to put together a profile of the actual man. Goebbels was also deemed to be a high level psychopath, which would help to give an accurate replication of Hitler's tendencies, and in public. It was all rather perfect.

She couldn't wait to tell Sam but she would have to return home this evening just to get familiar with the place where she was supposed to be living and, besides, she had a strong feeling that Clive might actually be home from London. She had a strong feeling that he would be home for a reason she couldn't explain other than that she wanted him to be home so that she could start work on getting at the source of the Hitler communiques at best and, at worst, start to get an idea of how the British were going to manipulate the FDR 'unconditional surrender' decree. She had told Sam that if she didn't return to the cottage that night she would have become tied up with something and would see him the next day.

As she turned onto the crushed rock circular drive of the red brick Victorian that she and Clive lived in, just off the base in Aldershot, she could see the faint wisp of blue grey smoke coming from the front right corner of the house where the terrace chairs were located.

It was a chilly and damp late February day which had already grown dark as she pulled up in front of the great door, shivering slightly from the chill in the night and the fact that Clive's little red 1939 MG TA did not offer much warmth even with the top pulled over the usually open two-seater. The mechanism that started the shiver was the realization that it was Clive sitting in a whicker chair in his army greatcoat, which she had once been corrected to call 'British warm', smoking his cut Meerschaum pipe which had been passed down by his father and had grown a light pink, from its original white, over the years of smoking. The motif on the pipe was that of a fox hunt and Clive smoked that pipe only when he was content with himself or when something 'smashing good' or absolutely 'wizard' had happened with his 'work'.

"Alow, alow Maddi", he stammered slightly, "so what brings you this way?"

"The essence of Balkan Sabran tobacco only as it comes from a properly aged Meerschaum pipe. What is the good news? I take it that it is good news with that pipe in one hand and a single malt in the other."

"Ever the observant one. Am I that transparent?"

"Not really, I'm just taking a wild guess and I'm sure that it's something that you deserve to celebrate over." She said as she walked over to him and kissed him on the top of the head and took the whicker chair next to his separated only by a matching whicker table. The table held a rare bottle of 25-year-old Lagavulin single malt scotch whiskey and an ash tray from the Stork club from when he'd been in the States on a fact finding mission for the British Army back in 1940. He also had a pack of Lucky Strikes sitting unopened next to the ashtray.

"I didn't know you smoked cigarettes Clive; if I'm so observant you'd think I would have known."

"I don't but I thought I'd try them as I like the pack; it's rather brilliant don't you think?"

"What's brilliant about a package of Lucky Strike cigarettes, except that they're old"

"The packaging is green, bloody brilliant these Yanks. The buggers have dyed it green and camouflaged it. I should have to try these. Those bloody Yanks." Clive slightly stammered proud of himself for the observation. "What do you mean old?"

"The packaging is now white to save the ingredients of green for the war effort, and by the way I am one of those bloody Yanks Clive."

"Oh, yes, yes that's right but I got these from Ike himself I shall have to try one camouflaged or not."

"So you were at the headquarters in London. I take it that everything went well."

"Smashing my dear, just smashing, although I am a bit flogged."

"'Smashing', not considering yesterday and Kasserine Pass."

"That is something quite altogether different, you Yanks sure made a mess of it; you came a cropper."

"Well, we learn quickly and hopefully in the future we won't have British leadership over our heads to deal with."

"I would suggest my dear that you would be lucky to have British leadership."

"From both a tactical and strategic standpoint, God help us and I will do everything in my power to make sure that American forces are lead by overall American command headed on the road to American developed strategy. After all, that is why your Sandhurst was patterned after our West Point but you still don't get it."

"Get what my dear?"

"Because you were born in the upper class does not mean that you will be good at leading men in battle."

Removing his pipe from his mouth Clive stated in a serious tone, "Only the upper class have the proper up-bringing, education, and ability to make such decisions as how and when to commit men to battle."

"I seriously don't hope that you believe that statement, you are smarter than that."

"And that is precisely my point."

Changing subjects knowing this conversation would not be productive Madison continued, " So, what brings out the 'fox hunt'?"

Looking confused for one brief second then taking his pipe down from his mouth and looking at it he said, with a smile, "Oh, this: three days ago the Combined Chiefs rejected Eisenhower's decision to invade Sicily in July, they want the timetable moved up a month. The Prime Minister threw in his two pence as well and said that we would be the laughing stock if we didn't have British and American troops firing at German and Italian troops in Sicily by late spring early summer. Ike has to confirm by March 1 that the invasion can take place before an August moon. The sooner the better."

"You mean Operation HUSKY."

"Why my dear, you even have clearance as high as knowing the operational name."

"I should, I worked on the analysis."

"Ah, this should draw more Germans away from 'Ali Baba' and make 'Glyptic' happy, as well as get the Turks on the right side this time around."

"So, that's part of the concern, Churchill is still living WWI and is fixated on winning over the Turks."

"Well you could say that is part of it, yes, but just an added benefit."

"So the 'Ali Baba' or the Russians and 'Glyptic' or Stalin will be given relief at the expense of American and British troops, and predominately American as we will represent the bulk of the force."

"Oh my dear, I prefer to talk using their code names, but yes I suppose that you are right."

"Well, we've already committed to the whole Mediterranean campaign from fighting the Vichy French, and now up through Sicily and probably beyond. It will be long and bloody, and unnecessary........... And to think, Churchill is half American through Jennie Jerome," Madison added as a quiet aside.

"Dear Madison, it is the only way to get this done............. and as far as Winston being half American, we don't talk about that."

"Maybe," continued Madison not recognizing Clive's follow-up remark with regard to Churchill's mother, "How will 'unconditional surrender' be viewed once we head in the direction of Italy?"

"Well, we in British command are against that doctrine but the Russians are quite comfortable with it. It has kept them off our backs to some extent."

"So the policy has its benefits."

"Quite, from a political standpoint that is; but from a strategical standpoint, quite the different story."

"And how is that, as you are a better authority than I on European interpretation and reaction within a geo-political and military context?"

"Well, that is the mouthful my dear but strategically it is just incorrect, though from a political standpoint we will use it in future planning."

"How do you mean use it Clive?"

"Well, for the benefit of the Allies to give us the leverage to get certain operations approved beyond the conceptual stage."

"You mean the British Army."

"Yes, quite. We can use 'unconditional surrender' to legitimize extra-ordinary steps using the vast wealth of your great country my dear."

"And how might that work? This could actually help in my understanding of current European military thinking past the dusty text books that I have always lived with."

"Well, we could threaten the heart of Germany with a massed drive of force much like a spear that would get them to capitulate unconditionally. It would not be an attack on a broad front with flanking movement but it would be one bold move by a bold officer such as our Monty. The mass fire bombing and area bombing of German cities would add into this too as it would create more refugees, kill the German spirit and create scorched earth, unlike the Yanks' daylight strategic target bombing."

"But this has not worked with the bombing of London."

"Ah, but the Hun is different. He understands no quarter and we learned this from the first war, that you Yanks came in on late."

"We do that, don't we. We broke the word of our Founding Fathers never to get involved in Europe's wars."

"But they are your wars too."

"Maybe you need a history lesson and then maybe you are right but tell me what is the basis for the argument against 'unconditional surrender', it may help me better interpret the analyses going back to U.S. Military intelligence and the State Department?"

"Simply this: That it will inadvertently bring the German Officer Corp more in line with Adolf Hitler forcing the Allies to serve a crushing blow after reducing their forces' numbers and destroying their cities."

"That's quite a large order Clive and do you actually believe that this is forcing the German Officer Corp to align itself more closely with Hitler?"

"Well that is the way we see it," he hesitated slightly, " no matter what."

"I would assume then that you are seeing the same communiqués that I'm seeing from Hitler to the field."

"Yes, indeed my dear." He said as he sipped his single malt and just looked off into the night with his pipe sitting idly in the Stork Club ashtray.

"I would love to get my hands on more of those communiqués in the original German text and even any personal communiqués, which would be beneficial; and it might be productive to talk with the source. It would all help me to back up your notion of the German Officer Corp coming more into line with him, which is a frightening scenario."

"Well, if it is 'love' for you to see these things we shall have to see what we can do as you are at the highest clearance level as it is and I do have some contact with the source."

"When can we set this up?"

"I do love you Madison but you Yanks are always in such a hurry, the war isn't going anyplace."

"Maybe that's the problem," Madison said with a little frustration in her voice.

"You are the impatient one aren't you."

"Just part of why you love me Clive."

"Ah, yes, you are right. There is something about this American in you besides your intelligence and charm that captured me the first time we met. Maybe I'm envious of your get up and go attitude, it is rather dashing in a woman rather appealing; and you seem to be spot on with many of your assessments."

"Clive, you have it inside yourself as well you just don't look at the clock enough and your ancestors didn't have to build a nation from scratch."

"We are your ancestors."

"Once removed."

"Touché dear Maddi." He said warmly with respect in his voice and a bit more sincerity. "I will be away again tomorrow at o' five hundred; this time for a fortnight but I will set something up with regard to the Hitler communiqués, over the next week; if I can."

"Thank you Clive and I'll give you any special interpretation that I feel I've found through my German so you can give me your input, especially with regard to the ill-effects of 'unconditional surrender". She said this knowing she was deceiving the man who had come to her rescue but this was war and not a game and he was doing the same thing with her.

She and Sam had also sent the final "Hitler Attempts" analysis up the intelligence chain of command just the previous Friday. They had delayed longer than they had intended while waiting for some additional corroborating data. It was sent up without fanfare and without response, as of yet. They of course sent the analysis assuming that both the first attempt and the second would fail which would give them more credibility in the depth and perception of their analysis and create a directive for closer attention to their future analysis on the subject. If the attempt, or attempts, succeeded they would immediately put forward the appropriate analysis, which had already been prepared, and they felt that this would not affect their credibility to any significant degree. They had decided not to put out the analyses of all three possible scenarios together which would include the first attempt failing and the second one succeeding or the first one succeeding. They decided not to send these two scenarios along with the analysis that they did send as this would reduce their credibility. They needed to roll the dice to some extent. Madison had not informed Clive of this as well and not because he did not have the clearance but these theories debunked the British criticism of the 'unconditional surrender' doctrine. Her analysis under 'Commodore' might at some point trickle down to him but she also knew that he would typically receive only 'Commodore's' strategic and tactical military analysis and in most cases as part of a general overall briefing and not singled out as having come from 'Commodore'.

When this was all over she hoped that she could sit in the same chair across this whicker table from Clive and be close friends laughing at some of the things that they took too seriously in the past.

◆   ◆   ◆

The next day was a Tuesday and, even with a war on, people were headed for the Fleet train station at 8:00 in the morning as Madison drove the little red MG TA down Elvetham Road. She had just turned off Fleet Road and past the entrance to the train station and then she took the left hand bend which had put her on Elvetham and the road that would take her to the cottage and to Sam.

It was again a chilly day as she turned right, onto the gravel of the small drive and pulled around the back of the cottage turning the engine off and setting the handbrake with a re-assuring short staccato clicking sound. She sat there for a moment and shook off a chill from the air that was enhanced by the thoughts that came from her conversation with Clive the night before.

She looked up just in time to see Sam through the back window lowering a cup of coffee from his lips as he smiled at her. She smiled back at him the warmth of the situation ruined by what she knew she would have to discuss, about the direction this war might take, with the man that she loved beyond everything else. They would be on the front lines with their intelligence in trying to keep the British under control.

As she opened the back door Sam just stood there with his coffee cup in hand and waited for her to speak. Sam was a smart man when it came to Madison. She knew it was because he loved her and listened to her that he knew her so well. He knew by her expression not to go to the back door and open it for her. She was in that mood where he needed to let her control the situation and say what was on her mind when she was ready. He knew her well and respected her even more and she loved him for it.

She just tossed her thin briefcase on the counter opposite the door and, before unbuttoning her coat, went up to Sam without looking him in the eyes, because she didn't need to, and wrapped her arms around him as he held her.

"Clive is going to get me to the source of the Hitler communiqués," she whispered, her head tucked into that warm and safe crook between his neck and shoulder.

"That sounds promising," he said flatly without emotion knowing there was more and she needed to control the emotion. Madison was complicated like this but she was also brilliant and Sam knew that they went hand-in-hand.

"The Brits are also going to use 'unconditional surrender' as a means to get their operations, or an operation, past the concept stage when they most want it and what frightens me is that General Montgomery's name came up. They actually believe in the doctrine from the way Clive spoke mentioning Ali Baba but they intend to use it in a 'dastardly' way to quote FDR or 'Victor'."

"The forty thieves, and the Russians that come with them."

"Yes, and they want to pacify them. The Russians like the doctrine, which makes the Brits happy because they can keep them at bay with it. And if this is any indication they may use this to get us to do even more to pacify 'Ali Baba' and 'Glyptic", in the future, along the lines of tactics or overall strategy that they deem important for themselves. And 'Victor' will fall for it because 'Colonel Warden' will talk him into it."

"Since when are we calling FDR and Churchill by their code names although 'warden' does seem to fit Churchill with regard to his relationship to FDR."

"Since this became a circus of the macabre; and it would appear that someone had a prophetic sense of humor."

"Well, I guess this job is not all that it was cracked up to be." Said Sam pulling back and looking down into Madison's eyes with a smile.

"I guess not." She said feeling the tension leave her. "I guess the pay-off is getting to tackle this problem which is multi-faceted."

"I'm assuming that the operations that are implied are center stage and not broad based."

"Yes, my feeling is that, like the Mediterranean campaign, they will want to come up with a campaign on the next front that will focus the spotlight on them to the detriment of the entire war campaign and if it fails it will prolong the war. And in the meantime they will want carte blanche on their area bombing of Germany and the German civilian population."

"They want pay-back."

"Yes and they will use 'unconditional surrender' as the excuse. Clive implied that this will give them the excuse for 'scorched earth' and they will also endeavor to increase the numbers of refugees in Germany. The Treaty of Versailles was payback and look where it got us, not to mention the loss of civilian life which has been unparalleled in this war. We're taking heavy casualties in the daylight bombing of military targets that the 8th Air Force is hitting just so we can hit those military targets and avoid civilians as much as possible and the Brits just want to fire up their cities."

"There is not much we can do about that except stick with the separate policy that Spaatz bought us, as best as possible."

"I met 'Bomber' Harris at a meeting with the RAF command and this man would never be in a position to head up US bomber command the way he heads up RAF Bomber Command; he seems to have a personal vendetta against the 'Hun'."

"We are going to find certain patterns through ground operations and equipment usage that will give us road signs to the German Army's overall strategy once the puzzle pieces start coming together more. As more operations get underway we'll be able to formulate firm models. The more that the German Army becomes involved in multiple operations the more we'll see." Stated Sam trying to get Madison to calm down through focusing.

"I know Sam but what happens when we see them going right and the Brits say they are going left on a major front strategically."

"We'll have to do our homework and use your powers of persuasion even if we have to go up to 'Victor' himself."

"My powers and your numbers Mr. 26," She smiled.

Sam laughed then, heading into the living room, he went to the right side of the fireplace saying, "I have something for you."

As Madison entered the room she saw Sam bending down over something and then she heard the unmistakable amplified crackle of the needle of a Victrola falling into the first grove of a record, and before she could say anything the mesmerizing French voice of Edith Piaf came out of the small brass horn that caught her eye as Sam stepped back with a smile. It wasn't a Victrola but it was a Singer, made in Chicago, and Sam found some humor in this.

"Where did you get that and where did you find that record?"

"Don't ask and I also have Glen Miller, Artie Shaw and a couple of others."

"I never have to wonder why I love you."

"Should I take that as a compliment?"

"Take it however you want", she said as she once again wrapped her arms around him kicking off her low heels as they started to turn slowly to the voice of Edith Piaf and her 'French Blues' as Madison called it.

Whispering in her ear Sam said, "Do you remember what you told me about your summers as a child on Nauset Heights, on Cape Cod; about looking down over the bluffs at the glistening water not knowing why you were so mesmerized until your parents finally took you down those long stairs to the beach? I remember you telling me how you were frightened the first time they took you down those steep wooden steps until you were at the waters edge with your toes barely touching the edge of the foamy ocean as the tide started to work its way in. You told me that once you felt the sea and heard its voice that day you were no longer afraid of the steps down because you knew that everything would be okay and that the steps where part of the journey to that mystery of the sea that so captivated you."

"How do you remember all of that, it was once that I told you that, one night after we first met."

"I never forgot it because you gave that experience to me that night in the way that you told it. You gave me something special that night and you didn't know it. You make a difference to more than just yourself, you make a difference to the lives around you in a way that you will never know but you do. I wrote this for you last night when I missed you so and had only the freesia for company. I wrote you about that mystery in the manner in which you inspired my thought that night. I want to read it to you while you're here in my arms listening to Edith Piaf."

And she said nothing but just looked up at him as he pulled a folded paper from his pocket unfolding it with one hand while he held her with the other. Pulling her back against his chest softly and still moving slowly to the music he read quietly just above the voice of Edith Piaf:

The sea knows no bounds until against the beach does it repose.
It runs itself relentlessly against the beach with the same
familiar crashing song, or a whisper, which is always new sweet
music to the ears.
The beach is fresh and new to me as a familiar friend once was
with every beat of its surf to heart it meets with song of future's
hope alive.
The ocean's color is cobalt blue at night, it is said, but the stars
do dapple over darkened sea to disappear and leave the blue
for morning's child; calm and new the canvas starts again with
ceaseless pounding of the heart such force is life of life itself
and sucks us like a moth to flame but to quench our thirst for
life reborn not to burn in a pyre from whence we came.
On the beach my feet do slow and childlike and naked they go
to carry me slowly to the water's edge which creeps forward at
my approach as if to cradle me to my birth before the warmth
of the womb I left telling me in the whisper of the surf that here
all men are children again with clear thought of whence it came
and where it will go again.
Good-bye dear surf that anoint my feet and rush headlong out to
sea only to come back to another's feet in this circle of life it is
meant to be.
Your wondrous body in a storm does crash the beach in a lover's
rage but in the calm to make such love against the beach which
swoons true lovers and alike to peace of heart and soul and
mind.

It is the beach and the ocean together that stand as God's true

lovers of Mankind.
Farewell this beach of mine I've shared, it is not sorrow that I
seek for the rapid fires of time you will quench and bring me
home once more.

    Sam could feel her tears as they warmed his neck and he found himself with tears in his eyes for the tears she needed to shed.

    After a moment she pulled her head from his shoulder and, looking him in the eyes, reached up and kissed him and then kissed him again and they feel into each other's arms to the pleading words of Edith Piaf's love lost.

Sunday, March 14, 1943

It was Sunday morning March 14, 1943. Clive was still away, actually longer than planned but he had delivered to Madison the one request she had of him and that was the source of the Hitler communiques. The source name was 'Fagin' at what she now, after a very recent security briefing, knew to be the top secret Ultra code breaking team but she did not know that it was located at Bletchley Park, 60 miles north of London, and she remained curious about the location, being an analyst. She had a secure line to him but for the most part they had used military couriers. The relationship started exactly two weeks ago Friday when she received a call in the lair of the Commodore Group.

Her direct and secure line rang that late afternoon near the end of the day for most and when she picked it up the male voice on the other end had simply asked, "Madison?"

"Yes, who are you and how did you come by this number?"

"Clive sent me about a mutual friend with an abbreviated mustache, do you know the one?"

"Why yes, I think I do."

"I'll send a courier to 'Commodore' on Monday to verify everything. Also, please read and sign the document he will be carrying, my name is 'Fagin'", and the phone went dead.

This Sunday morning Madison was going over several weeks of information 'Fagin' had supplied her with and it was like looking through a looking glass with the full text in German as deciphered from code and as she had requested. She also knew, through her recent secret briefing, that the messages were going out through a military cipher machine code named 'Enigma' which weighed 26 pounds. Why the weight mattered in the briefing she didn't know but it put a curious smile on her face for her briefer to wonder about. The important fact about 'Enigma' was that it could only be interpreted by another machine with the proper settings. This told Madison that Hitler's communiqués were probably unedited, as only the chosen recipient would see them. It actually allowed him to rant and rave even more than when he had a larger audience. She was excited about what was being revealed so easily right in front of her, especially in some of the personal communiqués, which she had also requested. The Goebbels study that the 'head doctors' were running for her was now not as important but it did confirm that Goebbels was Hitler's doppelganger and this, as well, had its uses. Of course she couldn't tell Milton and his group that they were right on the money but she smiled to herself, that they were, as a compliment to their work.

She was still smiling when her secure line rang. She wondered who would be calling on a Sunday not knowing that she would be there. "Hello."

"This is 'Fagin', I have some news that couldn't wait."

"How did you know I was here." She said impressed.

"You are on the premises of the Home of the British Army." He calmly stated allowing for conversation instead of just a short cryptic communication as was usually the case.

"The biggest mistake is to miss the obvious." She admitted.

"Apparently you hit the target with the first half of your double attempt analysis."

Madison at first could not say a word, it had been just over three weeks since they had issued the 'Hitler Attempts' paper without one word back or request for a presentation. Usually an analysis of this importance would require a presentation in front of high ranking intelligence and military authorities but it hadn't generated a peep from higher up, in part, because it was sent up without a priority designation attached to it. So, she knew what he meant and she also knew that, by his words, the attempt had failed. She had been waiting for this as the first key to pushing the analysis heavily in the proper direction; the second key would be the result of the second attempt if it occurred, which she knew it would. "When?" was all she could say.

"Yesterday and the little man is not aware. I'm sending a courier your way, please be there, and you will be getting an expected surprise."

"Fagin."

"Yes Mum."

"Thank you."

"No Mum, thank you for the magic; It's been on my watch list since your analysis went out, cheers Mum." And he hung up.

She was elated that her analysis was put in the hands of what she now knew to be Ultra. It had that much importance without having to be legitimized through a presentation. She was also rewarded with the importance of the event to high command by the way 'Fagin' had, for a brief moment, been personal and complimentary. She couldn't wait for the courier to arrive. She also knew that the statement "……..the little man is not aware" had great importance. It also meant that she had a communiqué from one of the conspirators to another and no doubt it would be in very cryptic German, but Ultra was able to see it because, unknown to her until just now, she had them looking for it. She also knew from 'Fagin's' words that they probably would not have picked it up out of the communiques if not for the analysis that she and Sam had put together. Their paper had Ultra scrutinizing every communiqué that came in, no matter how trivial, for any connection.

The courier arrived an hour later on his motor bike and seemed to be out of breath as he greeted Madison, checked her ID and had her sign for the pouch.

She could not get back to her desk quickly enough to retrieve her corresponding key to the locked pouch. Sitting down on the old wooden swivel desk chair, that had been 'nicked' "…from a Guards maja ouh'll never know ot 'it em in the bum when e sits down," by her British orderly, she heard that old familiar squeak of reassurance. She sat in the wonderful gift and opened her middle right-hand draw to pull the key off of a small framing nail placed at the rear right side of the draw. This key had been a gift of the first courier two weeks before.

She unlocked the pouch and removed the 14"x9" gray envelope marked SECRET: MINISTRY OF DEFENSE and sealed with old-fashioned sealing wax which was red, hard brittle, and had to be broken by taking it in both hands and snapping it in half. With a snap of the Ministry seal Madison retrieved the documents still in German, as she always requested now so she would not receive someone else's interpretation. The communiqué was from a General Henning von Tresckow to Admiral Canaris. Her jaw just about dropped and her blood rushed, here was the expected surprise 'Fagin' had mentioned and she had let it pass as just part of the importance of the overall communiqué, no wonder he seemed excited as well. Canaris had finally come active in their analysis, they had been expecting it and 'Fagin' had been made aware of this.

Madison translated the 'old' more formal, non-colloquial, German text to simply read: *Dear Admiral thank you for the condolences on my Snowzer but fortunately he is still with us and is as stubborn as ever. Unfortunately the brandy to be delivered to Wolfsschanze, with Der Fuhrer, arrived broken. Der Fuhrer would appear not to be disturbed by this and was on time.*

Faithfully, Henning von Treschow

She found it interesting that the communiqué was signed in the familiar whether this was a slip or not; she assumed it was not as he was still a young man of 42 and was known to have been sharp when he was a stockbroker for a few years after WWI before rejoining the army in 1924. She and Sam were consuming as much research as they could with regard to members of the German general staff officer ranks and it was making it easier to see simple things that helped add up to a bigger picture.

The communiqué was also accompanied by a much longer handwritten note that had a red stamp over it which read: **DESTROY UPON READING**.

Commodore: *You should know that General von Tresckow's dog is named Adolf. We think that it is an inside joke, Germanic humor if you will, as Hitler hates smaller dogs and refers to them as " push dogs." He will not allow a picture* *to be taken of himself with any dog other than his Alsatian 'Blondi'. In 1941 a German army photographer snapped a photo of Hitler and von Ribbentrop, with Hitler sitting in a chair next to a wire-haired terrier on another chair, the photo was published; Hitler went into a rage about the army plotting against him hence the importance of the aforementioned dog. You should also know that General von Tresckow has been on our watch list for some time now as an anti-fascist. He has not come up in our communiqués until now. Along with some other highly classified information on this individual and the fact that a communiqué with Canaris makes little sense, as they have never appeared to be acquaintances and they do not work with each other, this communiqué can only mean one thing. Further to this it is a potentially provocative communiqué within German ranks for the same reasons I have previously listed. Being such, we feel that there may be an ongoing conspiracy with a second attempt lined up in case the first was a failure. Your analysis tied this all together and we now believe that this represents the first attempt and a second attempt is immanent within the next week as your analysis mentioned. We feel that a degree of risk was taken in sending this communique and it could only mean that Canaris may be an integral part in the second back-up attempt, not just one player among many. Again, we feel it will occur soon, following your paper, which was prepared assuming that failure of the first attempt would be discovered. The second attempt would have to occur quickly under the cover of chaos as your analysis so clearly points out and therefore it would have been planned along with the first plot. Although this first attempt has not as yet been discovered it is assumed that the second attempt will still follow shortly. We also think that the 'Brandy" refers to a bomb placed on Hitler's private plane which arrived safely at Wolfsschanze, or Hitler's military headquarters in East Prussian, yesterday 13 March, with our man on board. As indicated, please destroy this after reading. Thank you Commodore; well done.*

Admiral Canaris, head of German intelligence, was now an active player in this deadly game. As Sam would say '…he's thrown all of his chips into the pot,' but his cards were still unknown and Canaris was difficult at best to figure out. He was known to be an intelligent man of few words who worked quietly behind the scenes. That's why this communiqué was important as well. There was virtually no communication coming out of or going into his office so this held additional importance even if it was only directed to him personally and were truly just an innocuous personal greeting, but this wasn't. They had Canaris now in sight and they might get more communications which would let them see a little bit more into his world. The only insight that they had up to this point came through the communication he carried out second person with Bishop Bell of England after the invasion of Poland, and the communications from his offices to Hitler which appeared to be purposely misleading the Fuhrer. It had been thought that he would be part of an attempt, now it was known that he was probably a leader, as well he should be if involved.

Madison had just recently received what little background research she could on Admiral Wilhelm Canaris born on January 1, 1887 to a wealthy family in Aplerbeck, Germany. He had joined the German navy in 1905 reaching the rank of Lieutenant by 1911. He took part in the Battle of the Falklands and wound up in an internment camp where he escaped in August 1915. After returning to Germany in October 1915 he was sent to work for the intelligence service for U-boat operations in the Mediterranean where he worked as an undercover agent until finally getting command of a U-boat in 1917. After the war he was involved in secretly building the German U-boat force, as far as MI6 could tell, and in 1933 became head of German intelligence. The man had an interesting past but that is where the information on the man himself stopped.

The report she had read came from MI6 through British Military intelligence and due to her clearance it was unedited. They hadn't even paid attention to the fact that she was an American. Maybe it was checked out through British military intelligence under the clearance of 'Commodore' located in Aldershot, which had been set up by the British and therefore they were not concerned that anyone other than a British intelligence officer, with high clearance, would see it. The report indicated that MI6 had been actively working Canaris to become a British agent, which Madison found interesting but knew enough to know that the man was devoted to his country, if not his Furhrer. The report was in length and covered the activities of an MI6 agent up to his 'working' of Canaris. His history was in the report to establish his 'spy' pedigree and credentials. The report included information about this agent and his contacts back to March of 1938 when he had sent a directive to the then Prime Minister Neville Chamberlain stating that Hitler would be removed by the German military if the British stood behind Czechoslovakia. The report also indicated that this agent had warned Chamberlain in August of 1939 that Hitler had decided to attack Poland. In both cases the Prime Minister had totally ignored the information. This little bit of information once again sent warning signals to the core of Madison's being with regard to British war politics.

Sam and Madison where now waiting for the other shoe to drop and every day that passed, from that Sunday, was nerve racking as a second attempt within a week's time was important to prove that the plot was well planned, especially if the first attempt was not discovered as was the case, and that the plotters were many and highly placed. They needed this to occur to show that their analyses were well founded so that they would be moved to a higher level in the future planning of the Allies. If this did occur, which meant that the plotters were highly placed, it would make it dangerous for them all if the second attempt failed, and this second failure would no doubt extend the war but not adversely effect the benefits of 'unconditional surrender'. The doctrine of 'unconditional surrender' would have the German High Command at odds with Hitler and more concerned with the future of their country after the war with the fear of 'scorched earth' constantly in their thinking and influencing their moves.

Madison did not miss a day in her office while Sam toiled at the cottage putting the pieces of their analysis together to get a better reading on the German High Command and Army and to, at the end of the day, create a "crystal ball" which would allow them to see major German military moves before they occurred. 'Crystal Ball' was the private code that Sam and Madison used for the predictability, or end result, of the completed puzzles, partly determined by their models coming together, which would allow them to read major German movements and spot the eventual 'pinnacle'. 'Crystal Ball' was their private code as actually using this as an operational code would put doubt in the mind of the reader. To them 'Crystal Ball' was as real as could be and was a true time machine into the future and future operations of the enemy, better than H.G. Wells. Nothing like this had been accomplished before.

On Sunday March 21, 1943 at 07:00 Madison's private line rang once again and almost stopped her heart as she was deeply engrossed in some of the communications between Rommel and

Hitler. The North African campaign was on and Hitler had demanded that Rommel keep him informed everyday, which had benefited Montgomery earlier on in the North African campaign even before Operation TORCH had been launched. They knew Rommel's every move as a result and this became a wealth of information and an operational blueprint of how German armor was used for maneuver. They also received very thorough information on equipment and its state, which contributed to the manner of German maneuver and clearly related military maneuver to statistics for Sam. He was elated by the information Madison and her group were supplying to him through these communications.

She had been thinking of this when the phone rang and yanked her back to the present, sitting at her desk with a pile of classified documents that would have to be destroyed once the analysis was complete and recorded cryptically in notes which where kept under lock and key, and guard. The cryptic notes were taken to the cottage, which both she and Sam felt was secure, and translated and discussed with Sam who put it together with numbers for an overall report with vague reference to 'classified-U' reports, which meant that the information used was verified. Madison had been in the middle of this and the phone just sent her heart into a quick panic before she picked up the receiver.

"Hello."

"Fagin here, I have some news for you. The gang tried again yesterday but they did not make any noise; they seem to be related in more ways than one. I'll send another courier. You are bang on; Two for two, you seem to have a crystal ball"

Madison's heart jumped again when she heard the innocent use of the phrase with 'crystal ball' in it. How fitting. "It may be that we do Mr. Fagin."

"Well it would appear that you are my best thieves of the future, true Dickensian characters."

Madison chuckled, "So you're the leader of the gang."

'Fagin' laughed, "It would appear that the gang is leading me Mum, more magic. Have a good morning."

"And you," said Madison as he hung up.

Once again the courier arrived within an hour and Madison tried to think where Ultra was located by the travel time on a fast motorbike but then she knew that 'Fagin' would have already thought of that and called her when he knew the rider was near an hour out from her. He also knew she was there at 7 in the morning. She was no doubt being watched and no doubt they knew about the cottage and Sam, and this told her too that their work was assuredly secure. She wouldn't tell Sam as there would be no reason to and maybe they were safer with MI5 watching out over them and then too the memory of two faked fatal accidents that split she and Sam to begin with came back to her thoughts. They were important but they were expendable too, depending on whom they became more important to. She knew they would have to tread lightly with the presentation of their analysis, which would go counter to British thinking, as it started to carry more weight. And as a result to the double-'attempt' within a week the weight of their analysis was most likely established. They would have to tread lightly but this did not mean that they would not confront head-on something they thought was militarily ill-conceived with potentially disastrous consequences.

Madison was once again in a hurry to get back to her desk and that duplicate key hanging by the framing nail at the rear of the middle right-hand draw. She was not allowed to remove the key from her desk by protocol. She could only therefore open the pouches once she was seated at it. She could really do what she wanted but the protocol rules made sense, even though she did bring her cryptic notes 'home', or what was becoming home, to the cottage. Protocols were sort of like coming to a full stop at a stop sign even with no traffic in sight; good practice to prevent a future disaster.

Madison once again snapped the red seal of the Ministry of Defense on the 14"x9" grey envelope marked SECRET: MINISTRY OF DEFENSE and removed the documents.

She was curious about 'Fagin's' phraseology , "……but they did not make any noise;…." and, "…. they seem to be related in more ways than one."; but then she already had a good idea as to what this all meant.

As she pulled out the document, the German text was on top and once again it was cryptic but this time it was in familiar German. It was addressed to Field Marshall Hans Gunther von Kluge whose chief of staff was General Henning von Treschow who had sent the communiqué to Canaris about the first attempt. It read:

Herr Field Marshall
Our Leader decided to leave the exhibit at the arsenal early
today, which was unfortunate as he did not get a chance to see
everything.

On another topic; as you know, I have had trouble with my
meals and the anti-acid, that you suggested, has removed all
trace of any symptoms. It may, after all, be the field rations as
this seems to happen when I am with the troops. But then maybe
it is the high explosive one can experience in the field rather
suddenly but fortunately not in Berlin where since 1940 one at
least knows of the 'Tommy' in the sky before he arrives, with
little accuracy and not as of late. As an intelligence officer the
stress can manifest itself in many ways but the evidence as to
why is non-existent, even to your intelligence officer.

Once again, thank you for your personal help to a devoted
officer, I am sure that my work will be much more efficient and
effective in the future.

Colonel Rudolf von Gertsdorff.

This was accompanied again by handwritten note that had a red stamp over it which read: **DESTROY UPON READING**.

Commodore: *The enclosed communiqué was received yesterday, 20 March, and we know that Hitler was in Berlin at the Zeughaus or the old arsenal which, as you may know, is now a museum to the Great War as an undeserved defeat and the center of Nazi propaganda. Colonel Rudolf von Gertsdorff is chief of intelligence for Field Marshall Hans Gunther von Kluge. General Henning von Treschow is the Field Marshall's chief of staff and as you will notice all three by the 'von' prefix are aristocratic. This 'plot' seems to be taking form and it seems* *to be well established in the higher echelons of the Old German Officer Corp and those that represent its tradition and core just as your analysis indicated. We believe this represents your 'second attempt' for several reasons. The connection to the Field Marshall's staff is the first one and this is also the first non-official communique that we can detect between the Field Marshall and his head of intelligence. Secondly, the communiqué is also uncharacteristically in the familiar form for a junior officer, albeit a colonel, to write to a general officer in the German Army. Thirdly, the letter is somewhat inane for this particular intelligence officer, or for any intelligence officer for that matter, to write and we believe that it was the quickest means to communicate to the Field Marshall, and the rest of the plotters, that Hitler is not aware of the attempt and that there is no evidence to reveal such an attempt. This communiqué would not stand out to any German counter-intelligence group and particularly not Canaris's as we feel that Canaris would squelch, to use a Yank term, any such suspicion. We also feel that the Gestapo would not be alerted as this communiqué would never reach them unless deemed suspicious by Canaris's group or a specialized group set up by the Gestapo itself to intercept such transmissions, a specialized group of which we have no evidence. Further to this and lastly, the colonel does not spend time in the field and the reference to Berlin being bombed by the RAF in 1940 is a sore point with German general officers as we have noticed due to the promise by Goering and Hitler, before the event, that it would never happen. The first bombing of Berlin seems to be a watershed of enlightenment among other events that started to bring the plotters together and galvanize them. We assume that the plotters are safe up to this point and that at some future date another attempt may take place. We agree with your analysis that in order to keep the attempts compartmentalized and secure that only two attempts were planned together, the first one on 13 March and the this attempt on 20 March. They were putting their odds on success. As both attempts have seemed to have gone undetected we assume that another plot will, as mentioned in your analysis, be planned sometime in the future. We can only assume that because the plot went undetected, and that it may have been based on time, as it references Hitler leaving early, along with the subtle and obvious but cryptic mention of explosives, that it was another bomb plot. As indicated, please destroy this after reading. Thank you, and again, well done Commodore.*

Madison was elated as well as concerned. The two attempts had given more credence to the reports that she and Sam were issuing and therefore more latitude with regard to their analyses and conclusions. But the two actual attempts also changed the dynamics of their "Hitler Attempts" analysis as the analysis did not take into account the possibility that the attempts would go undetected. The analysis relied heavily on the fact that at least one of the two would be revealed if not both and that Hitler would take retribution on a segment of the Officer Corp. They would have to revise their analyses but this would be productive in that it would get some fresh analysis in front of faces that were now acutely aware of the effectiveness of such analysis coming out of 'Commodore'. It would also seem that the plotters were protected for another attempt which if it came soon would leave much of their analysis intact, but Madison knew that it probably wouldn't come for many months as the plotters tried to re-group while maintaining security. They would have to insure security by laying low for some time and watching, and once they knew they were clear from suspicion they would have to start re-communicating with each other which meant reestablishing the network almost from scratch to prevent suspicion from arising and, more importantly, to prevent leaks. Madison knew that it would take a long, long time.

'Fagin' had indicated that the 1940 bombing of Berlin was a 'watershed' event for the plotters. This flew, somewhat, in the face of the 'assassination attempts' analysis of which 'Fagin' no doubt had a complete copy. The analysis indicated that the 'unconditional surrender' doctrine was the catalyst. She believed that the 1940 bombing of Berlin became a rallying cry, if you will, for the plotters, over two years after the initial bombing, after the doctrine of 'unconditional surrender' had been revealed at the end of January.

Madison also felt that the conspiracy had reached the heights of the core of the Old Prussian or German Officer Corp, or the elite of the Officer Corp, and that there was no turning back. She believed that this penetration, to those levels of aristocratic power and influence, which were indicated to be better than they expected, might have already achieved what their paper said a purge would achieve as a result of one of the attempts being discovered. She would have to trouble shoot this with Sam and game out the possibilities and its potential in relationship to their initial document.

It seemed Clive might be away for the duration of the war as he was still not home well past his fortnight prediction. The only time that she knew of his whereabouts was on that rare occasion that he was at Eisenhower's headquarters, the rest, as he would say, was, "….rather hush-hush as you know my dear." She wondered why then the Eisenhower visits were not as well 'hush-hush' as the frequency and placing of visits to that headquarters by a colonel in his situation could reveal a great deal to someone with her knowledge. It really didn't matter but she knew that he would mention these meetings to try to use her to clarify something in the meeting that he needed to have an answer or response to for his superiors and what better person than his wife who was not only a Yank but as well one of their " desk spyglasses" as he would affectionately refer to her once and a while.

She headed straight to the cottage late in the day, actually almost suppertime, after finishing up with the correspondence between Rommel and Hitler. She had correlated their attitudes and comments with not only the statistics on equipment that Rommel was giving Hitler in that correspondence, or reporting, but as well with the statistics that her group had put together during the previous week. Sam would find this a wealth of valuable information in modeling the German Army and its responses, which would allow them to put the puzzle pieces together as they went along on the way to determining the 'pinnacle', or the high water mark of the war and the beginning of the end.

◆   ◆   ◆

The familiar soft cascading sound of her tires moving slowly over the small pebbles and pushing them forward as she drove over the short driveway to the back of the cottage was an ever sweet melody to her ears these days because she knew that she was truly home and that Sam would be at the other end waiting for her.

She pulled up in the MG TA crunching to a stop as the little car slowed and settled on the pebbles. She could see Sam through the back window working with a bottle and a corkscrew and she knew that he was opening one of her favorite wines. She also noticed the glass martini pitcher sitting on the counter with its glass stir rod resting in the clear liquid.

As she came through the door and once again tossed her thin briefcase, with classified research, on the counter Sam turned and had a martini glass in his hand and a smile on his face.

"I never know quite when to expect you but I am getting trained to be intuitive, actually you are starting to form a statistical pattern so I used both to give me a jump on making some rather dry, dry martini's; have to go sparingly with the vermouth as you never know when we'll get a another bottle with a war on and all. And I have a nice hard to get Merlot Bordeaux breathing for you, rich and dark as you like it."

"That's the best excuse for trying to get me drunk, and by-the-way you can hear this MG half way to the Links Pub from here?"

"I've been found out on two accounts."

"And I love you for it," she said softly as he handed her the martini.

"I have a steak that I got from a madman professor I know at Cambridge who won't say anything other than that a Yank met his daughter in London and gave him several steaks earmarked for a general. He said, ' The lad has a gift of making things appear magically and he said the general would rather like us to enjoy a bit of America through these steaks straight from Texas.' I can probably guess that there is one steaming general right about now as it would appear that the 'lad' made a whole box of these disappear. He also threw in a couple of cartons of Home Run cigarettes for the professor; and who knows where those came from but you know they had to be special ordered for someone important as we only see Luckys."

They both laughed and then Madison observed, " Besides the 50,000 some odd troops that came through here drawn from the three American divisions already in Britain and added to those shipping directly from Virginia for TORCH I guess our build-up here is starting to be noticeable."

"I would say and with that we become less noticeable."

"That's true," she said with a smile on her face.

"What's up, why the little talk and the smile."

"It's happened, they tried again."

"When?"

"Yesterday and it failed."

"So events will start to unfold."

"Not quite, this attempt as well went undetected."

"How could that be?"

"It appears to have been another bomb that didn't go off."

"Well, the bombs make sense as it is the most covert way to assassinate someone and you don't have to be present or anywhere near the site but timing and the complexity of any bomb vs. a gun leaves too much room for failure. We'll just have to rework our analysis, the outcome will be the same."

"That's just it, the outcome will be the same and it has been made easier for us to determine that as the officer who made this attempt is from the aristocratic side of the German military or part of the foundation or core of the German Officer Corp just like the last officer, and they are both on the staff of Field Marshal von Kluge."

"So it would appear that the Officer Corp, or at least the Old Prussian Officer Corp, is united and squarely behind this without the necessity of a purge as we had predicted. So we have skipped that step and actually jumped ahead because it will keep more players in the game who might have been killed in a purge."

"Exactly my thinking and we can put this in a follow-up paper in such a way as to further support our theory on 'unconditional surrender' and as well form some of our models around this end goal even if Hitler remains viable to the end."

"So it's a good day." Said Sam as he picked up his martini and touched it to Madison's, which was raised.

They both sipped their martinis and just looked at each other. Then Madison spoke first after a few seconds. "I have some interesting, unadulterated, equipment statistics for you accompanied by comments from two of the best professors on the subject that you can have: Irwin Rommel and Hitler himself."

Sam's eyebrow just went up, he looked at her then took another sip while contemplating the glass with a far off look then he smiled and looked at her again and swallowed the sip of martini.

"I knew you'd appreciate that and I have it all in the briefcase." as she nodded toward the case on the counter while taking a sip of her martini.

"You've got me on the edge of my statistician's seat but first this steak and the Merlot that I have breathing for you, before it goes to vinegar."

"Now you know I'd never let a good bottle go to vinegar."

"I seem to recall…"

"I know the story, no need to repeat it."

"I never want to put anything on hold with you again not even a bottle of wine because like that wine it will go away from us before we know, especially in this world of ours."

"You're sounding more philosophical than pragmatic the way a statistician is supposed to think but I know, and you're right. I'm thinking too far ahead to ending this all and being in New York City and on the Hudson with you again that I'm missing these little islands that we have in this chaotic stream."

"Now who's being philosophical? I tell you what, we can start that little magazine we discussed just after we first met and use that for our practical outlet and the rest of our time can be spent making sure that good wine doesn't go to vinegar, good bread doesn't go stale and the beauty of the seasons are not missed."

"'The Pragmatist' I had almost forgotten about that dream but wasn't that our romantic way of saving this world from itself and preserving 'Freedom of Speech' which does fine on its own in the States?"

"And what's wrong with romance," Sam responded and then adding a little more weight to the conversation, "and freedom of speech in America, unlike Nazi German?"

"Absolutely nothing," said Madison as she started to feel the giddy lightheadedness of a strong martini on an empty stomach because, as usual, she had forgotten to eat all day.

"I'm so glad you agree so how about that steak and then some real romance by the fire, if you're lucky."

"Whaddaya mean if Uh'm lucky."

"That's just what I said because, as I see it, if I don't get that dinner done quickly your one martini may turn into one tee many martoonies."

And with this she just started laughing and stammered between laughs, "Thaas jus like the 'where the fugouwee tribe.'" And she started laughing some more.

"You see what I mean, I either cut you off right now or feed you quickly or both. Ah, the joy of simple humor," he stated as he worked on the dinner. He had pre-prepared everything except the steak and short of a grill he pan fried it in an old American cast iron grill pan with ridging. He had found the pan in a second hand shop and the owner had told him that it was ironic because the pan had been in his shop since the end of the first World War when an American soldier left it there for sale before returning home and that now another Yank was going to buy it, so he gave it to Sam without charge.

The dinner was set in no time and Madison was able to eat before the martini won the battle.

They sat and shared this wonderful 38oz. Porterhouse Steak with Glen Miller's Moonlight Serenade playing in the background and it reminded them of a time before the war when they had gone to Peter Luger's in Brooklyn. It was so reminiscent of home as they both had their Merlot and where enjoying their shared steak.

"As soon as we get home we'll have to go back to Brooklyn," subtly remarked Sam while concentrating on the steak and not Madison.

"Don't tell me that you've become a Dodgers fan," said Madison with feigned disbelief in her voice.

"What?", blurted Sam looking up from his steak.

"A Brooklyn Dodgers fan, you were talking about becoming one?" joked Madison.

"A what? Brooklyn, Luger's then the Bronx and Yankee Stadium", smiled Sam.

"I miss home."

"So do I", added Sam as he got up to change the record.

"Maybe spring will come early this year at home, it's almost April."

Sam turned after putting on some Arty Shaw and came back to her, while she looked at him, leaned over kissed her on the forehead and then the lips, "Baby, we'll make our own spring here, the daffodils will be up in no time, from what I remember from last year. It's beautiful the way they pop up in all the towns; we can imagine that we're home for moments at a time."

"But we'll still have the war right here in our laps."

   With this Sam pulled her up from her chair and started to dance with her to Arty Shaw then he pulled back and looked into her beautiful gray-green eyes and kissed her softly and briefly, then again and again until they were in a soft embrace and the dishes would stay where they were for the night.

Sunday, March 22, 1943 ---- The Chimney Sweep Cottage

Sam awoke early the next morning and just watched the serenity on Madison's face as she slept, at least she seemed to be at peace in her sleep. He didn't want to disturb her but she could feel him looking at her and she started to smile as she slowly opened her eyes.

"Morning handsome, is that what they call sweeping a girl right off her feet?"

"It was Arty Shaw," he said with a smile as he ran his fingers through her hair.

With her eyes now closed again and delight in her voice from his fingers titillating her scalp she said, "I think it was the martini, the Merlot and the statistician."

"I told you that martini would get you into trouble," laughed Sam.

"I was given the wrong information. I was once told that statisticians do it strictly by the numbers." She stated with a devious giggle, "I think you break the rule book."

"And I think you let the martini get to your head," he responded with a chuckle.

"It did do that and I have a headache."

"Ah, too dry."

"Funny."

"Stay here and I'll make some coffee and I want you to have some breakfast."

"Uck."

"That was intelligent, your professors would be proud."

"Speaking of which, we need to go through the works of professors Rommel and Hitler this morning before I head back to the group."

"We'll need to do that then I have to head up to Cambridge for the next two days to do some catch-up but I'll go through everything that your team has given me recently along with your new material."

"Sounds like a plan."

"And you'll also have something to eat while we go over things, I need you healthy and alert; you can't just live on black coffee and, should I say, martinis."

And with that she caught him in the face with the pillow as he now stood in the doorway in his blue and white striped boxer shorts with his legs crossed at the ankles.

"Are my boxers that bad?" he said with a nonplused straight face.

"I love you." She laughed as he turned and headed down the narrow and step stairway to the kitchen.

◆   ◆   ◆

Sam went over the papers that were in her briefcase while Madison munched on her toast tentatively and had pure Columbian black coffee, no sugar, out of an old Buffalo Ware dinner's mug that she loved. She loved it partly because it reminded her of home.

"This is absolutely magnificent stuff. Not only do they give me the numbers of equipment that is in North Africa now but I'm getting what both of them deem to be necessary. As this relationship goes on Rommel, along with other generals and field officers, will start to get their needs in line with what Hitler deems appropriate. There will eventually be a synergy to this. They will meet halfway and by the looks of it Hitler is reformulating what is currently an effective force structure in the German Army and this will eventually hold true for both the Wehrmacht and the SS Panzer units. A pattern will evolve out of all of this. Whose brilliant idea was it that Rommel would communicate his daily moves to Hitler; don't tell me professor Adolf. They're actually starting to give us a primer, or Rosetta Stone to interpret our two models working together much quicker than if we were to look at them separately and try to pull out anomalies or specific patterns, especially with one model having active neuroses. If we get a primer to work with then our puzzle pieces will jump together."

Madison just smiled over the top of her coffee mug as she warmed both hands around its broad and shaped sides, "I see that you're happy with yourself."

"I couldn't be more so, these guys are giving away the farm and they don't know it. What do you think of Hitler's reaction to Rommel?"

"Well, I read it in the German original and I could see it even more clearly; there is a degree of respect and admiration from Hitler that I haven't seen before, quite the opposite of communiqués with General Paulus even if that were not a losing situation. That communication was perfunctory at best with regard to Paulus and his men, this is almost dependant as though Hitler is putting his last hope in the man."

"I got the same feeling, I'd say that Irwin Rommel is our boy and is key to other events."

"I would agree. I'd really like to have Milton's team see this but I can't. What I can do is have them keep an eye on Goebbels and get his attitude on Rommel and we may get a little of the doppelganger effect so that they can confirm this."

"That sounds good. Can you give me a ride to the station? I have to catch the 9:10 into London."

"Are you sure you can fit alright, maybe you want to take your bicycle?", she said with a grin as he always deferred to his bicycle saying the MG was too cramped when she asked him if he wanted a ride.

"My knee is bothering me again."

"Didn't your teachers tell you not to run cross-country."

"They were just jealous and this dampness is killing it."

"I think I can give an old guy like you a ride."

"Gee, thanks, that made it feel better."

She went up to him kissed him on the lips touched his knee, then moved her hand up while he was rinsing the two plates of the last of the cheese residue and toast crumbs, "Now does that feel better."

"That's trouble, but the knee does feel better," he said as he put the second plate in the dryer and dried his hands on the white dishtowel hanging from a small towel stand next to the sink.

"It just needs a little warmth. Going my way now?," she smiled as she started to put her coat on.

"I'm helplessly in your care."

She leaned back with a serious face and kissed him, and said, "I love you."

"I love you too baby."

"Please be safe."

"There aren't too many dangers in Cambridge maybe with the exception of that madman professor and his connection with a general."

"I mean in London as you pass through."

"Baby the Blitz ended two years ago."

"Bethnal Green Station, 173 people died there 19 days ago and 62 were children," she said as tears started to form in her eyes at the thought of the children.

"That was a freak accident, they panicked and couldn't see and the stairway down to the tube had no railing; it was a new station."

"I don't care, the war brought this about and I don't want to lose you."

"You won't lose me, this knee couldn't take the hike to 6/26/01 right now so I'm staying right here."

And she laughed through tears because he remembered and she knew that promise was important to him because it was important to her.

They held each other by the car for a few minutes and he gently rocked her back and forth, then he lowered his 6'2" frame into the MG, which wasn't bad once you were sitting with your legs extended. Then they drove to the station and Sam marveled at the fact that Madison was a better driver than most men he knew. She could probably race that MG TA and win in its class if there were such a thing. His daydreaming of this stopped as she turned into the station parking lot.

They kissed, said their good-byes, to last for the next couple of days, and then Sam hoisted himself out of the now comfortable

MG seat, apologetically stepped on the seat, opened the door and stepped out.

"A shoe print to remember you by for the next two days, I won't wash it off," she said with a laugh knowing that there was no mark or dirt left behind on the seat.

"I love you too baby, see you in a couple of days.

And with that Sam shut the door, turned, and headed toward the front of the station. He turned to look back just in time to see Madison smile lovingly at him in a way only she could do and then put the little MG in gear and pull out of the parking lot moving through the gears on the car with perfect precision. Then he turned back towards the station and headed for the platform to catch his train to London and then on to Cambridge from there.

Spring 1943

On April 18, Prime Minister John Curin of Australia was critical of the "Europe First" policy with regard to the war in the Pacific by stating "…the Australian Government accepts the global strategy… but it does not accept a flow of war material, notably aircraft, that does not measure up to the requirements of a holding war." Both Sam and Madison had been against the "Europe First" or The Rainbow–5 war plan as designated by the Americans which was dictated, in a sense, by the December 7, 1940 letter from Churchill to FDR and reaffirmed during the ARCADIA Conference in January. But that was water long over the dam from their standpoint as they had moved to supporting ROUNDUP or the early cross-channel invasion of the European continent which was most likely going to be by-passed as well, at least for 1943, for Churchill's Mediterranean 'policy'. Some parts of Rainow-5 they agreed with in the context of BOLERO or building up troops in England and sending relief to the Pacific but instead they got TORCH and the Mediterranean.

On Monday April 19, Milton Lennox's team confirmed, through the Goebbels doppelganger view of Adolf Hilter, that Irwin Rommel was Hitler's golden boy and that they could expect that wherever Irwin Rommel popped up Adolf Hitler had his focus for one reason or another. They qualified this by saying that the focus could be intense and primary and it could also change abruptly, such was the individual of Adolf Hitler.

On April 21, a neutral source confirmed American intelligence in the Pacific that the Japanese were executing American prisoners of war. Madison, reading the intelligence which was passed along as a warning of what might come once Americans were in Europe, screamed inside and crumpled the document once again angry about the "Europe First" policy which left thousands of American and Filipino troops to die on the vine and rot in Japanese hell holes. There were confirmations in the intelligence community that hundreds of American prisoners had been bayoneted by the Japanese while being marched to POW camps after the fall of Bataan and Corregidor. Australia was now in the middle of it and the Prime Minister was a little bit more than concerned about the policy on the other side of the world.

Again, BOLERO could have taken place in England while the Germans and Russians occupied themselves. The buildup could have occurred while the U.S. sent more forces earlier to back up troops in the Philippines and places like Wake Island. BOLERO could have taken place with the end result of ROUNDUP taking place in this current year but that possibility for 1943 was still in debate, mostly for appearances' sake, while American prisoners were brutalized and executed in the Philippines. The only solace that Madison had was that the Doolittle Raid, in April 1942, on Tokyo and Nagoya Japan with 16 USAAF B-25 Mitchell medium bombers launched from the deck of the USS Hornet had precipitated the Battle of Midway on June 4, 1942, as far as intelligence could now tell these many months later. Midway was an early turning point for the war in the Pacific and the Japanese were all but on the run. The idea of the Raid had come from Navy Captain Francis Lowe; this also had been heartening as the powers that be would hear out a Navy captain who just happened to have a good idea for a solution to a problem that the President wanted solved, and that was how to attack the Japanese mainland.

On Thursday April 22, 1943 the first daffodils started coming up. Madison awoke to find that the many of the street corners in an around Fleet and Aldershot had been mysteriously planted with daffodils overnight, the same thought she had had when she had first seen them the previous spring though she knew that they had been first planted years before. Sam was right, they were beautiful and even more so than she had remembered from the previous year. She also found them along the road to Aldershot as she had once again stayed in the cottage with Sam while Clive was still away from home.

On April 23; Good Friday, Clive finally returned back to Aldeshot.

On April 25, Madison attended Easter Sunday at the Saint-Michael-and-Saint-George   Catholic church down on the flats skirting the military base of Aldershot by the narrow Basingstoke Canal that borders Aldershot and adjacent to a large set of pitches belonging to a boys school. Madison was impressed with the red-brick spire of this 1892 church while she also smiled to herself that they had named the church after both the highland patron St. Michael and the lowland patron St. George; they were trying to cover all of their bases by taking both options, which could be a bad approach in the field with combatants. Clive was a member of the Church of England and Madison was Episcopalian which were one in the same but they were attending the Catholic service as one of Clive's non-commissioned officers from the regiment was having his child christened at the same time. It was a wartime christening on Easter and maybe hope for this new member of the next generation on the day of resurrection thought Madison.

Easter Sunday found Sam with the Madman professor, his wife and daughter and the Yank 'magician', who turned out to be a young sergeant, in Cambridge at King's College Chapel with its incredible vaulting. Sam had never seen such splendid ceiling vaulting. It was so mathematical in its beauty. The symmetry was mesmerizing. The vaulting fanned out overhead to form these wonderful overlapping cones that radiated out towards the center of the great long cathedral like the ripple effect of dropping a pebble in a placid pond. This was all bathed in the soft light coming in through the tall stained glass windows ten on each side of the chapel. It seemed that these windows comprised 80% of the two outside walls making up this long cathedral. It gave Sam a strange but comforting feeling of a greater power, something beyond all that was going on around them and one that would get them all through this period of time and deliver them to a better place. For the first time he truly knew that there was nothing that would ever separate he and Madison, not time nor death itself. Sam also could not take his eyes off of the two angels topping both sides of the great organ. They were heralding something greater than what was now controlling their world. He could only wish that Madison was here to share this with him. He had visited the chapel when he had first arrived months ago but he had never noticed it in this light as the sermon on the Resurrection gained a soft cadence to it. Things would be better, and they would end this war.

On May 11, 1943 Churchill arrived in Washington, D.C. for the TRIDENT Conference. Madison had contributed to intelligence that pushed for a buildup to execute Operation ROUNDUP in 1943. She feared, and had actually felt for the previous month or so, that the peripheral approach to the continent through the Mediterranean campaign, with an invasion of Italy, would prevail although the analyses coming from 'Commodore' had gained more stature recently due to the 'Hitler Attempts'. "The Med and Italy are Churchill's 'pets'......", as Madison would put it angrily when discussing it with her team.

On May 12, General Jurgen von Arnim surrendered all Axis forces in North Africa. Madison and Sam realized that this could not have been timed better to add more fuel to the invasion of Italy.

On May 19, Churchill addressed a joint session of Congress where he stated, that the final triumph, in spite of the recent victory in Tunisia, would come only after battles as difficult and costly as those that had followed the pivotal Battle of Gettysburg in the American Civil War. Madison was horrified when she heard these historical references as she knew that North Africa was not pivotal, as implied, but only the warm-up for potentially a much bloodier campaign. She knew that the Germans would fight a protracted and bloody defense of the Italian Peninsula. She knew from a tactical standpoint that fighting up through the boot of Italy would be more reminiscent of the three bloody days of Gettysburg in that hot July of 1863 where there were somewhere just over 51,000 casualties.

She knew it would be reminiscent of 'Longstreet's Grand Assault' or "Pickett's Charge" on Cemetery Ridge, one of the bloodiest events in American history. It was the last day of the battle at Gettysburg. Twelve Thousand Five Hundred Confederate troops charged that ridge that day and over 6,500 fell with 1,123 killed on the field. The

Union Army had 1,500 casualties. Madison remembered reading from one of the survivors that the air rippled and vibrated not from the heat of that hot July day but from the lead in the air, it was like a slaughter house he said but they kept on going and actually held the Ridge for a brief moment. She remembered visiting the field with her father when she was 12. It was a wet drizzly day and the mud was red and she remembered looking up the hill as tears came down her checks mixing with the drizzle. Her father had respected her emotions and held an umbrella for both of them as he watched his daughter from the corner of his eye, appreciating what she was feeling. She remembered that she had made sure that none of that red mud clung to her to be taken away, she made sure that it stayed on that hill where it belonged; hallowed with the blood of a generation, the blood that made America as great as she was. Madison had remembered what she had seen in the museum in Gettysburg that day that had marked the intensity of that one charge. She remembered seeing Confederate mini-balls and Union bullets that had met in mid flight and become one. There were many of them and they all had been found on the field of Pickett's Charge.

On May 27, TRIDENT ended and so did Madison's hopes for an earlier end to the war. The British felt, through their interpretation of Ultra intercepts, that Hitler would not defend Sicily or Italy and that it would be a walk in the park. 'Commodore' knew differently. Madison was receiving many of the same intercepts and interpreting them, for analysis, in the German. These interpretations were going into the puzzle to give them models on how Hitler and the German military, as two separate parts, would combine to form a 'particular action' under specific circumstances. The 'particular action' was two dimensional as it was made up of characteristics of the pure military model and characteristics of the Hitler geopolitical model. The Rommel/Hitler communiqués had given them the Rosetta Stone they needed to determine when the two separate models would be able to accommodate each other to form a synergetic action. You could not interpret one separate from the other as Sam and Madison had come to realize and that is what the British were doing. They had also said that Hitler would not fight on two fronts and they had been wrong. TRIDENT concluded poorly from the standpoint of

'Commodore'. They were moving forward with Sicily and, no doubt, Italy and they had postponed the cross-channel attack until May of 1944. ROUNDUP was finally dead and so too were many American troops by this decision, and again Madison took it personally.

On Monday June 7, 1943 Madison found herself at her desk in the 'Dome' bright and early as Clive was off to areas unknown at 5AM and she had decided to have a breakfast for him before he left. She didn't know where he was off to but she could only assume that it had to do with the final stages for the assault on Sicily. When asked he had simply referred to his intelligence team and said, "The buggers have a problem and they can't seem to fix it without my expertise. I should once again be gone for a fortnight or more."

Madison had said, "Ah, a fortnight or more for a problem. A big problem I would assume." And then she had smiled knowingly thinking that her naively coated input, over the past several months, about 'unconditional surrender' had let her know, in advance, that the British were going to use it with subtly to push for the invasion of Sicily and Italy, at the TRIDENT Conference, so they could stay on their Mediterranean path. She had known by Clive's responses, over the past month, that the British would say that Hitler would not defend Sicily and Italy in deference to France, Belgium and the Netherlands, which fronted Germany on a broad front and further, that the Italians would just surrender. Clive implied that due to 'unconditional surrender' the Allies would have to secure the Mediterranean to bottle up Germany for the cross-channel attack as the Germans would now fight with a scorched earth policy in hand. Clive had made no mention of the attempts on Hitler and what they had meant and Madison knew that he had access to the same reports but ironically not 'Commodore's' reports. Anything that was relayed to him that came from 'Commodore' was part of another report. Although he had been 'Commodore's' liaison officer in the beginning he no longer was and he was not necessarily in line to see their original reports before they were reviewed and dissected, and then disseminated by higher intelligence.

Madison had used this knowledge in the analysis that she and Sam had put together for the American General Staff to use at the conference to push for the by-pass of Sicily and Italy and the drive for ROUNDUP in 1943. They did this to no avail as FDR sided once again with his 'older brother', as Madison would look at it.

Clive had kissed her and said, "It's 'much ado about nothing' really. They seem to have a bit of a problem with the boffins meeting a proper schedule."

"What do scientists have to do with military intelligence?" Madison had known that the boffins probably referred to meteorologists that were involved in predicting the winds and sea for first an airborne drop then multiple beach landings on the island of Sicily.

"It is the world turned upside down my dear, mine '..not to reason why............'" and he had just smiled and turned to head out the door to the waiting Jeep with his driver sitting behind the wheel.

"........ours '..but to do and die'." Madison had finished as he headed across the drive to the idling American made Jeep; the world was certainly upside down.

She now sat at her desk in the 'Dome' knowing that the invasion of Sicily was on its way and that the invasion of Italy would more than likely follow on its heels.

She was reading through a myriad of recent communiqués from Ultra with a list of criteria in hand when her private line rang.

She picked it up and said, "Fagin."

"No, me," came Sam's voice from the other end. "I hope you haven't been reading Dickens these days, I really need you to concentrate on the woes of the Twentieth Century."

Madison laughed, "I thought you were someone else."

"I hope you don't have a second job of slight of hand that I don't know about."

"Are you implying that this one is slight of hand?"

"If you add the politics, which seems to be the main ingredient."

"You've never used this line before, what do you have to say for yourself?," she said with mock accusation.

"What, a mug like me?"

"No the statistician slash historian."

"We've got something, I have two events both of which meet the combined model criteria for German Army reaction and Hitler influence. We have the two models meeting synergetically to create a specific and 'particular action'. We have a 'Crystal Ball'."

"I'll be over in ten minutes. I want to see this."

"Don't race, it's too early and you'll be noticed," chuckled Sam.

"You won't hear me coming."

"Oh, I doubt that."

"See you in a few minutes."

Madison raced the little red MG down Fleet Road to Fleet and then left down Elvetham Road. Sam could just about hear her downshift into the left-hand turn at the Links Pub onto Elvetham as she pumped the gas like a race car double-clutching, and then the MG boomed to life as she shifted back up through the gears after making the turn. She started downshifting 50 yards before getting to the driveway like she was driving a race car, again pumping the gas to catch the gears as she moved down through the two lower gears. She had the car comfortably in first gear as she crossed the property line in front of the cottage and then put the clutch in to perfectly make the sharp right turn onto the short pebble drive as smooth as if the car were on a rail.

She rushed into the kitchen through the back door out of breath to see Sam standing there with a smile on his face and a cup of steaming Columbian black coffee in his right hand. "Gee, that was quiet. I thought I was in the pits of Le Mans for minute.'

She just smiled, put her hands around the cup he was holding, took a sip and then looked up at him and said, " Well, that's what you do to me with all that fancy analytical talk."

"You're going to be well trained for the New York State Police when we get home, the motorcycle cops are gonna love you."

"And right now I'd give any of them a big hug just to see them."

"Don't do that when we get home."

"Is this going to help us to get there?"

"I don't know but it proves two things; or let's just say that it comes in two parts. The first part is that the German High Command is going to launch a new summer offensive in Russia."

"After the defeat in Stalingrad?"

"Precisely why; the westward retreat of the German Army has to stop to prove that Germany's military was not dealt a fatal blow at Stalingrad. Also a retreating army is easy prey. They also want to pick up German moral. They as well know that if they pull off a successful offensive it might destroy the relationship that the Russians have with the Allies in the west as Stalin has been calling for a second front against the Germans, or the cross-channel attack. It's no secret and the Abwehr is fully aware of this which gives us a third ingredient other than Hitler and the German High Command."

"What's the third ingredient?"

"Canaris"

"This is getting complicated."

"To simplify it Canaris is using Hitler's personality and pushing the buttons we have taken a great deal of time to understand. He's pushing the buttons that he knows will work with the German High Command, or he is helping to control the two models that we watch for a cross-over. He is helping to some degree to align the moons of Hitler and the German High Command if you will. I think he has them convinced that an offensive will not only boost moral and create a great defense by creating a great offense but he, most importantly, may think that he might force the Allies into the cross-channel invasion, which is what he wants. Canaris wants to bring this war to an end and the effects of 'unconditional surrender' on Hitler has him trying to manipulate this in that direction."

"Can we prove this?"

"To one degree, yes and in other ways we can only show the correlation with historical reactions by some of the key players with Hitler at the center; we are very limited on information on Canaris as you know. The only reference we can make to Canaris are the way his intelligence reports are presented to Hitler pieced together from some of the intercepts we've received and that is weak at best to anyone other you, myself and the rest of the 'Commodore' team; who no one seems to know exists beyond you. The one item that stands out is equipment and its movement."

"Your equipment statistics are coming into play?"

"Clearly. I've been able to determine that the Germans have doubled their production of medium and heavy tanks from close to 6,000 in 1942 to 12,000 this year due to the fact that many of our daylight bombers have been diverted by Churchill's Mediterranean plans. They've been talking about new equipment and one can only surmise that these are tanks and self-propelled guns. These people are having no problem in the heavy equipment category and this equipment is on the move to the eastern front with Russia. There doesn't seem to be a problem with trained crews for the equipment either. I estimate that a whole two thirds of the German Army is in Russia right now and I know what they are going to hit."

Sam pulled out a map and on that map were three railroad junctions with the main junction in the middle of a bulge which was outlined in red and pushed out with the town of Orel at the top of the bulge and the town of Kharov at the bottom and in the center was a third where Sam's right forefinger rested, Madison knew what it was.

As he raised his finger he said, "Kursk, they are going to try to retake Kursk. They are going to hit this bulge with one great wallop right at this major east west north south rail crossing. It is too tempting a target for their panzer units and Hitler wants it back, he had it for 15 months. This type of strategic and tactical target combined fits the model that we've developed. Hitler wants it politically and the German High Command sees it tactically as ripe but dangerous. The two models have met with all their requirements in the middle and Canaris has pushed them over the top. They are going to hit Kursk hard and hit it with everything they have. And this is only part one of two parts."

"I can't wait for the second part, now everything makes sense, even though it doesn't make sense to try to retake Kursk," as Madison could see because she knew the figures and the communiques that Sam was putting together as she had worked on it all. It all made complete sense in the end. "I know the second part of this has to do with Hitler as the predominate factor."

"Your money is on the right horse. No matter where the German Army winds up in this offensive Hitler will do just what the British say he won't do."

"He can't let the Allies have Sicily and Italy."

"Precisely, it would be an embarrassment and an insult and I know you understand that one. It's similar to some of his need to retake Kursk. That's the first model and it's simple knowing our man the way we now do. The second model lines up perfectly too as the German High Command would feel that the Allies could come up through Italy or, as Churchill himself has admitted, '..the underbelly of Europe', to Austria and France and create two fronts with Switzerland as a buffer but more importantly they see it as an ideal way to wear the Allies down with a protracted defense up the narrow Italian Peninsula with the help of the Apennine Mountain Range and the Alps to create defensive belts to beat up the Allies. The geographical layout of Italy suits a perfect defense and reduces any flanking maneuver by an invading army other than the use of additional landings, which are difficult at best. The Germans also know that this would over-burden our supply lines from America and as well add the burden of the care for the Italian population, which they know the Americans would maintain. They wouldn't hesitate stopping an offensive in full flight, such as Kursk, no matter what the state of that offensive, in order to be able move troops into Italy to oppose the western Allies. The two models align perfectly with this second part without having to bend to become synergetic."

"Sam, you don't have to go into more detail, I can see the complete picture including the statistics I've been getting to you and the models we've pieced together. It makes too much sense but can we sell it enough to get around the politics and stop the invasions?"

"Well, the machinery is well underway and even with the best and clearest intelligence in the world, such as an announcement from the other side, it will be hard to stop but there is a chance. Worst case the planners don't budge but we get our analysis in front of the powers that be and that may give our next argument more credence."

"We have to make them see this clearly and we have to get them to react positively."

"I'm with you on this. I gave you the worst case reaction but we can sure as hell try. It's like baseball, there's nothing like a late inning comeback especially started by a Texas Leaguer."

"If you can make this convincing enough for them to react the Yankees game is on me, along with Peter Luger's, when we get home and then I'll ask you to explain what a Texas Leaguer is," she said with a conspiratorial smile which made Sam subconsciously hesitate in his response for one second.

"You've got a deal. If we can sell this, as we keep saying, maybe we'll get home sooner."

"The ultimate prize."

"Brother you can say that again."

"I hope I'm not your brother."

His voice lowered and became soft as Sam looked directly into Madison's eyes and said, "I don't think there would be any confusion there even if I had a brother but I can tell you one thing and that's that not only are you my lover but you are closer than any sibling, twin or other could possibly ever be. You are like my female doppelganger. I hear you in my voice and my thoughts are in your voice, I feel your touch in my touch when I touch something purely out of curiosity and I feel your soul in my sight when I look at something for the first time and this has all made me hear myself better, feel more and see with new and more vibrant colors."

She didn't say a thing she just put her arms around him and let him hold her with her head in that familiar and safe place on his shoulder and in the crook of his neck. She knew that she would have to have 'Commodore' declare an emergency meeting at Eisenhower's headquarters and she also knew that she would have to bring Sam in for the first time, which was technically a security breach as they had initially been kept compartmentalized to protect both of their functions. Madison knew that at some point she was going to have to use Sam as back up. She also knew that MI5 or maybe it was MI6 for in-country surveillance of intelligence groups, as they were very good having remained invisible all these months, probably already reported this working relationship.

She felt this new burden intensely as though it were her responsibility if the Allies went ahead with Sicily and Italy and it prolonged the war and killed more Americans among other allies, enemy and civilians. It was quite a weight and she needed Sam to make love to her this night before it came down on her and crushed her.

She quietly took his hand, turned and walked him to the stairs up to the second floor and their private island away from the rest of the world. As she walked into the room a warm smile came over her face as she noticed the fresh daffodils in the Mason Jar, which this late in the season were becoming rare. She turned to Sam smiled again and said, "I love you for that, how did I get you?"

Sam pulled her close to him and whispered to himself, "How did I get you?"

They quietly undressed each other, held each other in the warmth of that room with a mild June morning breeze tickling their bodies and they spent the next several hours making love.

By 10 AM they were facing reality again sitting at the dining room table sipping coffee and discussing the briefing they intended to give Eisenhower and his staff at their Goodge Street headquarters. Goodge Street was classified and if it were viewed from the outside someone would think it was a bomb shelter except that it was closed and guarded on the inside of the two entrances.

"Can we use any members of your Commodore team to back up the significance of our data with regard to statistical patterns? Come to think of it, I know very little about your team other than what you told me that day on the platform and knowing you that has a distinct characteristic of government secrecy. I've almost come to think that you are Commodore in total."

"Well, I guess I'm doing part of my job well," sighed Madison projecting forward and worrying over the imminent landings on Sicily and Italy. "The team, as you know, is made up of two Americans, both men and posing as research doctors. That's all I can say to anyone with clearance as they are 'moveable assets'. I can tell you that you have unknowingly met one of them, Al."

"Moveable assets?", Sam said with a cynical frown remembering an American 'medical' doctor he had met at Fleet station some months ago by the name of Al.

"Great term isn't it. It simply means that due to their pedigree and rarity I may lose them to another team or operation so the less known about them, even at high levels of clearance, the better."

"Well, it makes sense; and we can't use them. But I don't think they'll be happy to see that we've linked up even though the Brits may have already reported it to Donovan himself now that we're all part of his Office of Strategic Services and officially foreign intelligence. It might have been a lot easier if we were pure military intelligence, and sometimes I think that holds more clout with the Chiefs of Staff anyway."

"You may be right; but with regard to them possibly knowing about us I would just put it down to our superior ability as intelligence analysts that nothing has been said so far, if they do know. If they do know and haven't yet said a word it further illustrates that they may think we are probably so good together that we can discover things as though we have a 'Crystal Ball'.

"Ah great. Let's hope that we don't hear about it and, God, let's not mention the phrase 'Crystal Ball'."

Madison laughed, "Are you afraid of divulging your powers Merlin?"

"Ah, funny girl. You say that, after they look at us like we each have a third eye."

"Do you think we can convince them of Kursk and tie that into Hitler moving against the Allies if they invade Sicily and Italy."

"Knowing what I think I know about Eisenhower we'll convince him of Kursk and I think he already believes that Hitler will reposition troops to strongly appose us in Italy. But we all may be hamstrung by the politics unless we can offer him a strong argument against Operation HUSKY and then the invasion of Italy, to give him and us that Texas Leaguer and a late inning comeback," Sam said referring to research he had done on several of the Allied generals in order to know how to position their analysis.

Madison knew that Sam was good at figuring out personalities and positioning their work in a manner that could even be complementary to the person they were trying to convince. Sam had tried this technique shortly after he had first met Madison in Boston. She was vexed over the personality of one of her undergraduate professors and the way in which he attacked her theoretic proposals on historical alternatives if one were to change the actions of some of the players. Sam had audited the class as an invited guest of one of his professors at Boston University so that he would not draw undo attention and then he had Madison put forward an unsolicited hypothesis of the outcome at Gallipoli with a different command structure in place. Churchill's Dardanelles 'adventure' was a topic which would always draw the attention of this professor as a paper he had written in 1922 was so well read by students that The Harry Elkins Widener Memorial Library's copy, at Harvard, was falling apart.

The professor slammed Madison that day even though her hypothesis could clearly have been drawn from his paper. Sam had him figured and just out of curiosity, and to help back some minor research into the dynamics of power and influence, they came up with an alternative hypothesis. The alternative hypothesis was clearly in direct conflict with his 1922 paper but Sam had Madison position the argument differently, in a more complimentary manner. It had worked like a charm. The professor agreed with her hypothesis and in doing so contradicted his 1922 analysis and opinion. It was a tool they had used on several occasions since and they would use it with Eisenhower and his staff in a bit different manner. Sam would position the analysis, which he knew that Eisenhower probably knew and agreed with in his heart, in a way where the general was moved to take an action which could put a halt to a plan that was near fruition, or Operation HUSKY.

Madison called her OSS contact on her secure phone in the 'Dome' later that day and declared a **'code Black'** in the name of 'Commodore' and that 'Commodore' needed to meet with 'Duckpin' which was Eisenhower's code name. She hung the phone up after the contact replied, "Duckpin will be notified of the 'code Black', I need you at this line for the next two hours, your green light will be 'backwash'" and he hung up.

She found that her palms were sweating. Sam was back in the cottage feverously working on the presentation they had agreed upon and for the first time she had used the words which declared an emergency: **'code Black'**. The code name for their green light to meet with Eisenhower for an emergency meeting was not all that comforting.

The phone rang again twenty minutes later while she was working through some minor communiqués that she needed to push herself through in order to find any usually indiscernible clues that might lead her to more important information. It was all in German so that the clues would be left in tact. The ring of the phone startled her so much so that she broke the tip of the herringbone designed Royal Challenger Parker fountain

pen that had been a gift from Sam before the war, it had been his pen in undergraduate school and she cherished it. "Damn;......... bad luck", she muttered as the phone rang again and she went for the receiver.

"Hello!"

"With whom am I speaking."

"Bell at Commodore."

"You have 'backwash'; an olive drab 4 door Plymouth will be at your location at 2100 hours. Do you have any other passengers?"

"Yes, one."

"What is the name and reference?"

"Dr. Samuel Harbour, OSS"

"Hold one," commanded the voice on the other end and the phone went on hold before Madison could respond.

A minute later the voice came back on the line, "The car will pick you both up, please have all ID's readily available for the driver. Have a good trip Commodore" and the phone hung up.

So, they would leave just after dark to be taken to Goodge Street in London some 45 miles or so from Aldershot.

As she dashed out of the front of the hospital with her thin briefcase in tow she hoped that Sam was near completion on his presentation and for the first time she thought of the rule against running out of the hospital, '..... so as not to draw undo attention to oneself.' This was part of her original indoctrination these many months ago now by a British security officer. It now seemed so ridiculous as she hopped into the MG and turned over the engine with a bit too much of a roar as her foot was down a little too firmly on the accelerator. "Maybe I do need to calm down," she muttered to herself has she put the car in reverse and put her left arm on the back of the seat as she looked behind to back out.

She backed out in a hurry and was off to Fleet in a slight haze of light blue/gray smoke which cleared quickly as she disappeared from in front of the hospital moving through the gears with perfect precision, shifting instinctively at the highest RPM for each particular gear.

Sam could once again hear her coming and smiled while still concentrating on his presentation.

He heard the MG roll to a stop on the pebble drive and the engine die just seconds before hearing her come through the back door in a hurry.

"How's the presentation?"

"Almost there."

"They're sending a staff car to pick us up at 9 o'clock."

Sam looking at his watch said, " a little over four hours " and trying to calm her he looked up and said with a grin on his face, "ya wanna fool around?"

Madison just smiled, calmed down and put her arms around him.

They spent the next four hours going over their presentation and then headed for the MG in the back of the cottage.

"Now I get the luxury of experiencing a fast woman on the left-hand side of the road and maybe a new land speed record," Sam said closing the door behind them.

"You love fast women."

"That number is one."

Madison stopped in her tracks and came back to Sam and kissed him on the lips.

"What was that for?"

"For being you," she said as she headed back to the right side of the car.

Just as her rear wheels cleared the pebbles, she straightened out on Elvetham Road and hit the accelerator making the MG TA come to life with a roar as it jumped forward heading towards the Links Pub. As she approached the pub she downshifted from fourth to third and then, in quick succession, third to second gear with a quick pump of the accelerator just before the right hand turn towards Fleet Road. She moved smoothly as always back up through each gear taking the engine to the top of its RPM's for that gear before moving into the next.

As they headed down Fleet Road Sam, wrapped in the cool June air flowing in around him, looked at Madison and smiled to himself impressed with her ability to become one with the MG as though it were an extension of her body. She had a smile on her face and always seemed happy when she was traveling at high speed with everything in her control. He marveled at this with even more appreciation than he had for her genius for historical analysis.

She turned briefly and smiled at him, without taking her concentration off of the road, just as they passed the large ancient English oak on their right that marked the end of the long portion of Fleet Road just before they bore left which would head them towards Saint-Michael-and-Saint-George Catholic church and another right hand turn and then a left onto Queens Avenue past the small 1906 observatory, on the right, and the beginning of the Aldershot military complex.

She downshifted into each turn and then shifted the car back up through each gear before downshifting again for the last left hand turn into the hospital grounds. She did it with such fluidity that Sam felt exhilarated and realized for the first time the joy of being in a car like this when it was driven at the top range of its performance. He loved her for the experience.

They found themselves in front of the hospital with five minutes to spare.

In a few minutes they could see the outline of an American sedan with its two flat pinpoint beams of blackout lights punctuating the night with authority as it came up the hill and just past the front gate of the military base before turning right and into the hospital grounds.

The staff car came past them, in the hospital grounds, and made a U-Turn so that the driver's door wound up directly in front of them and no more than six feet away.

Two men stepped out and Madison could see that they wore American Army uniforms and both, as far as she could tell, seemed to have Staff Sergeant chevrons, three above with one below, on their sleeves. The driver, who was of medium build came towards them as the other man, a big stocky man, walked in front of the car and held an M1A1 Thompson submachine gun at the ready. This made Madison a little nervous but she understood the need for such security.

"Evenin' Mam." Said the driver as he stopped in front of her nodding his head slightly and at the same time touching the front peak of his garrison cap, or what she had recently heard them call a "piss-cutter", between his thumb and forefinger. She had noticed that he had removed it from under his right shoulder epaulet and put it on just after stepping out of the car. They had a comforting polite discipline about them which made her feel safe and reminded her of home.

"Good evening Sergeant."

"Mam, can you tell me who you are?"

"I'm 'Commodore' and you are 'backwash'."

"Yes Mam, can I see your ID's?"

Having them at the ready as directed Madison extends them toward the Sergeant, "Here you go Sergeant."

"Thank you Mam," replied the sergeant taking his flashlight and looking at the ID's and photos, and by the light of the quarter moon looking at their faces for a match.

"Everything seems in order Mam, would you like to get in?" he said as he motioned her towards the car and then preceded her to open the back rear door.

The second Sergeant stayed where he was with his eyes alert and searching the entire perimeter until both she and Sam were in the car and their door had been closed by the driver. The driver then got in followed by the second Sergeant.

As the Plymouth headed out the gate and turned left into Aldershot the second Sergeant said without turning around, "Sorry about the gun Mam but we're just trying to be safe."

"No apologies necessary Sergeant, I actually feel safer in your presence and as strange as it may sound it feels nice to be in an American car again."

"I take it you've been here for sometime then Mam."

"Long enough Sergeant."

The driver then spoke up saying, "Sorry about the late meeting with the General but the cover of darkness gives us a little more security and better ability to see if we're being followed."

"We understand Sergeant," said Madison and trying to make them feel more comfortable she noted the patches on their left shoulders by saying, "Is your Division from Texas? It looks like a bull." Madison said this knowing full well what division they were and where they were from.

"No Mam, we're not from Texas but we are the Red Bull Division or the 34th. They call us the 'palace guard' 'cause Ike chose us for his security."

"That's an honor," harped in Sam for the first time.

"Yes Sir, it is."

"Well I've never been to Texas myself but I'd like to see it someday," said Sam.

"Yes Sir," responded the sergeant, not correcting him.

"Where are you boys from?," asked Sam in a brotherly tone not really paying attention to the fact that he wasn't all that much older than they were.

"I'm from Minnesota. Jim over there is from Missouri."

"Nice to meet you boys. I'm from New York and 'Commodore' over here is from New Jersey. You boys are making me homesick," said Sam bringing up childhood memories of his Father who was originally from a small town in Missouri called Kennett, but he didn't tell the other sergeant this.

They gave Sam's comment a warm laugh and the trip into London went quietly from then on until they came to the junction of Chenies Street and North Crescent and the car came to a stop in front of an elongated low structure with two cylinders like large pill boxes at either end. The lower pillbox structure was truly cylindrical and had a small square blockhouse on its roof with two vent ports at the top. It was obvious to both Madison and Sam that this was the entrance to Eisenhower's underground headquarters or 'Goodge Street' which was built off of the underground system.

"Well Mam we're here."

"So who is the dominant figure here or is it just your great looks," Sam whispered to Madison referring to the sergeant addressing her alone.

Both sergeants hopped out of the car. The sergeant with the Thompson held the gun in a less conspicuous position than he did in Aldershot while the sergeant from Minnesota quickly opened their rear door and stood aside as they got out. It was 10:30 in the evening, 'on the nose' as Sam would say on occasion.

"Mam, just head to the front doors of that building; the guards inside know you are coming at this specific time and they will direct you, we'll be here to take you back to Aldershot after the meeting," said the Minnesotan.

"Thank you sergeant," said Madison as they headed towards the doors at the front of the elongated low rectangular structure connecting the two pillboxes. It was obvious where to head. She also knew that the car that had delivered them at the precise hour would disappear from sight and would be back again in front of the doors, just off of Alfred Square, at the appointed time of their departure.

As they walked towards the doors Madison muttered to Sam, "I hope it's 'Commodore' and not the 'great looks' that are eliciting deference to me as a 'Mam'." She then turned slightly to him and smiled in the dim light of the quarter moon.

Just as they approached the doors one opened and another sergeant stepped out while still another sergeant stood behind him with a Thompson at the ready. It was a world of sergeants and as it should be thought Madison, as the army was truly run by them.

"Mam, can I have your ID's and can you both please stand here while I check them."

"Certainly Sergeant," said Madison as she collected Sam's ID and once again handed them both to a sergeant with a red bull on his shoulder.

The first sergeant disappeared into the structure while the second sergeant stood by the door with his weapon remaining at the ready. The first sergeant was back in a matter of seconds as he was just checking the ID's with a flashlight inside the doorway in order to preserve light discipline in a blacked out London.

Returning he glanced at their faces in the minimal moonlight, handed the ID's back to Madison and then directed them into the dark enclosure with the sound of a heavy door closing behind them. This had all taken place in a matter of ten seconds.

As soon as the door closed a light came on revealing the two sergeants. Inside the building now the sergeant who had checked their ID's requested their briefcases and checked both.

Then the sergeants directed them to the left and the elevator which occupied part of the cylindrical pillbox structure that they had seen from the outside. To the side of the elevator was a double spiral staircase split in two with an obvious up-stairway and a down-stairway. They headed for the elevator.

The sergeant who had checked their ID's noticing Sam looking at the stairway smiled and said, "It would be a long walk sir, we're at the 32 floor of what you might want to think of as an inverted skyscraper."

Sam was impressed, "Well sergeant I guess we're not in Kansas anymore."

"No sir." He said smartly with a smile as he directed them onto the elevator.

The only thing Sam could figure was that this Goodge Street station had to be off of the Northern Line due to its location. He didn't ask any questions as he felt they probably wouldn't be answered. But he would test the sergeant just the same. The only information was the declaration of 32 floors and they did not know what level they were on once the lift stopped but Sam could feel the pressure in his ears and had to swallow to clear them. He assumed that there was only one level and that was deep.

"A man could get the bends down here Sergeant," said Sam looking at the sergeant and Madison, who stood just behind the man and to his left.

"Yes sir", said the sergeant, and nothing more. The second sergeant had remained on the street level where Sam had noticed two other men at the other side of the rectangular building at the far side of the other pillbox structure.

Within minutes they were at their destination and the sergeant guided them off the elevator and down a dimly lit hall. At the end of the hall they came to a steel door raised several inches from the floor, and shaped like the door of a warship's passageway, where the sergeant stopped them. He knocked on the door and the word, "Texas" came from the other side.

The sergeant replied, "leaguer" and the steel door opened, without so much as a squeak, which one would expect just looking at it.

Sam and Madison looked at each other for one brief moment with mouths partly open and Madison said in mocked seriousness, " I guess I need to pay more attention next time we go to a ball game, especially for a Texas Leaguer."

Sam followed, "Ya, and I guess someone or something is telling me I should check out the Lone Star state."

"This way, please", directed the sergeant as he ushered them through the steel door that, noticeably up close, had a rubber gasket around it which told Sam that this part of the underground complex was sealed against a gas attack and that they were getting closer to their destination. As the door closed behind them the light in the intersecting hallway went from dim to bright and they were led to the right and down to a lower level. They walked a good hundred yards on this lower level before they were led, through another steel door, into a conference room on their left that was set up to be completely sealed and self-sufficient, if needed, in case of a gas attack. Sam had seen such a room once before, near the old U.S. Naval Observatory in Foggy Bottom in Washington, D.C., just before he had left for England. It had been a place that he was told to forget.

The room that they now found themselves in was oak paneled with nothing hanging on the walls for any type of adornment. It was mostly taken up by a long oak conference table at its center with eight chairs up either side and one at each end. They were not in the room more than a minute, after being taken to two seats at the end of table, when the door on the opposite side of the room opened.

Walking in with a quick pace and an instant air of authority, which caught them both off guard, was Ike himself with three members of his staff directly behind him. The man had a presence thought Sam as both he and Madison stood. Sam had heard of people with such presence but he had never experienced it before. He knew that part of it was his knowledge of the man who, was in many ways, low keyed and humble but knew his stuff besides being a good manager of people, especially generals with inflated egos such as Montgomery was turning out to be.

"Please be seated," he said as he nodded to both Madison and Sam.

As they seated themselves, which included Ike and the three members of his staff, both Madison and Sam pulled up their briefcases to pull the papers needed for their presentation.

The General, leaning forward, lit a cigarette and in that comforting Midwestern voice said, " Miss Bell I have read much of your material including your paper in early 1939 predicting the invasion of Poland and quite frankly I trust whatever you say without a great deal of paperwork to back it up."

They both pulled their papers and just rested them on the table and Sam smiled inside. Madison glanced at him briefly as this was what Sam had predicted and she knew the presentation that Sam had prepared could empower Eisenhower to make a call on the invasion of Sicily, and then probably the Italian Peninsula, at a higher level. She felt this knowing that Eisenhower had been put in charge of coming up with the plan for Operation HUSKY or the invasion of Sicily. She also felt extremely proud from the general's remarks and Sam could feel that and also felt proud of her.

They proceeded to first outline their models and how the Hitler model and the German High Command model had to cross, or come together, to create a predictable event.

The general was not hard to convince as Madison and Sam felt that he thought along the same lines as they but balanced a fine line between good military strategy and the politics involved which had to be dealt with in order to get things done. Madison could feel the pressure on this man as he asked his questions. She was impressed that he did not show it and that he was calm and direct in his questioning and he was also personable. She felt that his cigarette smoking might be one of the ways that he subdued some of this pressure as he smoked heavily and the ashtray would be full by the time that they would leave.

Eisenhower was somewhat amazed at the equipment numbers Sam was talking about and Sam made a mental note to get more definitive numbers of equipment. These numbers would include repaired and not fully usable equipment and their varying states of condition along with substitute equipment such as horses which were a large part of the German Army transport, instead of trucks.

The retaking of Kursk made complete sense to him after a brief discussion and he indicated that they would try to warn the Russians in a way that would not compromise their intelligence asset as the Russians had been warned that Germany would attack them in June of 1941 but they had been paranoid about the Allies and distrusted the warning, and in the aftermath almost compromised the security of the Allied intelligence gathering methods.

Ike also knew that the British were fooling themselves if they thought Italy would be a walk in the park. He agreed with Madison and Sam's analysis and fell a little quiet and reflective for a brief moment while his worst nightmare of a slugfest up the Italian Peninsula was confirmed.

"American boys are going to take the brunt of this and it's now firmly a political issue. It was actually a political issue before its inception. I'll see what I can do with your analysis," said the general with concern in his voice.

Before finishing Sam put forward the "Point-Blank Doctrine" and the need to have it executed. This was a simple straightforward doctrine that 'Commodore' had deemed necessary with invasion forces on the ground in Europe. It dealt with air supremacy over the battlefield and called for daylight bombing of aircraft factors and the destruction of the Luftwaffe's fighter arm by, as well, pulling the fighters up into aerial combat.

Ike agreed with 'Point-Blank' and he would push through its execution even with the continual protest of the British with regard to daylight bombing. "It will be American boys risking their lives for other American boys on the ground and the British will have to get over their embarrassment of the eventual effectiveness of American daylight air operations." He made this statement and punctuated it by putting a cigarette out in the ashtray on the oak conference table and the meeting was concluded.

Ike thanked them for their analysis and told them it would be put to use. He also said that, as a result, 'Commodore' would have greater priority in his future intelligence briefings.

As they left, Sam, glancing back, could see the general with one hand on his hip and the other bringing another cigarette to his mouth as he looked down and looked worried. Sam knew that his worst fears had been verified and he knew that this was a soldier's general and that he would do the best that he could for his men. Sam felt briefly ashamed for the pressure that he and Madison felt in doing their job better than well; this man had the world on his shoulders and having been a graduate of West Point himself he probably saw those young newly minted second lieutenants clearly along with the men under them and bore the weight of responsibility for them all. Sam also knew from his research that the general had a son by the name of John who was due to graduate from the academy in just a year, scheduled for June 6th, with the class of 1944.

Feeling Ike's pressure Sam felt that it was time that he and Madison took a break from all of this madness, and now that it would definitely be known by the OSS that they had reconnected it might be a good time to slip out from under the MI5 or MI6 man that they knew was probably watching them before a second operator from the OSS showed up. The OSS would surely be coming out to Aldershot to take a look at two dead people who found each other alive.

The meeting had lasted just over an hour and both Madison and Sam found the general and his staff members easy to talk with even with regard to the historical references as they knew they had been students of military history, if they had attended the United States Military Academy at West Point.

When they came out onto the street their two sergeants were waiting in the staff car that had probably just pulled up after being called. As Sam and Madison got closer to the car the two sergeants got out with the driver opening the back door and the second sergeant standing guard and looking around while they got into the Plymouth.

They all exchanged pleasantries and had a quiet ride back to Aldershot.

Both Sam and Madison had dozed off in the back seat of the Plymouth partly due to the long day and the adrenaline come down after the pre-meeting stress and partly due to the fact that the Plymouth felt and smelled like home. They woke as the Plymouth slowed and came to a complete stop in front of the hospital. Madison was amazed at how the end of the ride into Aldershot and into the hospital grounds had felt so familiar that both she and Sam started coming awake before the car started to slow. They had both been here a long time and with the stress of the war and their responsibilities, it was a lifetime.

The sergeant from Missouri got out to the right with his Thompson at the ready and the driver from Minnesota got out and opened their door. Madison exited; then Sam scooted over to the same door and exited. It seemed normal to both exit the same door with their security, in the hands of the Missourian, on the right side.

"Goodnight sergeants," said Madison, "Stay safe."

"Night Mam," said the driver then after a brief hesitation, "we'll try." Madison smiled with concern and the sergeant knew that she had meant it and that's why he had answered that they'd try.

"Thanks fellas," added Sam.

"Your welcome sir," said the Minnesotan as the sergeant with the Thompson kept an eye out; although security was not really needed at this stage of meeting with the heavily armed sergeant just following protocol.

Then the driver got in, followed by the big Missourian and the staff car was off down to the hospital exit; turned left, past the gates to the base, and into Aldershot before heading back to London. Both Sam and Madison had stared until the car was gone from view in the night and they had just lingered there for a few moments before turning to each other. It was 1:26 in the morning of the 8th.

"26," said Sam looking at the luminous dials of his watch, "Well there's that pesky number again."

"You timed our arrival right to that minute by taking longer to get back in the car in London," Madison said as she laughed.

"And you are delirious or just plan ol' tired."

"I almost feel more tired than I have ever been."

"I think we both need a break and with possibly another shadowy, invisible figure snooping around here to oversee us, I would assume after our joint appearance, it may be a good time to sneak away for a couple of days."

"What do you mean, and not tell anyone?"

"My plan precisely."

"Count me in. It would be like hitting a Texas Leaguer and fooling both the infield and the outfield with the ball dropping between them."

Sam stopped and slowly looked around at her found this big teeth-baring smile on her face, then he smiled and said, "You always do know more than you let on."

"How do you think a girl like me got in a place like this."

"You volunteered," and they both laughed.

They mounted the MG and Sam had a nighttime experience he wouldn't soon forget. Clive was away again for a fortnight or more and Madison had free wheel again with his car, which he never seemed to drive even when he was home. She gunned the little car after turning right, out of the hospital entrance, and past the 1906 observatory; she then double-clutched the car by pumping the gas and downshifted into second gear as she glided into another right hand turn, then briefly up through the gears and downshifting again into a lefthander that put her on Fleet and she came back up through the gears again and flew down Fleet. The big ancient oak tree on the left, as they hit the straight road, went by Sam's eyes in a ghostly blur protected by the night and kept company by all the other nightly objects out there. Madison could have awoken the dead as she throttled that little MG up as high as she could.

She downshifted at the Links and then came up through the gears again on Elvetham and downshifted nicely just before she entered the property perimeter hitting the throttle between each gear to really wake the neighbors.

As Sam climbed out, after they parked, he ran his hands through his hair and said, "Well I guess they all know where the party is."

"That wonderful heart of yours loves it."

"Yah, well right about now it's trying to get out and find another home," he said as she came around the car to him and then wrapped her arms around him.

"Your heart belongs to me and it's not going anywhere; it's simply rejoicing in being in my company.".

"Well the first bit is true, as the Brits like to say, but the second one brings me conversations in the middle of my sleep; this little guy shows up with a steel helmet mounted on a trophy stand and then lectures me on the value of the damned thing every time you burn a lot of gas."

"What do you tell him."

"That he just doesn't understand the value of flying unencumbered with Madison Bell. And then he storms off in a huff. It never fails. I think he's expecting me to say something different every time but it will always be the same answer."

"Ya wanna get crazy?"

"I thought you were dog tired."

"I am and most of it is the mental strain but the thought of upsetting that little man some more sounds like fun."

"Always out to start some trouble," Sam said with a smile of mocked concern.

They headed to the little bedroom that evening with daffodils still in the Mason Jar. They went to that secret island together and then fell asleep in each other's arms.

Later that week the Allies warned the Russians of a potential attack by the Germans, at Kursk, to retake the city, even though there were no Ultra communiqués specifically discussing it. It was presented to the Russians as a military guess by the build up that could be discerned from the side of the western Allies. The Russians apparently accepted the information with a degree of mistrust in the same manner that they had accepted the information from the Allies about Operation BARBAROSA or the German invasion of Russia in June of 1941. They were warned, whatever they chose to do with it.

General Eisenhower also spoke over a secured line with The President of The United States later on in the week, after putting some more intelligence together and at the request of Army Chief of Staff George C. Marshall. He told the President that his belief that the German priority would become Italy once Sicily was invaded was corroborated. He just envisioned a slugfest up the Italian spine even though their operations would be well laid out. Even if the plans for the invasion of Italy were executed properly and successfully, for the initial foothold into Italy, it would simply be the start to a long drawn out and bloody battle northward through the mountains of the Apennine Range with the final obstacle being the Julian Alps. He also explained his concern with regard to tying up too many assets in Italy to properly execute a cross-channel invasion at the earliest possible date. FDR could see his point but the operations would have to continue and the Mediterranean campaign of Churchill and the British would be carried out.

And on Friday of that week Madison and Sam had decided to sneak off to London and take the first bus they could get to the Cotswolds; Clive would be away for weeks still. They would have to ditch their tail, which they hadn't seen but they knew he was watching as he had to be. If they managed to lose their tail they could only stay for a weekend as anything longer than that would set off a manhunt due to their level of security clearance.

They decided to play hooky and leave Friday afternoon; they would spoil themselves with a little of their family money and stay at the Savoy. The poor 'tail'. Staying at the Savoy would not only give them an early start on the Cotswolds but it would make it easier to spot a lurking man if there was one. Madison thought that this could be fun. As they got ready to leave she threw on her old blue jeans, western shirt and topped it off with her Yankee ball cap and came downstairs to meet Sam for a late lunch. The coffee smelled even better now then it did in the morning and she knew that it was going to be a wonderful day.

As she trotted down the stairs Sam looked back and smiled then back at what he was doing, and then he quickly turned back again for a double-take, "Now, how are we going to lose our man if we have the bat boy for the New York Yankees along?"

"Does this look like a boy to you?," said Madison as she playfully and jokingly took a pose and ran her hands up her legs and over the shape of her rear end and then, over the top and smiled with her eyes closed.

"No I would guess not," laughed Sam, "but even dress slacks may stand out over here outside of a factory right now and the amount of material and buttons used may not fall within the ration limits set by the English Board of Trade."

"You've got to be kidding," said Madison giving him a feigned stern look.

Sam just smiled with an 'I gotcha' smile, "Actually you look sexier than the first time that I saw you in that get-up, but maybe just a little too sexy and too American. Women over here probably won't wear American jeans for the next couple of generations."

Madison just put her head down in a mocked frown and headed back off upstairs.

Sam yelled up after her, "I'll take you to the first game once we get home and you can wear what you want."

He heard a "Weee" of glee from upstairs then , "You have no idea what you just got yourself into Mr. Harbour."

Sam smiled and muttered to himself, "Oh I know that.............. and I can't wait."

Fifteen minutes later Madison came down in a plain summer dress which was off-white with small nondescript flowers on it that looked like a bouquet from heaven with her wearing it.

"That'll do but what do we do about you; the rose that you are stands out amongst the most beautiful of roses."

Madison almost blushing like a schoolgirl, and as a result looking even more alluring, said; "That is wholly unfair to all other women but I'll take it if just for a day."

Sam now did not want to leave the house but escape to their island with this wonderful woman, but he knew they had to get away.

After a light lunch of bread and cheese they walked together down Elvetham on the asphalt path on the right side of the road with its root bumps for added character. It was so peaceful and quiet with only the birds for company and the one train that passed heading towards the cottage and in the direction of Basingstoke and then Winchester, the home of the Wessex monarchs and early capital of all of England, before London. Sam thinking about all of these things at once realized that they just didn't walk down Elvetham together everyday and it was a pleasure that he would keep in mind. It had also been months since they had had a drink in the Links and the bartender was probably wondering about his Americans whose vodka he was safeguarding.

It was one of those rare days where the air was perfect and the light was beautiful and the company was enchanting. It was one of those days that it seemed he could count on only one hand, at least recently. They both felt young and alive like college kids again. They felt carefree for the first time in a long time even with the war looming in the background. Sam could not get over how beautiful Madison was and his love was so great for her that he felt it might all come out in an uncontrollable deluge of metaphors and similes and weak attempts at poetry. He felt all of this, but he knew that he would keep it in the jar that gave Madison the love that kept her warm in the cold world of military analysis that she lived in most of the time.

Madison skipped ahead and then came running back to fall in his arms and then she'd run ahead again and twirl around like a ballerina and get mesmerized by the kaleidoscope of dappled light coming through the grand oak leaves as she looked up to catch the sky.

Things couldn't be better and the world was just the two of them and this was the thought she had just as Sam caught up with her and she fell onto his arm at the end of her last twirl. They were two young lovers on a country lane not in a rush to catch their train. Madison was almost a child again.

They caught the 14:10 or the 2:10 PM 'slammer' to London's Waterloo Station then they took the Bakerloo Line of the Underground to Embankment station where they got off and walked along Victoria Embankment towards Waterloo Bridge and the Savoy.

As if in a great spy game they had been keeping their eyes open for any stranger following them and they had been joking about it quietly until Madison noticed a man for the second time. Then it became real and a bit unnerving. She noticed him for the second time as they made the turn to the front door of the Savoy, which was set back a bit from the street down a wide ally. The man kept walking past.

She had first noticed him after they had stepped off the 'slammer' at Waterloo Station when she had looked back down the platform to check the time on the platform clock. There was nothing unusual about him other than that he was young, handsome and not in uniform. She noticed him for this in passing and paid no attention to it until they turned the corner from The Strand to the Savoy and she had looked back from where they had come in nervous reaction to a car's backfire. He saw her look at him but not in a way that indicated that she had recognized him, at least so he thought. As they continued to walk down the alley enclave leading to the front of the hotel with the large Art Deco lettering SAVOY on the stainless steel marquee Madison squeezed Sam's hand in a death grip without even realizing it.

Sam rebounded, " What are you trying to do, break my hand bones?.," as she squeezed his hand even more tightly in reaction to the delayed realization that someone really was following them and it was no longer a game.

Looking straight ahead but whispering in his direction she said, "I saw him."

"Who did you see, 'him'?, whispered Sam with a warm smile.

"Not so loud", she whispered as she entered the revolving door of the Savoy just before him and hearing him say, "You mea…" just as the door revolved in with her enclosed.

As Sam's portion of the door revolved around to the lobby where Madison now stood, she heard, "You mean our bodyguard?"

"If that's what you want to call him. I find it rather unnerving to realize that someone is actually following us."

Sam just chuckled.

"What's so funny?"

Sam leaned over to her and whispered, "One of the best military analysts that the Allies have is shocked to realize that counter-intelligence is actually looking out for her."

"You're right but the realization just takes some getting used to."

Sam checked them in as Dr. and Mrs. Harbour and once again flashed his Cambridge ID card and once again, thankfully, they did not ask for passports.

The next morning they had an early breakfast delivered by room service. They both loved the dinning room looking out to the Thames but Madison did not want to see their 'bodyguard' at breakfast so they viewed the river from their room with a nice private breakfast.

"Well, I hope MI5 or 6 or whoever they are don't have a line into Clive or if they do I hope they're smart about it because now they surely know that we're having an affair. It can't be written off as it might have been with the cottage. At least with the cottage they could think that we were just working late and that we probably slept separately because of our late work hours and the fact that it has two bedrooms. After all the cottage was probably looked at as a work location with low security and that's why they were there, to look out for the bad guys who may be lurking," stated Madison.

"Slow down; I'm sure they figured that out a while ago, or at least I hope they did or I'll be worried about our security."

"Oh God, you're right", whispered Madison to no one in particular thinking of Clive's emotional threat those many months ago before she even knew Sam was alive, his threat to use his service revolver.

"They also would not, I hope, be dumb enough to tell Clive and open up a whole can of worms with all that is on the line right now. They would probably work hard to keep it from coming out, at least until the war is over."

Realizing the truth of Sam's statement Madison sighed, "You're so smart."

"No, just practical; you know, numbers and all of that." Then he smiled; picked up her hand; held it to his nose; took a breath through his nose, as though it were in a bed of roses, and exhaling continued, " That is until I get this close to you and drink in your intoxication and become a complete idiot."

"Oh, so that's what I do to you then, make you an idiot."

"Yah, and it's great."

◆   ◆   ◆

The rest of their breakfast went cold as they made love with the great Thames in the background.

They checked out that morning, a little later than expected, and as they left the Savoy Madison had her eye out for their 'bodyguard' but did not see him.

They walked to the Underground for the District Line to Victoria Station where they would head on to the Victoria Coach Station at the corner of Buckingham Palace Road and Elizabeth Street.

They were not on the Underground platform of the District Line for more than 20 seconds when Madison saw the bodyguard step out onto the same platform. She just happened to be looking in that direction when he appeared and looked over at them to check where they were. Madison could not help but look right at him and he knew, this time, that he had been made. He smiled at her sheepishly as she smiled back with a bit of a humorous grin. When Sam and Madison stepped on the train their 'bodyguard' stayed on the platform. As the door closed Madison chuckled.

"What's so funny?", queried Sam as the train started up.

"I just smiled at our 'bodyguard'."

"Where?"

As the train started to move, "Right in front of you."

Sam looked right at the man through the glass and back several feet on the platform as Madison smiled again and the young man smiled back and tipped his head ever so slightly and then he was gone.

"You have a friend," said Sam.

"I hope he doesn't."

"I wouldn't think we are that type of priority especially as stretched as everyone is, at least through the weekend; if we are still missing on Monday then we will have stepped on a hornets nest knowing what we know about 'things'," whispered Sam.

"I hope you're right," said Madison starting to get lost in thought.

"Trust me," replied Sam looking at her warmly.

Madison just smiled and grasped his hand tenderly in reply.

◆   ◆   ◆

In no time they were walking out of the front of Victoria Station into the early morning sun and off to their left, backed by a large oak tree, was a statue of a man on a horse.

"Look at old Marshal Foch there frozen in time on his horse. His war ended with Versailles, let's hope ours ends better than his," said Sam drolly nodding his head in the statue's direction. "The man set forth the burdening terms for the future of Germany", continued Sam, "and actually said, 'This is not a peace. It is an Armistice for 20 years', well he got what he set forth and here we are again."

"How did you know that was Foch?", asked Madison as she glanced at the statue once again as they started to turn left up the side of the station towards Elizabeth Street. She could barely make out the face of a man she held little to no respect for historically.

"Believe it or not I read it in some mundane statistical book years ago that correlated types and numbers of statues and their dates of erection with economics and politics. It was a strange little book that was somewhat humorous but being a historian as well this statue stood out and gave me an added bit of humor", smiled Sam.

"I always knew that you had a 'strangely' interesting sense of humor, for a statistician," laughed Madison.

Sam just smiled back at her as they headed for the bus station two blocks away.

The Victoria Coach Station was two blocks up from Victoria Station on the right and it was a beautiful Art Deco design from the early thirties. It sat on the corner of the two intersecting streets and had a great corner entrance with a flat tower Art Deco structure presenting it. It looked like it could have been lifted right out of downtown L.A. or Manhattan. It actually reminded them both a little bit of home and, in particular, of the McGraw-Hill building in New York minus the blue-green terracotta. They just stopped, while holding each others hand, and looked at it for a brief moment before heading for its doors.

Inside they asked for the first bus to the Cotswolds and where sold tickets for the Cheltenham Spa bus and directed to its gate. It was one of the few buses still running as the buses of the Green Line Coaches Limited of the London General Country Service had, for the most part, been turned into ambulances, troop carriers or mobile canteens by 1943. Cheltenham was deemed important as a center of education and culture as well as being a spa and was kept open and maintained by Black & White Motorways Ltd. They were looking forward to the trip.

The bus was a two-tone colored bus. Most of the lower portion was white and the roof, down to the base of the windows, was black. At the peak of the roof, at the front of the bus and centered, was a winged logo with a large W superimposed over a smaller B on a rectangular frame with rounded corners. They couldn't recall having been on a long-distance bus trip together and it was a nice first.

By late morning they had made several stops along the way while Madison napped against Sam's shoulder as he dozed. The next to last stop before Cheltenham was called out by the driver as Madison started to wake and she thought she had heard Siren Sisters, which stuck as a name of a place that they might want to visit after the war when the word siren would have a less dramatic and more romantic tone to it. But as she checked the schedule, which she had picked up at the coach station, she noticed it was Cirencester. She liked her name better.

Some distance out of Cirencester Sam woke as they turned right onto a mild incline towards Cheltenham and on their right was a grass field filled with rabbits popping in and out of their burrows; they had never seen such a large warren and it was rather humorous.

Further on up the road they passed fields of bright yellow, again, down to their right and it was spectacular under the pre-summer sun. It was mythically gold and it reminded Madison of the Romans and the Greeks and the beauty and strength of their mythology. Sam loved the same mythology and thought of being with Madison as always bright and warm like the season when Ceres had Proserpina, it was never the season of winter when she would be with Hades in the cold underworld. Looking at her with the yellow beauty painted behind her, as the bus moved on, Sam was thankful for every second he had with her, war or no war.

They arrived in Cheltenham well before noon and de-bused at an Art Deco station, which again reminded them of home. The building was finished in smooth white stucco almost as if it were terracotta. Coming out from the main building was a wide overhang with rectangular support columns and then a canopy extended beyond that which afforded the buses shelter from the elements as they loaded and unloaded. The building was three stories and to the right of the main structure, and attached, was a café which was one level with three large glass paned areas surrounding three separate entrances. There must have been 40 large panes of glass in each section and it was inviting as it was opened up to the daylight. They walked in through the entrance with another, larger, winged crest above it similar to the one on the bus. After the long ride they needed to get a cup of whatever they could get at this point in the war in England. They stopped just past the entrance, before taking a seat, to admire the floor that was a checkerboard of large black and white tiles. They were the size of the linoleum tiles Sam had once seen on an American submarine he had quietly visited while in school in Boston when the Navy was trying to woo him into intelligence, just before he had met Madison. The floor for some reason had a relaxing effect on them and they started to put London, Fleet and Aldershot further behind them.

Tea was the drink of the day and they relaxed for awhile to get rid of the bus ride wishing they each had a real cup of strong 'joe' instead of weak tea.

While they sat there an old dilapidated London cab pulled up and parked outside the café window in front of a wooden bench. It was just post WWI and a bit worse for wear, and they loved the look of it. They paid their bill and walked out. They approached the driver, who was leaning up again the old cab, and, as Madison noticed, wore the insignia of the British 1st Infantry Division along with the Back Badge of the Gloucestershire Regiment.

"Excuse me Sir, could you tell me where we might find an inn for the night?", queried Sam as he approached the driver.

"Ah gov'na oy was only a lowly private not a Sir en ya sound a bit Biblical for a Yank; or is it Canadian?"

"It's Yank and I can get that way at times,… and you would understand if you were to know my wife," stated Sam as he nodded over to Madison at his side.

"Ah, a Yank with a sense au humor, excuse me Miss," he said turning his glance from Sam and nodding over to Madison.

"You're both excused", said Madison in a mockingly stern voice. "So you were with the 1st Brigade of the 1st Infantry Division Royal Glosters," Madison smiled at the man.

"Blimey, you're a mind reeda ya ar," he said looking at her, eyes wide open.

"No, I just read too much and I've always liked that badge with the Sphinx and the laurel leaves of victory that you have on your arm," and she smiled.

Looking at Sam he said, "Ya got yaself a fine one er mate, a fine one endeed," and he smiled with admiration.

Looking at them both he continued, "Since oy got ta know your lot qoyt well in the last war oy've missed 'earin' that accent. A great tyme ta be 'ere on a uneymoon."

"Ah, a Brit with a sense of humor."

"Oy dare ask but you're not on the run from the coppers?"

"I hope not."

"Well then, both get in n' Jimmy 'ere ell take ya ta the best place 'n town or jus' before ya get inta town. Ya passed it comin' in. The Swan."

Jimmy drove them to the Swan that day; he would adopt them for the rest of the weekend.

After they checked in they were shown one of two rooms available above the pub. The building was several hundred years old and cozy. It was set just back from the road as it dipped down off a hill, of early summer wheat filled with pheasants, into the outskirts of town just before the large cricket field belonging to Cheltenham College. The cricket field was on the left side of the road with a chapel, which reminded Sam of King's College Chapel, at the end of it and the town's general hospital across the street. Right next to the inn was a fenced pasture with lambs bleating for their mother's milk. It was pastoral and romantic and no one knew where they were other than that they were last seen at the Embankment tube station in London. They were free with each other for the first time since being together before their last, disrupted, meeting at the Commodore which seemed too many years in the past now.

They were with each other and Jimmy intuitively knew that they were under some extraordinary stress from the war. He probably knew that they were involved in war work and he was kind enough not to ask but drove them to special places so that they would never forget this area of the Cotswolds.

He drove them back in time three hundred years to a town by the name of Painswick and they fell in love with the town and with each other again in a place so removed from where they had been. They almost fooled themselves into believing that they had escaped the war to an island where no one would find them again. They sat in the churchyard of St. Mary's Church surrounded by sculpted yew trees and listened to the solitude. They couldn't shake their curiosity as historians and walked the churchyard reading the headstones.

"Thomas Heague, The Square, 23 September 1821 aged 53: *Mourn not my wife and children, I am not dead but sleeping here, my debt is paid a grave you see, stay but awhile you will follow me;* Mary, wife 15 June 1826 aged 52. Well she didn't make it much longer after he was gone," noted Sam reading the only stone to actually have a somewhat poetic inscription.

"John Bartlett, of this parish, Yeoman 24 April 1826, aged 50", read Madison. "Both Mary and John left us in 1826 around the same age. I wonder if these three had a similar problem to ours? And there's '26' again."

"Enough of history, we'll make our own and it won't end on an all but forgotten stone, although this is the most beautiful and tranquil spot to be forgotten in. Let's take a walk.", Sam said warmly as he stretched his hand out to Madison on the other side of John Bartlett's headstone.

They walked the cobbled ways and viewed the green valley that bordered the town on one side. They spent what was left of Saturday in the town and had a wonderful trout dinner in the small pub located in the middle of town almost on the side of the hill overlooking the valley. Jimmy had told them that he would be by to pick them up at 8PM in the evening by the church and that suited them just fine.

By the time they were in the cab with Jimmy at the wheel and headed back to The Swan they had the weight of the world removed from their shoulders. They hadn't thought of their meeting with General Eisenhower or the fears that they had over the Italian campaign, it had all drained out of them for this brief moment in time.

They made love quietly that night and in a way that was ethereal and peaceful in a world of its own away from the madness of the world they had come from. They then fell asleep in each other's arms and slept a sleep they had both been searching for since they each thought the other was dead.

They woke late and had breakfast just inside the front door of The Swan with the late morning sun falling in through the doorway and slowly spreading to bring everything back to life after a night bathed in the warm glow of a half moon. The song birds were filling the air with a morning cantata and Sam and Madison just held hands across the table and stared and smiled at each other like first time lovers.

After breakfast they walked the cricket field, just down the road across from the hospital. At the far end of the field they walked into the chapel and sat holding each other's hand. They held hands for the time that it took for them to realize that they were both thinking the same thoughts; then they squeezed each other's hand looking at each other with a conspiratorial smile of acknowledgement. The war was still with the world this wondrous morning and God help them all.

They walked downtown and past the fountain of Neptune with his trident; which gave them an initial chuckle, being out here in the Cotswolds, and at the same time reminding them of what they saw as a failure coming out of the TRIDENT Conference. They looked at each other briefly with sarcastic smiles as though someone with a strange sense of humor had put the statue there just for them to see, then they turned right at the fountain and walked down the short boulevard into the main part of town. At noon they walked to the bus station and met Jimmy who wanted to drive them around the outskirts of town and show them the Rococo Gardens from the 18th Century before taking them back to The Swan to collect their overnight valises, and then back to catch the 16:30 or 4:30 PM bus to London.

They said their sad good-byes just before four o'clock and Jimmy made them promise to return, which they said they would and that they would someday tell him why they were having a 'honeymoon' here in the middle of a war.

Jimmy just smiled at them clenched mouth and sad as their bus pulled away, and they were gone.

They passed the golden fields now on their left as the June sun of late day was setting them aglow and again they marveled at the beauty and the power of it all and then they were over the rise in the hill and down the other side and on their way to London.

They caught the third to last train out of Waterloo back to Fleet, on the wartime schedule, at 21:07.

As they exited the old Victorian gate, to their far right, at Fleet station, after having their tickets checked by the station master, they noticed, by the almost three quarters full moon, their 'bodyguard' leaning up again a small billboard in the parking lot advertising Guinness stout; he was being obvious and out in the open. They saw each other and Sam and Madison hesitated. He looked at his watch, looked back at them and nodded and smiled and they smiled back. If they could have they would have offered him a pint at the Links but they kept walking over the hill and across the street and over the next rise to the back of the Links and then onto Elvetham Road. They now knew that it was MI5 as he was not as good as the MI6 foreign espionage boys were purported to be. He was definitely an Englishman and in no way resembled an American OSS agent, as was obvious on their first close encounter in the Underground.

They headed straight to the cottage, bolted the door and headed for the little island with the daffodils still clinging on in the Mason Jar but now past their prime. They were back again and the war would start for them again the next day.

Late that night Sam snuck down to their small dinning table and wrote the following which he then put in her briefcase behind some mundane papers:

The flowers are sun so brilliant, to jacket these fields no photo can capture outside of Cheltenham town.
The winding road, these golden fields do trace, which one does take to London or another far off place with yellow flowers to embrace the memory of this splendid place with trout in nearby river grace, this winding road from Cheltenham town.
Their blinding yellow brilliance is painful beauty to the eye as brightness brighter will unfold around each turn in this winding road, from Cheltenham to the future behold.
It is the bus from Cheltenham to London, up so high above the road to view the yellow flowers in their greatest splendor and abundance do unfold.
This field to our left on this winding bus so brightly flashes by, broken by a country lane only to burst again with such yellow

flame.

*Prometheus and Ra together such fire of the sun to take, two
gods of two cultures join cunningly here to make.*

*Proserpina is in her day and Ceres does watch her play among
the yellow flowers with Hades kept at bay. No barren winter day
is there now in Proserpina's Springtime play and left behind
to winter's home is memory not finally kept but made of brittle
clay. Purple violets in her hair mark her dance a silver thread on
canvas made of gold in these fields of yellow flowers which we
feel and warmly hold.*

*Alatanta runs with glory in these fields of yellow gold looking
for bold Hippomenes and his golden apples of which, she has yet
to hold.*

*The Greeks were gods themselves and to these yellow fields of
brilliant sun they'd plain and simply say: Prometheus the gift of
fire do you give this day, this brilliance so abundant and yet so
plain to stay while Proserpina the Springtime and the flower, the
holder of the flame, is your child of wonder to the eyes and sense
of Man and Mankind while Alatanta does finally pick the apple
of her golden fame and Hippomenes the race does win and win
Alatanta just the same.*

*But the fields do see their seasons and the brightness does so
fade as Proserpina returns to Hades and the colors go to gray,
and Alatanta committed to the future here does so stay, and
turns for one last look alas with tear in eye to say good-bye
to the past and the last good-bye in Cheltenham town whose
memories she seems to amass.*

*These memories will always be with her never seeming to pass
and alas will never go away but in Cheltenham will stay.*

Sam finished by saying: 'Hades does not truly exist for us and
life will always be spring and summer when we once again return to
Cheltenham and sail the Hudson in a new day.'

July 1943 --- The Kursk Offensive

On July 5 the German offensive on Kursk started and the Russians were not so surprised.

On July 9, the first Allied airborne troops were dropped into Sicily with many men from the 505th Parachute Infantry Regiment and the 3rd Battalion of the 504th PIR of the American 82nd Airborne being widely scattered, some being dropped short and into the sea but the objectives were met.

On July 10, the main invasion of Sicily started at 2:45 AM local time and the Italian campaign, for all intents and purposes, was on although the invasion of the Italian Peninsula had not technically been agreed upon and therefore was not yet official. The landings by the American 7th Army and British 8th were a complete surprise. Operation HUSKY was underway. The occupation of Sicily was meant to secure lines of communications in the Mediterranean and pacify the British but Sam and Madison knew all too well that it would end with the invasion of Italy.

On July 11, the remaining Battalions of the 504th PIR were dropped in the vicinity of Gela, Sicily with heavy losses from both German and Allied antiaircraft fire.

On July 13, Hitler ordered a halt to the offensive on and around Kursk and began pulling troops out for redeployment to Italy as a result of the Sicily landings. Kursk, the largest tank battle in history, had been predicted by 'Commodore'.

The models that Sam and Madison had developed supported by equipment statistics and certain preceding events had proven their ability to predict when in line with each other, or when they became synergetic. 'Crystal Ball' had its first big success with predicting both strategy and tactics. The second major piece of analysis that they had presented to Eisenhower had as well, unfortunately, come to fruition. FDR/Churchill politics were proving too hard to influence. And once again; after reading the Ultra communiqué presented to her on the 14th, from Hitler, ordering a halt to the Kursk offensive and a redeployment of troops, Madison felt guilty that she had not done enough. She felt guilty while, at the same time, she was angry that politics were overriding 'pragmatic' analysis. Even though the landings on the Italian Peninsula were not committed to, as of yet, both Sam and Madison knew that the British would get their way against the solid opinion of the US Army Chief of Staff George C. Marshall. Even though they had armed Ike with what they called a 'Crystal Ball' on Kursk, to back a prediction of German troop movement into Italy as a result of the Sicily landings, they did not hold out much hope of stopping the British plan from being carried out. Madison had been affected by good solid analysis not being used properly and started to lose focus but Sam catered to her and had her back on track within a day, working even more tirelessly. He could start to see that she was getting worn down from the stress and the self-imposed responsibility for it all.

On July 16, FDR and Churchill released a joint statement telling the Italians they would suffer the consequences if they continued to tolerate a fascist regime. The Allies had unwittingly committed fully to the Italian campaign and Madison could see nothing coming from it other than great numbers of casualties on both sides. The British were the lead proponents of this madness, couldn't they just see the geography alone was forbidding, and now Hitler had committed troops to the defense of the peninsula, which they had said he would not do. Again, Madison was angry that the British were looking at all of this as though it were a grand game. The American Chiefs of Staff were not happy about opening up this campaign. BOLERO and ROUNDUP were gone. ROUNDUP would have to come in the next year with a new operational name.

On July 24-25; the British, under 'Bomber' Harris, hit the city of Hamburg at night with firebombs and committed the wholesale killing of civilians.

A day after the Hamburg raids Madison was horrified and wanted to put out a quick 'Flash' interpretation of the adverse consequences of such an attack on the effectiveness of the 'unconditional surrender' doctrine with regard to internal German politics. Not only was she personally horrified by the firebombing of civilians and wanted it stopped but she believed she could stop it with a good argument after sending out a 'Flash' communiqué, which was a general alert to the entire intelligence community at the highest level of clearance. She and Sam also agreed that such raids could adversely affect the doctrine from the civilian point of view, as the Allies would appear to be carrying out their own 'scorched earth' policy. In the end Madison had to agree with Sam that the argument was not strong enough and that it might compromise their influence, in the future, as the 'Flash' would be politically charged. The American military had warned the British not to area bomb and firebomb cities but the response had been that it would make more refugees and burden the Third Reich. 'Commodore' saw it as the result of two British policies; *nighttime bombing operations only*, which could only execute large area bombing and not strategic pinpoint bombings like the Americans, and just plan *destroy Germany* at all costs to its populous.

Madison and Sam could hear a vitriolic voice in the form of the commander of RAF Bomber Command Air Marshall Arthur 'Bomber' Harris. He wanted to destroy everything German and it did not matter that it did not make sense from a strategic standpoint. Both Madison and Sam looked at the historical backgrounds, as much as they could get, of individuals in power with whom they had to contend and 'Bomber' was one of them. His bombing of the beautiful medieval Hanseatic city of Lubeck in March of 1942 was pointless other than to destroy German heritage and kill civilians. It was almost carried out as retribution and was irrational and dangerous. Madison had noted that the after raid reports stated that the oldest carillon in German, built in 1508, was probably destroyed. It brought about Herman Goering's retaliatory response, which was the bombing of British cities such as Bath, Exeter and Norwich with the Baedeker Blitz. Harris was dangerous.

On Sunday, August 1, the oil refineries in Ploesti Romania were attacked by American B-24's in a low level attack. They were attacked on Sunday in order to minimize casualties among impressed workers at the refineries. Ploesti supplied almost half of Germany's refined petroleum products and its destruction would severely hamper Germany's ability to continue the war. The bombers paid a heavy toll with almost a third of the attack force lost. The Texaco refinery was hit first to show that America would destroy its own assets in the proper execution of the war. At the terminus of one of the bombing runs two damaged American aircraft were reported, by the new underground, to have been lost when the crews made a fatal turn, and stalled and crashed in order to avoid possibly hitting the orphanage they had been briefed about.

On August 5, Hitler ordered more troops in Russian to withdraw and re-deploy to Italy.

On August 6, German troops started flooding into Italy to take over its defense from the Italians.

On August 10, Churchill arrived in Quebec before the QUADRANT Conference in order to meet with the Canadian and Quebec Cabinets. Shortly afterward he headed to the Hyde Park, New York estate of FDR where he and the President meet for three days.

On August 17, the fight for Sicily ends as the Allies secure the island. In forty days of fighting the Allies suffer casualties of 23,934 killed, wounded or missing. The Axis suffers 29,000 killed wounded or missing. This represents a mere sample of what will take place if the peninsula is invaded.

On August 17-24, the QUADRANT Conference was held after FDR's arrival from Washington on the 17th. The meeting was held between FDR and Churchill and their advisors and Chiefs of Staff. Prime Minister of Canada Mackenzie King was also in attendance and the meetings were held at the Chateau Frontenac overlooking the city.

The first major topic was where and when the Allied invasion of Europe would occur. After three days of debate and, again, against the opinion of the George C. Marshall the British plan to invade the Italian Peninsula was agreed upon and finally became official. The new ROUNDUP plan, or cross-channel invasion, was agreed upon and Operations NEPTUNE and OVERLORD were officially born with a target date of May 1, 1944. The operational name of the invasion had moved from ROUNDUP to HAMMER and finally to NEPTUNE with the final lodgment on the continent codenamed OVERLORD. The Americans were worried that the Italian campaign would drain needed resources from the cross-channel invasion and after days of debate a compromise was reached and the two sides agreed that the Allied Forces would fight in Italy as long as "resources will be distributed and deployed with the main object of ensuring the success of 'Overlord'."

Churchill demanded that a prerequisite for the cross-channel invasion would be the destruction of the Luftwaffe, something that could only be achieved through daylight bombing which Churchill had fought against with the Americans. POINTBLANK, which had been put forward through Eisenhower's headquarters over two months earlier, specified the use of daylight bombing to gain air supremacy over the battlefield through the destruction of the Luftwaffe both on the ground and in the air. The American 8th Air Force would be taking the brunt of the casualties to achieve this, and achieve it with less resources as a result of the British push on the Mediterranean campaign.

Madison could only see the Prime Minister's politics as a dangerous contradiction within a contradiction within another contradiction. In the end it was a British lack of concern for American casualties. Here the Prime Minister of Great Britain was denying the Americans their operational needs and their operational approach but at the same time wanting the rewards that such operations would reap, which required their full implementation and full political support. He had fully embraced POINTBLANK and publicly made it his own. Madison even felt that the Prime Minister did not feel that complete air supremacy could be achieved and in so declaring a need for it gave himself a means of distancing himself from the reason for a cross-channel delay or setback, or even failure. She also knew that she could not afford to get too personally tied up in the politics of the Allies as it would affect her analyses. She could only try to positively affect politically charged policy as much as possible with pragmatically thorough analyses and hope for the best, even if she did blame herself when it did not work out well.

On September 3, a secret armistice was signed by the Italians with the Allies ending Italy's participation with the Axis and on the same day the British 8th Army landed at Reggio di Calabria on the Italian toe, as a feint to draw the growing German forces down from the area north of Naples. Field Marshall Albert von Kesselring sees it for what it is and does not move large forces against it.

On September 8, the Italian surrender is made public. It was delayed in order to give the Allies time to position troops for possible German response.

On September 9, the Italian campaign starts in earnest with the landings at Salerno of the US Fifth Army.

On September 10, German troops march into Rome and seized the capital.

On September 11, the heel of Italy falls to the British without much opposition as Kesselring is in a position to appose the landings at Salerno. The Italian slugfest is underway and 'Commodore' now focuses its analysis with the cross-channel invasion in mind. They have done all that they can do with regard to having an effect on the Mediterranean campaign and the Russian front. Madison and Sam now know that they have to use their models to bring about a 'Crystal Ball' in the areas that will be the target of NEPTUNE and/ or areas of future operations based off of the cross-channel foothold to be made in France with the establishment of OVERLORD. Their analyses leading up to a 'Crystal Ball' would come out in the form of advisories or, in the case of a lesser predictable event or warning it would come out as a 'Flash'. If it were to be a 'Crystal Ball' the analyses would go higher and would be directed with urgency possibly through the use of a **'code Black'**.

On September 12, 90 German glider borne troops, under Colonel Otto Skorzeny, rescued Mussolini from imprisonment at the Hotel Camp Imperatore in Abuzzi.

Shortly after this event 'Commodore' received intercepts, through Ultra, from Skorzeny to Hitler. Skorzeny put forward the proposition to kidnap both Yugoslavia's Tito and the Vichy government's Petain as a result of his success with the Mussolini operation. He appeared to have Hitler's ear and in one communiqué attacked Canaris's intelligence implying that he may not be trustworthy. Madison and Sam find this startling that a colonel would have so much power as to attack the head of the Ausland-Abwehr or foreign counter-intelligence and espionage. It also warned them that Admiral Canaris might be in jeopardy and if so the entire plot to kill Hitler and bring the war to an earlier end might be in jeopardy.

On October 14, B-17's of the American Eighth Air Force attacked the center of German ball bearing manufacture in Schweinfurt Germany. It was a daylight pinpoint raid to destroy the production of the one item that made the German war machine run and heavy casualties were taken when 60 bombers out of 291 were lost and 600 men did not return. There was aircraft debris littering the ground from coast-in to target and back out again and the landscape was dotted with white parachutes from the Eight Air Force and yellow parachutes from the Luftwaffe. It was 'Black Thursday' for the 'Mighty Eighth' Air Force. It was the type of risk that the American Air Force was taking with daylight bombing so that the German war industry could be shut down and the Luftwaffe would be removed as a factor during future operations, which would include the inevitable Operations NEPTUNE and OVERLORD. POINTBLANK hadn't yet been launched but the destruction of the Luftwaffe had become a priority on its own; POINTBLANK would just put the bull's-eye directly on the back of the Luftwaffe.

From October 19-30 American Secretary of State Cordell Hull, British Foreign Minister Anthony Eden and Stalin's Deputy Vyacheslav Molotov represented their governments in a series of Foreign Minister conferences in Moscow where the Russians were guaranteed that the cross-channel invasion would be staged in May of 1944. Also at these meetings the Russians' fears, or paranoia, of a separate armistice with Germany were put to rest by the U.S. and British agreement that the only surrender would be 'unconditional surrender'. They also agreed on plans for postwar Europe. The U.S. and British agreement over 'unconditional surrender' to appease Stalin reduced the use of this doctrine as leverage by British planners.

From November 28 to December 1 Stalin met with FDR and Churchill for the first time at the EUREKA Conference in Tehran, Iran where it was agreed that Operations OVERLORD and ANVIL, which was to be the invasion of Southern France after the D-Day landings, would receive the highest US and British priority.

Operation ANVIL had been set up to compliment what had first been called Operation HAMMER or what was now NEPTUNE and OVERLORD. American troops would land in Southern France between Cannes and Toulon. The objective would be to push German forces up from the south into easterly retreating German forces coming from the west as a result of OVERLORD. The idea was to cause confusion in the Wehrmacht ranks and allow the Allies to accelerate their advance. It would create a supporting force from the south to support any movement by OVERLORD troops further to the north and finally it would create another port of entry for supplies. Sam and Madison and 'Commodore' contributed a great deal of the work-up analysis for the second half of what they still referred to as ROUNDUP, as that is what the joint operation would help achieve by allowing the opportunity for an Allied encirclement of German troops and an early end to the war.

Churchill and the British were dead set against it. Churchill wanted all the resources he could get for the Italian campaign and to service his fixation with the Mediterranean. Eisenhower, backed by analysis from 'Commodore', stood his ground on this one and insisted that ANVIL was important to the success of OVERLORD because it would pin down German forces in southern France, slam German forces retreating from OVERLORD, and provide an additional port through which supplies could pass. He kept it simple.

Saturday morning December 4, 1943 found Sam and Madison at the 'chimney sweep cottage', which was becoming more and more like an office rather than a place to which they could escape. Clive was now gone most of the time and Sam and Madison were overly occupied with turning communiqués and data into effective analysis for the eventual invasion of France, and they had had a success: ANVIL.

"Churchill and the British are becoming an obstruction to proper analysis. I'm starting to interpret the communiqués and corresponding data in a way that would be acceptable to the British," worried Madison out loud.

Sam fully understanding what Madison was saying, but trying to alleviate the tension, chuckled and said, "Yah, it's worse than having to drink tea in the morning instead of coffee."

"This isn't funny Sam."

"I know it's not. Listen, we won one battle. We're getting ANVIL. This will give our forces the base they need to maneuver and potentially encircle an entire Army. It offers us a great deal of possibilities once we're on the ground in France."

"I see a problem with Churchill discounting it. If he manages to politically bury ANVIL so it can't be effectively used then what?"

"Eisenhower has stepped up to the plate; he didn't let them bury this one at the start or avoid it."

"So, we got a Texas Leaguer with a man on base in a tie ballgame; and it's still the top of the 9th inning with one man out. But I still feel that we're behind with crooked umpires and not playing on our home field."

Sam just stared at her, again in amazement, and then he smiled, "Yah, but we're the Yankees."

Madison smiled and then put her arms around him. She knew Sam's positive attitude was right and there were more factors in their favor than not. She would just have to put blinders on and interpret her data and come up with true analyses. She could let Sam position it with the magic he had when it came to understanding the bigger players in this game.

They had a workday in the cottage but evening came early and they would spend that in their own world. They were in England for another December and they seemed further away from home even though they were marching closer. They made love that night and they both separately dreamed of sailing the Hudson together in 'Whisper' on a warm summer afternoon, a summer afternoon from a lifetime ago which they would once again have.

The Italian campaign had run up against the collective German defensive line called the Winter Line south of Rome and it was running into snow and sub-zero temperatures. This defensive belt blocked any northern advance by the Allies, running from the Adriatic Sea across the width of Italy to the Tyrrhenian Sea. Madison and Sam knew that the worst was yet to come and then were would the priority lie. Troops and supplies were being tied up in Italy and the Allies were being bloodied. From an analyst's standpoint it was frustrating and from Madison's standpoint it was absolutely heartbreaking as well. She could feel the same feelings that had made her cry in the drizzle of that old far away battlefield at Gettysburg years ago when she was a child. 'Commodore' was working on intelligence for the coming cross-channel invasion but they were as well supplementing the tactical intelligence going out to the commanders in the field in Italy.

Madison and Sam, through 'Commodore', were able to visualize the defensive belts that the German Army was establishing, using the mountainous terrain to their benefit. The campaign would be nothing but bloody on both sides. Madison and 'Commodore' hoped that having greater input in the early planning stages of what was now known as NEPTUNE and OVERLORD would finally enable them to have a greater effect on an earlier end to the war with fewer casualties, even if they were momentarily shaken by Churchill's dismissive attitude with regard to ANVIL. The largest hurtle was always the British and both Madison and Sam saw that 'pompous little blowhard' in the name of General Bernard Law Montgomery as their key antagonist to getting the job done well; the Prime Minister was less of a threat. The British needed a hero and by default, and as a result of that shooting down of one particular Allied transport aircraft over the North African desert, by the Luftwaffe, Montgomery happened to be the only one standing on the stage when the dust settled. 'Commodore's' only leverage with Montgomery was the fact that they had discerned that the Prime Minister did not really like the man but put up with him as the accidental hero that the British population could tout as their 'sure bet'. This would be taken into account with specific analyses in which they knew the Prime Minister would be interested.

Their approach to Montgomery would be to try to feed him recommended solutions to potential tactical crises that would complement him. If they were able to do this they felt that they could get more of their intelligence recommendations implemented. They also felt that when a 'Crystal Ball' came up they might get a faster reaction with this man onboard and the way to do this was to make the intelligence coming from them beneficial to Montgomery's opinion of himself. This would no doubt prove to be as difficult a task as possible as the man was reminiscent of the American Civil War General of the Army of the Potomac McClellan. Madison, as an historian who lived history almost as much as if she were there, detested George Brinton McClellan "...who sat, asked for more troops, sat some more and let the war drone on," as Sam had heard her say on several occasions. Madison's fear was that McClellan had several chances to end the Civil War early and he hadn't taken them, and Monty sat in the same thrown of pomposity as McClellan had and would prove to be just as inept at commanding an aggressive army.

On December 12 Field Marshal Erwin Rommel was put in place as commander of the French coastal regions to set up a defense against an anticipated Allied cross-channel assault.

'Commodore' received a personal communiqué on December 13 from Hitler to Rommel which once again reconfirmed their belief that Rommel was the lead indicator for Hitler's primary concerns and focus, or fixation. Hitler had a respect and admiration for the man that allowed him to communicate his true strategic attitudes when communicating with him. The communiqué was overly exuberant about the appointment of the Field Marshal to 'guard the Atlantic Wall' to the point where it revealed a perceived weakness with the 'wall' on the part of Herr Hitler but that now he was relieved with Rommel in place. The Allies were anticipating that the cross-channel invasion would establish a foothold on the Continent from which to launch attacks on the weakening German Army. 'Commodore' perceived that the Atlantic Wall defenses were weaker than anticipated by the Allies, as a whole, even with the large delay in the invasion and that the invasion would be more than a foothold and could be a dash across Europe with the aid of ANVIL.

'Commodore' also saw a misperception of the true effectiveness of the Atlantic Wall as a lagging effect originating from the initial planners for the cross-channel invasion. The initial planners were British and lead by Lieutenant General Frederick E. Morgan. Their plan was first approved by the British Chiefs of Staff, who had both a past and a current predilection for underestimating Hitler and the ability of the German military to move major forces rapidly and, yet, what appeared to be a need to overestimate established German defenses. Even though the majority of the planning was now in the hands of G-5 Plans Section, headed by American Brigadier General Ray W. Barker, 'Commodore' saw this overestimation of fixed defenses and underestimation of troop mobility as a continual problem of the British that might inadvertently effect American planning. Madison felt that this British predilection was deeply ingrained and came from their experience in the fixed trenches of WWI, which was an altogether different war from the one that they were now fighting.

'Commodore' interpreted the appointment of Rommel, and the subsequent communiqué from Hitler, to give the first indications that Hitler was not going to bolster the French coast. 'Commodore' as a team felt that Hitler was putting too much trust in Rommel and the Atlantic Wall as it was. The initial planners felt that the 'Wall' was formidable and that they would concentrate on gaining a basic foothold from which they could launch attacks on the rest to the continent, or carry out follow-up operations. 'Commodore' felt that a major breakout could be made after successful landings catching Hitler off guard. His generals might anticipate Allied moves but Hitler controlled the movement of troops. With the establishment of Oberkommando der Wehrmacht, or the Armed Forces High Command in 1938, Hitler had decreed: "Command authority over the entire Armed Forces is from now on exercised directly by me personally."

'Commodore' felt that the breakout could be followed by a broad front movement deeper inland; then to be followed by two or three separate spearhead drives, backed up properly by logistics, to determine the point of greatest weakness. These spearheads would in effect be probing drives that would determine where the Allies would pile in and they could pile in through two separate corridors formed by the spearheads to overwhelm the German forces or encircle them. In their opinion the planning of OVERLORD, in concert with ANVIL, needed to keep this strategic concept in mind in order for the Allies to be set up to exploit such a situation if and when it were to occur; 'Commodore' believed it would occur.

On Tuesday December 14, 1943 'Commodore' issued a highly classified 'advisory' to Eisenhower's headquarters at Goodge Street that in part said '... *and with any future planning with regard to a potential cross-channel assault it is strongly advised that an aggressive broad front attack be planned for in order to probe for weaknesses in the German lines which can be exploited and in turn will naturally establish separate armor drives towards the heart of Germany. This will occur rapidly once a breakout from the beaches occurs. An aggressive defense by the enemy at the landing sites should be anticipated as well as a breakout from the beachheads that will catch the German Army off balance. The initial breakout from the beachheads will offer momentum against an off-balanced army which must be exploited. Any hesitation starts to afford German military doctrine an edge. Further, as mentioned earlier in this advisory, it cannot be stressed enough that a well implemented program for the purpose of misleading the German High Command, through deception, as to the actual time and place of such landings be given even greater focus than currently given. Misleading the enemy that such landings would take place in 1943 has had adverse effects which must be overcome...................'* COMMODORE

'Commodore' had also gone on to point out specific concerns with regard to the landings and one was that a major weakness in a plan by late spring 1944 would be the lack of Higgins boats. 'Commodore' felt that the procurement of landing craft had been overlooked with the requirements in the Pacific theatre and this was not quite figured into the equation.

'Commodore' would start compiling specific equipment statistics, again, according to Sam's earlier established and specific protocols. Sam would once again integrate these statistics with Madison and Commodore's analyses and accompanying data to come up with a potential event based on their models as affected by this data input. This could give them a 'Crystal Ball' or just enough overwhelming data to support a 'Flash' communiqué if it came to that, both of which could have a far reaching effect on the outcome of the cross-channel invasion.

On December 20 plans for an Allied amphibious assault on the west coast of Italy were cancelled due to lack of landing craft. Another factor for canceling the landing was that the Allies were now fully stalled at the German defensive Winter Line. Some of the fears of Madison and Sam were starting to play out.

On Christmas Eve day 1943 Eisenhower was appointed Supreme Allied Commander of Allied Expeditionary Forces with headquarters designated as Supreme Headquarters Allied Expeditionary Force or SHAEF for short. This was cause for a true Christmas Eve celebration. The only downside to this announcement was political in nature and that was that General Bernard Montgomery was named Commander Allied ground forces under Eisenhower.

Christmas Eve 1943, unlike Christmas Eve in 1942, found Madison and Sam together in the Fleet cottage, Clive being away for longer and longer periods of time no doubt involved in the cross-channel planning. Unknown to both of them, until now, was that during their getaway to Cheltenham Clive may have been close at hand as much of the British planning for the cross-channel invasion was carried out in that city. They seemed to have a 'coincidental type of luck' that Sam found statistically improbable, which he termed as 'exceedingly good luck' even for a statistician. He also now knew part of the reason that the buses still ran to Cheltenham and to him, as a statistician and intelligence officer, this was akin to a neon sign. If the Abwehr missed putting a man in Cheltenham, just to check it out, he would be amazed; but he couldn't worry himself with that possibility and he certainly would not mention it to Madison.

"My God, I can't believe it's another Christmas already," sighed Madison while snuggling up against Sam on the sofa in front of the coal fire with Bing Crosby's 'White Christmas' playing on the old Singer 'Victrola'.

"And this time we get to spend it together. And thank God you don't have to attend any parties around Fleet, you'd probably lose that genteel demeanor of yours over this appointment of Montgomery and blow our cover."

"What cover? With our friend from MI5 hanging around town everyone with the rank of colonel or above probably knows who we are."

"Ah, but they don't know how rambunctious we truly are."

"You're ridiculous." She smiled and then nuzzled into that cozy spot under his chin against his shoulder.

"And you're a lot of fun when you get rambunctious."

"I'll show you rambunctious," she said as she started to tickle him aggressively reminding him of the girl he knew way back when at the Commodore along the Hudson.

"Ah don't, don't I'll swallow my gum."

She stopped and looked at him quizzically, " I've noticed that recently, along with an opened package of Beemans gum here and there. You never chewed gum before."

"Nerves I guess, it calms me down. That sergeant up in Cambridge has been supplying me," Sam said sheepishly in a joking manner as he looked down at Madison.

"You're a child sometimes; a brilliant statistician, a great lover, a wonderful man and a child, and I love you for all of that. Now go spit your gum out, you're with me now and I'll take care of you," she scolded then smiled knowingly.

"I chew Black Jack on occasion too," he smiled jokingly.

"You're such a child," she said knowing that he was trying to downplay his abrupt confession to having stress.

Sam was starting to feel more stress lately as they both felt they hadn't gained any true control on having an effect on a quicker less costly execution of the war; even though they had some influence, mostly due to OVERLORD and Eisenhower. And now that Madison realized this, through this minor admittance by Sam of his new habit, she started to worry more. She had started to notice that he seemed to be a bit more tense than usual and she had noticed the new habit but she hadn't paid too much attention to it as Sam had never shown a weakness in the past. Sam was her rock. She was supposed to be the temperamental one and he was supposed to be the epitome of calm.

She just smiled up at him and started kissing him tenderly in front of the orange glow of the coal fire. She rubbed his neck and then moved her hand inside of his shirt and seduced him, in the most gentle of ways, on the small sofa in front of the chimney sweep's fireplace in the 'chimney sweep cottage' on Christmas Eve 1943.

On December 28th the British had talks with the Turks to bring them into the war on the side of the Allies. Churchill was still back in 1915 and the Dardanelles. The Allies did not need another WWI slaughter like Gallipoli but this British fixation on Italy was going to cause a lot more casualties for American troops than Gallipoli did for ANZAC troops and that was unacceptable. Gallipoli started on April 25, 1915 and ended at the beginning of January 1916. It accomplished nothing other than to create casualties. The conditions of the conflict were so bad that exact casualty figures were impossible for analysts, like Madison, to get; they didn't exist. The Allies suffered at total of between 142,000 and 175,000 casualties with around 44,000 killed. ANZAC troops accounted for somewhere around 34,000 of those casualties with over a third killed. On the other side, the Turks had a total of between 219,000 and 251,000 casualties with somewhere between 66,000 and 86,000 killed. The disparity in such large numbers, between the low estimate and the high estimate for both sides in the battle, had always been disturbing to Madison.

On New Years Day 1944 Erwin Rommel was made commander of Army Group B. This put him in direct command of all troops protecting the entire Atlantic Wall from Brittany to the Netherlands, or where the cross-channel landings were expected. While troops are being chewed up in Italy planners on both sides are focusing on the cross-channel move.

On January 11 American bombers took off on the first official mission of Operation POINTBLANK to cripple the German Aircraft industry. Aircraft factories were bombed in the daylight operations and heavy bomber losses were taken at the same time that the Luftwaffe was losing pilots in these aerial battles.

On January 15 U.S. forces captured Monte Trocchio reducing the Winter Line in the defensive belt traveling up the boot of Italy. The next and main line of the Winter Line was the Gustav Line anchored by Monte Cassino.

On January 16 Eisenhower assumed command of the Allied Expeditionary Forces.

On January 22 Allied forces, lead by Americans, landed at Anzio, 35 miles south of Rome, in a flanking maneuver. Operation

SHINGLE, as it was designated, was the brainchild of Winston Churchill and carried out against the arguments of the American command. Before the landings could be fully exploited the Germans moved the Hermann Goring Panzer Division in to attack the bridgehead. Other large German divisions were moved down from Northern Italy and casualties would be high.

On January 24 German forces formed stiff lines of resistance on the main Italian front when Hitler ordered the Gustave Line to be held at all costs.

The casualties that 'Commodore' had warned about would start to mount.

On January 27 the US military issued a report that Madison had been aware of and she was now satisfied that it was finally released. The report confirmed that the Japanese were committing atrocities on a large scale against US and Filipino prisoners captured after the fall of Bataan and Corregidor in 1942. She felt that this was part of the horrible cost of FDR pursuing the 'Europe First' policy.

On February 3 the Russians surrounded 10 German divisions, which was proof of Madison and Sam's theory, before the invasion of North Africa, that the Russians would tie up vast numbers of German troops to allow an earlier cross-channel attack. But now vast numbers of Allied troops where being held up and many were becoming casualties in Italy while the Allies worked feverishly to build up a supply and troop strength large enough to carry out the cross-channel attack in May.

On February 12 the Allies on Anzio beachhead fell back to a final defensive line and 83% of casualties were caused by devastating shrapnel wounds from artillery barrages being dropped on them. The first Allied assault on Monte Cassino was repulsed.

On February 15 the British theater commander in charge of the ground assault on Monte Cassino, General Harold Alexander, ordered the American 15th Air Force to bomb the 700 year old abbey. The Americans had refused twice, when first New Zealand General Bernard Freyberg had requested the bombing on February 12, before finally being ordered to do so. This order had originated from a request by two British ground commanders, Brigadier H.W. Dimoline and Major General Francis Tuker. The rubble of the great abbey gave the German airborne troops, on the mount, better protection and better hiding spots from which to fight. The taking of the abbey would be bloody and long and cause casualties among many different Allied nationalities as the German airborne troops had the high ground and the rubble for concealment. The irony of the Abbey was that left whole it afforded the German forces fewer fighting positions.

On February 20 POINTBLANK marched on as 1,000 bombers from the U.S. Eighth Air Force struck German aircraft factories centered in the Brunswick and Leipzig areas.

On February 22 Bombers from the U.S. Fifteenth Air Force in Italy joined in the daylight attacks on the German aircraft industry.

On February 24 German fighter attacks on U.S. bombers, bombing Schweinfurt and other strategic targets in Germany, intensified. Luftwaffe fighter aircraft losses were increasing.

On February 25 close to 20% of the bombers from the Fifteenth Air Force attacking Gegensburg aircraft factories were shot down. The fighter arm of the Luftwaffe took more losses.

American bombers disrupted a planned counteroffensive by German forces against the U.S. 3rd Division on Anzio Beach.

On March 3 the Anzio beachhead is secured and the American 3rd Division counterattacked and gained ground.

On March 4 the U.S. Eighth Air Force, for the first time in the war, attacks a German city directly and that city is Berlin. The capital of Berlin is now deemed a strategic target.

On March 8 590 bombers from the U.S. Eighth Air Force, accompanied by long range American P-51 fighters attack the Erkner ball-bearing factory in Berlin. The attack causes production slowdowns but thirty-seven American bombers are lost. The ball bearings are also a necessity for German fighter aircraft production. The Luftwaffe takes more fighter losses.

On March 15 Monte Cassino is bombed again to try to break the German defense but an assault by Indian and New Zealand troops, directly afterward, is repulsed.

On March 18 the heaviest air raid of the war, to date, is carried out at night by the RAF who area bomb the city of Frankfurt am Main.

On the same day an armored attack on the abbey of Monte Cassino by New Zealanders is repulsed with heavy losses.

Madison again found herself sitting at her desk in the 'Dome' feeling helpless. Here hundreds of civilians in a city were once again being slaughtered while young men died wholesale in Italy. These were two events that she had worked to prevent. She was a proponent of daylight strategic bombing and argued the adverse ramifications of night area bombing. Italy just should not have happened. She and Sam and 'Commodore' where now trying to put out analysis that would help to optimize 'the success' of the cross-channel landings, coming at them quickly now.

On March 22 Frankfurt an Main is attacked again killing just over 1000 civilians and this paled in comparison to the RAF firebombing of Hamburg in July of the previous year. Madison focuses on her immediate work.

On March 20-31 the RAF loses 95 planes out of 795 on a nighttime 'area raid' with 71 severely damaged and as a result the British suspend their long-range nighttime 'area raids'. International criticism is now growing with regard to the RAF's area bombing of German cities but the British government defends the raids as, '…. essential to the liberation of the peoples of western Europe.'

On April 5 U.S. planes once again strike at German oil targets and bomb rail facilities servicing the Ploesti, Romania refining center.

On April 13 the first actions in Operation NEPTUNE, or the cross-channel invasion, are carried out when Allied aircraft begin a series of attacks on German coastal artillery units in the Normandy area. Normandy is not the only area hit as other areas of the European coast are hit as well to camouflage Normandy. But, still, Madison is nervous every time an activity is covertly directed at the Normandy coast or what she knows to be the landing beaches of the Allied Expeditionary Force under General Dwight D. Eisenhower. The next day security is stepped up as the British restrict their own diplomatic privileges. Madison again is worried but in this case she is concerned that too much security at once could inadvertently reveal, to the enemy, something of great relevance to the success of the entire operation. Sam started her thinking this way as a mathematical or statistical idea: if you start shutting down anything that might reveal a specific objective then the types of communications shut down and their sequence of being shut down could point to that specific item or objective.

They were both feeling the increased stress and Sam was now always with his Beemans and was '…chewing gum like a shortstop playing in Yankee Stadium for the first time,' at least that's what Madison said worrying about him now and trying to lighten the atmosphere. She was starting to give Sam the support that he had always given her.

In April 'Commodore' was starting to pay closer attention to any communiqués with regard to German fighter strength. They were looking for the effects of Operation POINTBLANK with regard to degrading the Luftwaffe by the time the invasion forces were ready to land on the beaches. Sam found the statistics startling in that it appeared that fighter aircraft production had gone up while the amount of fighters that the Luftwaffe was putting up to meet the American daylight attacks had decreased.

Sam was both startled and worried. Was the Luftwaffe holding back forces in reserve waiting for the landings to occur before unleashing an onslaught from the air?

'Commodore' started looking at personnel statistics from the Luftwaffe and any communication whatsoever that popped up with regard to aircraft production, no matter how trivial. They even gave 'Fagin', at Ultra, a shopping list and invoked a 'pass phrase', which was to get them whatever they wanted in the run-up to NEPTUNE/ OVERLORD, no questions asked. When Madison was able to get the correct telephone connection directly to 'Fagin' using this phrase she dialed him. When he picked up she simple said: "Hi Fagin, it's Commodore and I have a shopping list and I'm going to pay for it with a *three pence broken candlestick*'. 'Fagin' had responded, "that currency sounds about right; what can I help you with?"

Madison had given 'Fagin' a shopping list from Sam. The items were as big as aircraft delivery times and places, as the Germans were great at keeping track of aircraft flying from one location to another almost as if they were filing a civilian flight plan, and there were smaller items. The items could be this big and as small as the delivery of ball bearings or specialized wire. He also needed to know about personnel and this could be anything from numbers coming from what were suspected to be pilot training facilities to pilots' death notices picked up by informants behind the lines. Intelligence sources feeding additional information into Ultra, for backup, were in contact with these informants throughout Europe, as 'Commodore' had recently learned.

On Friday, May 5, 'Commodore' came out with a 'Flash' analysis as SHAEF, or Eisenhower's command, and the planners were fully aware of the fact that German aircraft production was up. The 'Flash' read as follows: *German aircraft production is up due to the efficiency of daylight bombing and the bomb technology that has accompanied it. US bomb fusing for POINTBLANK has been set at 1/10th of a second in order to bring the roofs down on production equipment on direct hits and building collapses on near misses. It was felt that delayed action bombs would only be effective on direct hits and each bomb would be limited on its area of destruction. The feeling was that the 'quick' bombs would do the job more efficiently and the arming was carried out accordingly. The 8th and 15th Air Forces were efficient with their bomb accuracy and delayed action bombs would have shut production down. The 'quick' bombs, it appears, just buried equipment, which was dug out and moved, by the direction of Albert Speer (classified-U), to caves for protection and production reestablishment. Aircraft production has actually increased. Daylight bomber operations had a second effect on the Luftwaffe fighter arm besides accurate bombing of aircraft production facilities: it as well took a great toll on Luftwaffe pilots. The casualty rate for Luftwaffe fighter pilots has been high against the Eight Air Force and we more than strongly feel that they are currently undermanned and to fill this gap they are rushing under-trained pilots into combat. To back this up we had an analysis of Eight Air Force combat reports carried out. German fighter tactics have changed dramatically over the past couple of months showing more caution, while at the same time revealing a different skill level which is clearly showing up in the combat theatre. This group's fears of an enemy fighter build up for D-Day is alleviated and POINTBLANK has succeeded in its mission.*

This 'Flash' was well received by Eisenhower and SHAEF. The planners moved forward with less concern for the Luftwaffe built in to the operational plans of NEPTUNE.

On May 8, Eisenhower designated June 5 as D-Day.

On May 11, a major Allied offensive called Operation DIADEM was launched in central Italy to break through the Gustov Line, or the main defensive line of the Winter Line. The offensive began after nightfall at 23:00 with a massive artillery barrage from 1,600 guns followed by a frontal ground assault. The British general Alexander saw the operation as a way to tie down German forces in Italy during NEPTUNE and OVERLORD and capture Rome. Madison and Sam now see a complete transfer to Italy of what they initially held as the great importance of the Russian front, which was that of holding large amounts of German forces in check to aid the cross-channel invasion. It is a much bloodier scenario than they had envisioned two years earlier, much bloodier for all

combatants involved while extending, by a year, the actual date of the cross-channel invasion.

On May 12, Allied forces in Italy meet stiff German resistance as they advance on a broad front crossing the Rapido River.

On May 12; over 800 US bombers, with fighter escort, attack synthetic oil plants in Germany taking several out of production. Luftwaffe losses are heavy as nearly 200 of their fighters are shot down while 46 bombers and 10 Allied fighters are lost. The Luftwaffe losses help to back up the 'Commodore' 'Flash' of Friday May 5.

On Saturday May 13, with the U.S. 88th Infantry making progress against heavy resistance, the 4th Moroccan Mountain Division takes high ground overlooking the Liri Valley creating an initial breach in the Gustave Line. Seeing this initial breach American General Mark Clark's 85th Division joins with the 88th to smash into the German positions over rugged terrain and create a wide breach in the German lines.

On this Saturday the first daffodils come up more than two weeks later than the previous year and Madison had been waiting for their reassuring beauty of things renewed. When Sam looks at the daffodils he can only think of the smell of honeysuckles on a cool summer's evening back home with Madison; this is one scene of home that he was now living over and over again in his imagination. The war, so far, had been long and they had a long month in front of them. Not only were they running analysis but they were now part of the deception being created by the Allies.

As the German's were looking at Patton as the logical commander to lead the expected cross-channel invasion, and not Montgomery, it was decided to give Patton a fake army located in Dover, north of the actual invasion force. Dover would be the logical place to launch a cross-channel attack into the logical target Pas de Calais. Patton was put in charge of the First U.S. Army Group or **FUSAG**. He even went so far as to give rounds of speeches in the Dover area so that anyone watching would not miss him. This deception was code named Operation FORTITUDE with sub-plans named Operations QUICKSILVER I-VI. Commodore had input to QUICKSILVER II or the radio deception aspect of FORTITUDE dealing with phony Allied troop movement. Madison and Sam also supervised, from a distance, QUICKSILVER III and the establishment of dummy plywood landing craft along with the associated radio traffic, and signing of roads and special collection areas that would facilitate the movement of landing craft to the embarkation point. What was ironic to 'Commodore' was their warning to the planners of a severe lack of actual landing craft.

Against their better judgment 'Commodore' also sent out fictitious situation analyses to Patton's 'phony' staff. 'Commodore' was not identified but it still did not ensure their absolute security, which was paramount at this stage of the war.

The most disturbing order to Madison came to Sam from 'Wild Bill' Donovan himself. He wanted Sam to appear at Patton's headquarters as himself, as the analyst that he was. Donovan met with Sam and informed him that they had set Sam up with the high visibility arrival in England aboard the Yankee Clipper in order to establish his value, as far as Admiral Canaris would be concerned, to possibly be used at a later date for contact with the Admiral and head of the Abwehr. Sam had been kept low profile at Cambridge and was informed by Donovan that he had never been shadowed and that included to the cottage in Fleet, which got Sam to raise his eyebrows as Donovan smiled knowingly. He said that Sam had never been shadowed but that the dots would be connected when he appeared at Patton's headquarters in Dover, as it was being closely watched by the Abwehr with the graces of Allied counterintelligence. The Abwehr would finally establish his importance, confirmed by Canaris, therefore giving even more credence to the Dover crossing. He was also promised that security oversight would be put at a higher level for both he and Madison and 'Commodore' as a result.

The 'chimney sweep cottage' lost a great deal of the security and the seclusion that it offered them both from the war. The war was cornering them and they seemed to have no place to escape it except during their intimacies with each other.

On May 16, after savage fighting, the defenders of the Gustave Line fall back under the attacks from the American 85th and 88th Infantry Divisions. Heavy casualties are taken but the line is successfully and firmly breached, and U.S. forces start to take advantage of the fluid situation and to look toward a link up with American forces on the Anzio beachhead and a drive on Rome.

On Wednesday, May 18, Sam visited the headquarters of **FUSAG**. He never even met the general but sat with part of his phony staff and discussed possible German troop deployment in the Pas de Calais area. They were really keeping up appearances even behind closed doors. Sam had a good ol' American lunch of ham and cheese sandwiches and coffee topped off with a Hershey bar, which he found to be the highlight of the visit along with a couple of packs of Beemans gum. After lunch he was off; with his deception completed, and his credibility established and that of Patton's enhanced.

On May 18, German forces pull back from Monte Cassino as a result of the breach in the Gustav Line. Polish troops take the Casino and raise their flag over the ruins and the U.S. forces leading the breach link up with American forces on the Anzio beachhead so they can head to Rome. The struggle for the 700 year-old Benedictine monastery had lasted four brutal months and had been attacked by troops from 15 different nations. Twenty thousand had been killed in the battles of the Casino and another 100,000 had been wounded. The Italian campaign was growing costly for both sides. The Gustav Line had been breached and the next one in line is the Hitler Line, and the bloody Italian campaign continues on in its bitter struggle as the upcoming cross-channel invasion starts to take the spotlight and delegate the Italian campaign to a sideshow, and a brutal and bloody sideshow at that. The campaign of North Africa is no longer touted by Churchill as the pivotal campaign of the war like Gettysburg of the American Civil War.

On May 21, Allied fighters launch heavy attacks against Axis rail transport in France and Germany in preparation for the invasion. Intensive Allied bombing all month had already inflicted vast amounts of damage on the rail system that could feed logistical support into the potential landing sites along the French coast.

On May 25, American units breakout of the Anzio beachhead after four months of fighting and a link up is completed with Mark Clark's Fifth Army.

On May 29, heavy losses are incurred by the US 1st Armored and 34th Division on the approaches to Rome.

On May 31, Allied troops begin to board troop ships for the invasion of the Normandy coast.

On June 4, the U.S. Fifth Army enters Rome. Due to adverse weather Eisenhower orders a 24-hour postponement to the planned Normandy landing scheduled to take place on June 5th; all airborne units stand down while troops embarked remain on troop ships getting more sea sick by the hour. If the invasion is not launched on the night of the 5th and the morning of the 6th the next good day for tide and moon will be June 17. The Allies also need four good months of weather to gain the ground that they are looking to gain.

On June 5, with 175,000 troops embarked on ship and the weather report starting to look better for the next 24 to 36 hours Eisenhower simply says, "OK, we'll go," knowing that a delay could surely jeopardize security.

On June 5, all airborne units are given the green light. Men of the American 101st and 82nd Airborne are more than ready and have been training for two years for this night. Never have airborne units, or any other units for that matter, been at the elite level that these men are at now.

Eisenhower issues the message of the day, which reads:

Soldiers, Sailors and Airmen of the Allied Expeditionary Force!

You are about to embark upon the Great Crusade, toward which we have striven these many months. The eyes of the world are upon you. The hopes and prayers of liberty-loving people everywhere march with you. In company with our brave Allies and brother-in-arms on other Fronts, you will bring about the destruction of the German war machine, the elimination of Nazi tyranny over the oppressed peoples of Europe, and security for ourselves in a free world.

Your task will not be an easy one. Your enemy is well trained, well equipped and battle hardened. He will fight savagely.

But this is the year 1944! Much has happened since the Nazi triumphs of 1940-41. The United Nations have inflicted upon the Germans great defeats, in open battle, man-to-man. Our air offensive has seriously reduced their strength in the air and their capacity to wage war on the ground. Our Home Fronts have given us an overwhelming superiority in weapons and munitions of war, and placed at our disposal great reserves of trained fighting men. The tide has turned! The free men of the world are marching together to Victory!

I have full confidence in your courage and devotion to duty and skill in battle. We will accept nothing less than full Victory!

Good Luck! And let us beseech the blessing of Almighty God upon this great and noble undertaking.

SIGNED: Dwight D. Eisenhower

The airborne assault into Normandy in support of the landings on the 6th is the largest airborne assault to ever be massed to this point and is a primary element of Operation NEPTUNE. Sam had joked that as the early planners worked in Cheltenham they probably took the operational name from that 'impressive' fountain of Neptune they had seen.

The air armada is predominantly comprised of the U.S. 82nd 'All American' and 101st 'Screaming Eagles' Airborne Divisions, the British 6th Airborne Division, the 1st Canadian Parachute Battalion and elements of other Allied units. The total drop would be comprised of just over 20,000 men.

Paratroop elements of the 82nd and 101st Divisions comprising 6 regiments, along with parachute field artillery and engineers, number more than 13,000 men who will be ferried to the Cotentin Peninsula in 925 C-47's. Another 4,000 men from the two divisions, with supporting weapons and medical and signal units, will arrive in 500 gliders.

At 2215 on June 5, the first C-47's of the 432 being used by the 101st Airborne start their take-off rolls from seven different departure airdromes around England. The C-47's climb in a large rising circle like the tail of a comet as more and more take off and prepare to form up into the great air armada.

The airborne are the key to protecting the flanks of the sea borne beach landings. They are to secure crucial causeways and confuse and disrupt an organized defense by German forces.

Flying through heavy clouds and antiaircraft fire the C-47's carrying the 82nd and 101st drop troops all over the peninsula many at below minimum altitude and many more at higher than suggested speeds for a proper drop. Casualties are high from antiaircraft fire, much of it green 20MM tracers, and general ground fire directed at troops helplessly suspended under their parachute canopies. Many paratroopers drown under heavy equipment loads in fields flood by the German army.

The badly scattered airborne troops create confusion in the German lines and fighting as airborne troops, who are trained to fight in surrounded positions, they take their objectives to facilitate the success of the beach landings.

At 05:30 on June 6, 1944; the massive naval bombardment of the German defenses along the Normandy coast begins. Seven thousand ships and landing craft manned by 195,000 naval personnel from eight Allied countries take part.

At 06:30 troops start landing on the five beaches of Gold, Juno, Sword, and Omaha and Utah taking in a thirty-mile stretch of coastline. The Canadians land on Juno and the British on Sword and Gold. American forces land on Omaha and Utah beaches with American Rangers taking the heights at Pointe Du Hoc.

Omaha turned into the deadliest beach by 07:00. At least one veteran U.S. division is tasked to Omaha due to its difficulty and this is the 1st Division. The 1st Division along with the 29th Division and the 5th Ranger Battalion and 5th Engineer Special Brigade go up against a formidable defense. Omaha is unlike any of the other assault beaches in Normandy. It is the most defensible beach chosen for D-Day with its crescent curve and assortment of bluffs, cliffs and draws for optimum defense. It is the widest, at 6 miles, and the deepest of all beaches. Its five gullies, or draws, off the beach are covered by 14 Widerstandsnester or "resistance nests", which are heavily defended strongpoints. Also supporting the Widerstandsnesters and covering the draws and the beaches are over 85 machine gun nests. The approach to the bluffs are further protected by antitank walls, minefields and barbed wire.

The planners initially earmarked the beach as an unlikely landing beach due to its defensive terrain and the high ground above it. They determined that movements off the beach by invading forces would be funneled into narrow passages between the bluffs which could prove disastrous, and they also determined that to climb the bluffs would be more than difficult. For this reason, a year before the invasion, Brigadier General Norman Cota , Assistant Division Commander of the 29th, had suggested tactical surprise through a night landing; this was rejected.

Upon landing the American forces come under heavy enfilading fire. The naval bombardment had no effect on the beach as the beach's pillboxes are situated in the draws hidden from naval fires but positioned to stop movement on the beach. To compound the problem a full strength German infantry division is located directly behind the beach. The German 352nd Division is found in place and is known as one of the better trained infantry divisions in the Werhmacht.

There is no cover on 'Omaha' and seasick troops wet and weighted down with equipment are raked with machine gun fire. They carry out a frontal assault. Within ten minutes of the ramps on the landing crafts being dropped the leading company of the 1st Infantry Division losses all their officers and sergeants either dead or wounded.

At 6:36 that morning, right on schedule, Company A of the 1st Battalion of the 116th Infantry of the 29th Division lands on beach "Dog Green" on Omaha and are cut to pieces. Nineteen men from one town in Virginia are killed on or close to "Dog Green" that morning. These were General Cota's men. Cota, standing in full view of the enemy, would lead the remainder of his men off the beach this morning.

Towards the end of the morning the near impossible bluffs are scaled as the gullies between the bluffs are too deadly.

After 12 hours of fighting on "Bloody Omaha", and up the bluffs and across the plateau to attack enemy forces in the rear, the beach is secured and a bridgehead less than two miles deep is established. There are over 3,000 American casualties, over 1,000 of whom are dead.

By the end of the Day the Allies have their foothold on the coast of France.

Madison, Sam and 'Commodore' aware of the success of the day find themselves on this Tuesday, June 6, in Fleet at the cottage and in Aldershot at the 'Dome' still trying to jump ahead to predict the future on the battlefield in a way that will be utilized by the Allies to bring the conflict to a swifter and less bloodier close.

The Luftwaffe did not make a large appearance over the beaches as 'Commodore's' 'Flash' had predicted.

On Tuesday evening the 13th of June Sam hands Madison casualty numbers for the USAAF from January, and the start of POINTBLANK, through the beginning of June.

"1,434 Killed or missing, 326 wounded", muttered Madison to herself before looking up at Sam from the paper with tears starting. Sam noticed that she was starting to look more worn than ever and he also knew that she would take these numbers personally because of their push on POINTBLANK, but he wanted to give her the numbers before she received them from another source.

"POINTBLANK saved countless lives on the beaches and we now have a secure foothold on the Continent. It's the beginning of the end."

"I know, and I know that I'm an analyst and that I should look at all of this purely from an analytical standpoint but I can't. No matter how you cut it or slice it I am partly responsible for the missions that were deemed necessary to accomplish the goals of POINTBLANK. I can't simply get away from a degree of guilt, that would be too simple," she said as a tear dropped on the paper making a hollow sound just before the silence that followed.

Her face was stricken and Sam needed to give her a way out, "Don't you think that those airmen knew what they were doing, have you read any of the after action reports," he said with a degree of a feigned stern demeanor, his heart aching as he did so.

"Yes, but…"

"But nothing, give those young men credit. They knew exactly what they were doing and their debrief comments support that and the fact that they knew they were causing great attrition to the Luftwaffe both in men and material. They also knew the importance of this for the guys that would eventually be hitting the beaches."

She just put her arms around him and tucked her head up under his chin and against his chest, and wept quietly as Sam's heart broke. He would never purposely talk to her in this authoritative manner but he knew someplace inside of himself that this was the only way to snap her out of it, to make her feel guilty over her own guilt when these young men had suffered so much.

Before D-Day, General Bernard Law Montgomery was assigned the task of taking the key to the beach landings' breakout and that was the city of Caen. As Eisenhower's ground commander he guaranteed that he would have Caen on D-Day. It was key, as the gateway on the direct road to Paris, and it as well had all the airports in the region from where Allied aircraft could operate. When he was still just off the beaches a week later, he wasn't any closer to having Caen than in the first few hours of the landings.

On June 26, American forces cut off the Cherbourg Peninsula and captured it. The harbor had been destroyed by the surrendering German forces and would take a month to put back into some sort of workable shape.

On Wednesday July 4, 1944, Madison was at the 'Dome' and received a late day communique both in German and in the translated version from Ultra. The communiqué was in two parts with the first part coming from an unidentified source and the second communiqué from Hitler to all commands OB West; or Oberbefehlshaber West, the Commander in Chief West for Western Europe.

Sam was now a permanent fixture at the cottage and rarely returned to Cambridge. Things were happening too quickly to keep up the charade and by now the Allied intelligence services all knew that he and 'Commodore', or Madison, were working together out of the cottage. Neither Sam nor Madison worried about this as they knew they were surrounded by good security, mostly unseen. He was concentrating on new statistical data that had come in the day before when he heard the MG powering up through the gears after making the turn at the Links onto Elvetham. He just smiled and continued looking at the figures he had just worked out.

As the MG downshifted, just before the driveway, it backfired for the first time that he could remember and he laughed thinking that this was the extent of the 4th of July that they would get, and from a British car. "Ah, the irony", he chuckled to himself.

As Sam was heading to the small kitchen, to greet Madison at the back door, he heard that same door slam just as he saw her heading in his direction in more of a hurry than he had seen her in months.

"Whoa, slow down," he said as she breathlessly stopped in front of him with a smile on hear face.

"I have a fourth of July gift for you," she stammered anxiously as she handed him her briefcase which she had never done in the past.

"And I thought you had manipulated that car of yours to backfire for our celebration."

"Well maybe I did and in excitement over what's in the case," she said calmly, now watching him pull out the contents as he moved to his seat on the far side of their small dining room table. She then joined him and moved to her seat across from him.

As he looked over the first document he just said, "Wow."

"Is that all you can say?"

"Hitler's putting our old friend von Kluge in charge of OB West, or in command of the entire western army. It might be the perfect time for an assassination of Hitler. We know von Kluge wants to end this war and he had to have been involved in the two previous attempts. The pieces could be fitting in nicely."

"My thoughts as well, but look at the second communiqué and the reasoning behind the change in Command from von Rundstedt."

As Sam read through it he just muttered, "You're kidding.......... now this is a fourth of July gift." Looking up, Sam questioned, "Can this be verified?"

"Exactly what I thought and so did Ultra, and when I queried them, through 'Fagin', he said with some uncharacteristic joy in is voice, with regard to von Rundstedt, 'The good general was heard by several on July 1, in a phone conversation with Hitler's chief of staff Field Marshal Wilhelm Keitel, to say, in response to the chief of staff asking him what they should do about the Allied invasion in Normandy, "End the war, you fools. What else can you do?".' Fagin informed me that the original source was good and the confirming source was unidentified but highly placed and that it was verbatim, with the variance in translation of course."

"Now we're getting someplace. The key is the assassination of Hitler, he's the keystone that is keeping this all together. Now we have a chance of ending this thing sooner rather than later; no matter what influence that egocentric, defensive stance recidivist Montgomery wields."

"It would appear that way," said Madison a little more reserved than she had been, "especially with this indicator of spreading discontent with the continuation of the war at respected levels where military acumen resides and Prussian Military Tradition, such as von Rundstedt's, prevails. I also have no doubt that the 'unconditional surrender' doctrine is playing a part here by playing on the rational minds in the German High Command. And you have managed to expand the definition of recidivist," she finished trying to bring a little levity to the conversation.

"But what? I hear something in your voice," queried Sam, disregarding the last comment.

"All of the positive aspects of this change of events and state of the German High Command, and it's effect on the near term end to the war, balances on the elimination of Hitler and we've seen two failures already. The man has nine lives."

"Well, all we can hope for is a better approach than the use of a bomb and they may have figured this out by now."

"They may know that but a bomb is more feasible in more situations than a confrontation close in or at long range with a gun," stated Madison looking at him with concern in her eyes.

"Ah, Baby; you're doing everything you can and with our combined experience we both know that we've never seen a better set of events possibly leading to an earlier end to this war without having to deal with that interloper Montgomery."

"Oh Sam, I hope you're right.", she said looking at him and then after a brief pause with a light-hearted smile on her face she added, " 'Defensive stance recidivist' and 'interloper' who's the emotional one?"

" I'm allowed my times," said Sam with a sheepish smile.

They would put their joint analyses and potential scenarios together and send out a 'Flash' to SHAEF headquarters and qualify their source as 'classified-U', which would qualify them without having to identify them. At their level their use of 'classified-U' was unquestionable. They would send this out as soon as they finished their write up this evening.

After they put their 'Flash' together Madison jumped into the MG and at eight o'clock in the evening on July fourth gave her English neighbors a full throttle sound of an MG auditioning for Le Mans. She drove to the 'Dome' and called a courier who arrived on motorbike with an outrider, an outrider armed with a Thompson and another motorbike trailing behind. They were actually American troops on American Harley-Davidson WLA motorcycles this time and security was outwardly tight with the war moving along quickly. They were not tip-toeing around in the dark quietly and secretively now. The throaty pop-pop----pop-pop----pop-pop sound, made by the Harley's two pistons being tied into one pin on the crankshaft, was reassuring to Madison as they departed the Cambridge Military hospital with the 'Flash' message. As she smiled to herself about her mechanical knowledge, with regard to the Harleys, she knew that she wouldn't let Sam know until sometime after the war as she didn't want to scare him. He did know by know that she surely had a love for fast cars but not that she had such mechanical intimacy with anything motorized.

Sam could hear Madison make the turn onto Elvetham at 9:45 PM and, as she was downshifting just before hitting the boundary of the property, she backfired the MG.

Sam laughed and muttered, "I'll be damned, she did do it on purpose; happy 4th Baby."

That night they listened to Al Jolson to celebrate the Fourth of July in a foreign country. And then they made love in front to the fire with Edith Piaf lamenting sadly and beautifully in the background while their 'Singer' grew more distant as they became lost in each other in ways they never could have imagined years earlier, before they first met in the Boston Gardens.

A month after the landings 'Monty' is still sitting outside of the city of Caen within artillery support of the ships, which had initially backed up the landings. While 'Monty' is sitting outside of this key objective for the success of the invasion, the Americans are slugging it out in the hedgerows of Normandy; they are making things happen. The fact that 'Monty' had not delivered as advertised and is still sitting in a defensive mode while the American forces are trying to breakout sends bad tremors to Madison, Sam and 'Commodore' who are in the process of developing a 'Crystal Ball' analysis, which they still had not officially named 'Crystal Ball' for fear of creating a lack of credibility. The precise fear that they had developed when Montgomery was made an accidental hero in North Africa was here and unfortunately due to politics this man was in charge of ground forces in Normandy. American lives were being lost to pick up the slack from Montgomery's failure in order to protect the landings and bring about a success.

On the night of July 7, the British turned Caen into rubble with the start of Operation CHARNWOOD devised to take the city. The city was bombed so badly that the surviving populous did not recognize it while British Bomber Command had completed its first tactical bombing.

"My God, didn't they learn from Monte Cassino? They've killed large numbers of civilians and the Germans will just return to the rubble in the city and create better fighting positions," Madison stated with force.

"We have a problem in our midst with Montgomery and the only way to handle this is to project 'Crystal Ball' out as far as we can once a breakout is established and the German formations get repositioned. We'll have to do this and call a **'code Black'** or try to go even higher", stated Sam.

"By higher do you mean the President?", queried Madison while she stared down at a condensed map with estimated troop displacements in and around the Normandy beaches.

From the other side of the small dining room table in the cottage Sam just replied, "Yes."

The following day, July 8 the delayed attack of Operation CHARNWOOD is launched by Montgomery and British and Canadian forces. Heavy French casualties have been inflicted by the bombing and the delayed attack negates any shock value for the German troops holding the city. British and Canadian troops trying to enter Caen find it difficult to move through the rubble created by the bombing, which has now become a fortress for German forces inside the city.

Ten days after British and Canadian forces enter the city of Caen it is still controlled by German forces.

On July 18 Operation GOODWOOD is launched to clear Caen and the British lose a large amount of tanks, and get hit on their right flank. Montgomery promised once again he would take the key to the success of the cross-channel landings, or Caen.

Operation COBRA is launched on July 24 and American forces under Bradley finally break out of the hedgerows after bloody fighting and turn left to relieve Montgomery's right flank outside of Caen.

General George S. Patton's 3rd Army arrives in theatre just after the breakout and starts to capitalize on it.

Montgomery makes a statement that the American breakout was due to his effort and that he actually deliberately held a defensive position outside Caen to draw the German forces away from the Americans.

This comment sends up the red flag for 'Commodore'. They are dealing with, "….a 'military demagogue' and egocentric liar in a place of high military command", as Madison put it. She had never seen anything like it before, other than some similarities with the American general Douglas MacArthur, for whom she did not have high praise. This was trouble and now part of the work of 'Commodore' was to understand this individual, as they would an adversary, and to work with his character until they could get higher authority to agree with them over Montgomery.

The final frustration was the first true butting of heads between George Patton and this little tyrant. Patton's Third Army was loose and on the run.

Patton wanted to circle around Paris and encircle the entire German Army in France and end the war sooner. This was purely an American approach to the problem. You make bold quick armor moves to end hostilities sooner and reduce casualties. Montgomery's method was the opposite. His methodology was to sit in a defensive position and let the enemy come at you until you have overwhelming forces and supplies and then you attack on a smaller manageable scale, which leads to piecemeal movement and higher casualties.

General Patton's idea was shot down by the overall ground commander Montgomery, who has ground command authority over all Americans. Montgomery is ground commander and Patton had to do what he was told. Montgomery wanted to bottle up the German forces at a town called Falaise using U.S. and Canadian, and British troops. It would certainly catch a sizable amount of the German Army in France but it would not 'bag' the whole army as Patton's plan had intended and it would not do it with limited casualties on both sides. The encirclement of this pocket is not completed in a timely manner and the massacre that started taking place on August 15th in the Falaise Gap is wholesale slaughter of what is left of the

German Seventh Army and Fifth Panzer Army, and sickens many of the American forces that take part. Patton's larger encirclement would have been cleaner and more effective with less loss of life in the long run.

'Commodore' war gamed both approaches for future analytical backup to use against Montgomery when the time came. Through the war gaming they found that Caen should have been taken within two to three days after landing with the troops available to Montgomery and that if Patton's encirclement had succeeded, and they gave it a 92% chance of success, the war would end in September 1944. 'Commodore' saw another opportunity to end the war vanish before they could even have an effect on the strategic decision-making. Again they would have to reach as far into the future as possible to be able to a positive effect on an outcome.

They also added, to their support analysis, that had Montgomery taken Caen, as he was expected to on D-Day, the bloody fighting that the Americans suffered in the hedgerows would have been prevented; bloody fighting with high numbers of casualties. In the end, instead of leading the breakout, Montgomery was rescued by embattled American forces who made their own breakout.

Bold strokes would have to be the order of the day to win quickly not the over caution of General Bernard Law Montgomery.

On top of this Montgomery showed his total disregard for American forces by discounting their fight through the hedgerows a fight, which as many troops agreed, 'saved his bacon'. The Field Marshall was becoming an annoying liability but the politics were strong.

The final horror of the breakout, or the Falaise Gap, was the human and material remains of the absolute slaughter of German forces by rocket and machine-gun firing fighter aircraft. Ten thousand German troops lay dead among hundreds of dead horses, used for transport, and burning equipment. Thousands of trapped German troops had been allowed to escape through a whole in the encirclement by the Allies, which in the end lead to this slaughter. Patton's Third Army had out-paced Montgomery's timetable and was halted in its run north before the trap was complete and it took ground commander Montgomery 24 hours to set them on the move again, by which time it was too late to tie the enemy forces up for potential surrender. American forces knew that if an army had a backdoor out the odds of mass surrender were much less. Montgomery could not even complete this smaller double envelopment to surround these German forces and force their surrender.

In the latter part of July Ultra picked up an intercept from von Kluge to Hitler stating, in part, "The whole western front has been ripped open…….." Von Kluge wanted to displace troops but Hitler's 'no withdrawal' order was preventing this.

Most Allied analysts were anticipating an imminent collapse of the German Army with the end of the war in sight. 'Commodore' was not seeing the same evidence and they were looking beyond the obvious and hoping for a major break to occur inside the German High Command.

On July 20 an attempt was made on Hitler's life at his command post for the Eastern Front or the 'Wolf's Lair' headquarters in Rastenburg, East Prussia. The officer held immediately responsible was Colonel Claus Schenk Graf von Stauffenberg. He placed a bomb in Hitler's planning room above ground, and not in his bunker, where the meeting was to be held due to the heat of the day. Four were killed and everyone in the room was wounded; Hitler was wounded slightly. If the meeting had been held underground in the bunker, where it was usually held, the explosive force of the bomb may have been more effective.

'Commodore' learned of this the next day, Friday July 21. Once again the plotters had used a bomb and it had failed. From what they could gather, there had been a coup set in motion and it had failed. Colonel von Stauffenberg was picked up in Berlin the night of the 20th and, along with three other officers, was shot that night by firing squad in the courtyard of the headquarters of the Army High Command or the Bendler Block. Hitler was starting a purge.

On Saturday morning July 22, 1944 Sam and Madison found themselves sitting at the small dining room table in the Fleet cottage, once again, re-evaluating the new turn of events.

"Hitler is going to purge this situation, which is either going to force a coup with him still alive or shut down the conspirators and prolong the war. From what we have and know only Admiral

Canaris seems a viable source of a coup and even though he heads the Abwehr that communiqué from Skorzeny tells me Hitler has lost trust him as well", stated Madison.

"I'd have to agree and with that in mind we'll have to concentrate on German military movement, come up with a 'Crystal Ball' and make SHAEF react appropriately while massaging and manipulating Montgomery's ego. Did I forget anything?"

"Well, we're back to this nightmare. I thought there might be hope but three strikes we're out with the ninth inning coming up."

Sam just looked up from his paper wryly with his eyes squinting for effect, "I thought I was the baseball metaphorian, what's going on over there on the other side of the table?"

"Metaphorian?"

"It's the only thing I could come up with on short notice."

"How about, how do we control this guy?," she asked with a humorous smile.

"And you mean General Bernard Law Montgomery by this guy?! We're going to have to come up with a solid 'Crystal Ball' that wraps everything up and if need be declare a **'code Black'** for the President. Hell, at this point we have nothing to loose and have to roll the dice," Sam summed up.

"I thought you were a statistician and not a gambler."

"We're playing politics now and we'll have to position this analysis as best we can but it's going to attack part of the political status quo and we will not be popular, but I guess this is what we've been waiting for since we started working together and you asked for my support in any showdown with the brass. Our numbers and analyses may come up together so perfect and the models so clear that the prediction is obvious to the layman and they still may shoot us down."

"Mr. 'Optimistic'. I'm usually the pessimist."

"Well, I thought I'd run with those scissors for a bit and take the burden off of you."

"Oh, that's sweet."

"I thought you'd appreciate that; we do have a problem on our hands. We were both briefly hoping this war had come to the point were it would end itself and solve our problems but the man is still alive after another lousy bomb and when he gets done, unlike the last two events which he didn't know about, there will be few people standing who can bring about a quick 'unconditional' end to this mess."

"So where do we start?"

"Troop numbers across all fronts and equipment and type, also start paying closer attention to reports coming off the continent from civilian and underground sources along with the German military communications traffic."

"So, do you think you can handle professor 'Monty' like you handled my professors?" said Madison with a warm smile.

"You keep smiling at me like that and I'd handle Hercules with one hand behind my back; we'll have to convince 'Monty's' 'Victor', or FDR, in the end and that may mean going home the quick way if we have to."

"So you'd fly a gal like me first class."

"Only the best and with the U.S. Navy owning those Clippers we may have an in."

"That's swell, just so you don't tell them I get air sick," joked Madison.

"I'll let you surprise them."

Madison just smiled and shook her head gently as Sam walked over to her and then took her in his arms.

"Do you think we can do this Sam?" she half whispered as she put her head in that safe place on his shoulder just under his chin.

"I know we can get it right but whether or not we can get the powers that be to react only God knows; but we're going to give it everything even if it means that, after this is all over, they'll ban us from being analysts for the government."

"Then we'll just have to start The Pragmatist", said Madison as she pulled her head off of his shoulder with a smile and looked at him.

"Then they'd surely hate us."

"But just think of the fun we'll have. We can sit at our table in the Commodore, gobble down ice cream and think of ways to get them all crazy."

"And then run down to the "Whisper" and sail into the setting sun."

"You're such a romantic for a statistician."

"Ah, you know that I know the right numbers"

Turning serious for a moment Madison, half beckoning in her manner and in her voice, said, "And don't ever forget the one in the next century with 26 in it."

Looking into her gray-green eyes he smiled warmly and whispered, "I'll never forget." And she tucked her head into the crook of his neck, up against his shoulder, once more.

August 1944 on The Continent

By August the British Second Army and the US First Army were driving through Belgium towards Holland under Montgomery and south of the Ardennes Patton's Armor of the Third Army was driving rapidly towards Metz, and the Saar and Frankfurt. Patton was outrunning his supply lines and with both army groups being supplied through Cherbourg, over 400 miles away, and across the original beachheads, the Allied advance seemed doomed for a halt. All the other major ports are still in German hands.

On August 15 three American divisions, reinforced by a French armored division, landed in the south of France with Saint-Tropez at its center. 'Commodore's' one success, ANVIL, became a success of its own as it started to push German forces north as predicted. By August 16 all German divisions in the region started a general withdrawal, under pressure, north. American forces of ANVIL, stretching their supply lines, ran north to push enemy forces into the German forces retreating from OVERLORD and then up against the Allied forces moving rapidly east. A classic hammer and anvil was achieved and the Allies would have more ports through which to move supplies. By August 16 ANVIL was becoming a huge success as Churchill tried to play it down, out of political embarrassment. American logistics determined that at least one third of supplies needed in northern France could be moved through the beachheads of ANVIL, which was now called DRAGOON. The third benefit realized by 'Commodore' and SHAEF was that the Allies now had a third army group opposite the German border.

On August 19 Field Marshall Hans Gunther von Kluge took is own life near Metz, France after being ordered to return to Berlin. Earlier, on the 17th, he had been replaced by Field Marshall Walter Model.

On Saturday, August 19, Ultra relayed what information they had on the von Kluge situation to 'Commodore', via special messenger, as von Kluge had been on the watch list as '...of special interest for 'Commodore'. Madison met the courier at the 'Dome' and briefly noted, with some sadness, that the rider was not an American on a throaty Harley.

The message was from the German High Command announcing the fact that the Field Marshall had died in the field and it was still in its original German. Attached was a note from 'Fagin' again with a red stamp over it saying: **DESTROY UPON READING.**

Commodore: *It is believed that the Field Marshall was implicated in the 20 July assassination attempt on Hitler and that he became part of the purge and committed suicide by poison on 18 August instead of returning to Berlin for trial. It is also believed (classified-U) that the Field Marshall may have penned a letter to the Fuhrer imploring him to put an end to the war.*

A pity, really. Fagin
As indicated please destroy this after reading.

'Fagin' actually showed some emotion towards the Field Marshal, who he had been following for months, for 'Commodore'.

While she held the communiqué over an ashtray and held a Zippo lighter under it, supplied by the Cambridge sergeant, she knew that any potential coup was now just the stuff of dreams. After cleaning up the ashes and making sure that there was nothing left behind she locked her desk and headed out past the two members of 'Commodore' who where in the 'Dome' seven days a week, and slept in the 'Dome' more often than not. She did not need to inform them of the communiqué about the Field Marshall as it did not affect the material that they were working on. Sam would be as unhappy about this as she was even though they really did not expect to see a coup, it was just that every bang against its even remote possibility was deafening to the spirit.

The supply situation, with the two main Allied thrusts on a broad front, was starting to take its toll as equipment was taken off equipment carriers in lieu of gasoline and ammunition.

To top it off; 1,400 of Montgomery's British lorries were useless as they were manufactured with faulty pistons, so it fell to the Americans to run more of his supplies to him and from the original landing beaches and the captured port of Cherbourg, now up and running under full American control. Something had to be done quickly.

On August 21 American initiative and know how set up the Red Ball Express, 75% of whose drivers were Black American troops, and they started to run supplies around the clock. They were even known to fuel and re-arm tanks with enemy troops within 100 yards of their trucks and on many occasions, shooting.

Eisenhower knew that Antwerp was an imperative. The port had to be taken and all intelligence stressed the importance of this port. The logistics coming across the beachheads of DRAGOON were offering some additional resources but not enough as they strove to increase volume over these beaches in order to meet a projected third of the Allied resources heading into northern France.

On August 23, against his better judgment, General Eisenhower brought George Patton's dash across Europe to a standstill and left the Third Army to cannibalize their own equipment for parts and use captured enemy equipment and stores to continue there advance. He did this to supply Montgomery with the bulk of the supplies coming onto the Continent with the command to Montgomery to take the port of Antwerp at all costs. Eisenhower also promised Montgomery the use of the Allied First Airborne Army in England. This was the only reserve that SHAEF had at the time. Montgomery was also given control of the US First Army on his right flank if he needed it. He was given everything and he started to behave even more as though he were actually commander of all Allied forces west of Italy, which was still raging and was still bloody and taking up huge amounts of resources as 'Commodore' had warned.

Eisenhower had made the decision to take supplies away from his bold and aggressive commander, one who could recognize an opportunity and exploit it, and give those supplies to a commander who was slow and conservative and who would lose the opportunity if one presented itself. He had maintained a broad front with Patton in the lead headed to Frankfurt and now he had to weaken his main drive because he needed Antwerp before winter set in. He needed Antwerp to keep his front on the move and prevent what was left of the German military from re-grouping.

Montgomery was finally going to get his way. He had been ill-mannered when it came to the Supreme Commander and the Americans and demanded the lions' share of the supplies coming onto the Continent. He had been so abrasive that most of the British staff at SHAEF couldn't stand the man. Now he would be insufferable with regard to command control but Eisenhower and the Allies needed the port of Antwerp desperately.

Finally on September 4, the British 11th Armored Division captured the port of Antwerp but did not finish the job. Before Montgomery's army even attempted to clear the German stronghold on the Schelde Estuary, or the seaward approaches to the port, Montgomery turned the Second British Army east away from the estuary to use Patton's supplies in order to head towards Holland and the prize, Germany.

The entire German 15th Army under General von Zangen was trapped. The army was comprised of 86,000 men, more than 600 artillery pieces, better than 6,000 vehicles, 6000 horses and a vast supply of miscellaneous material. This was the grand army that Hitler had set up in Pas de Calais to appose Patton's fake invasion force, which never came.

Montgomery turned his back on this trapped army as well and headed east and then stopped. He was trying again to put his plan across for a single mighty thrust into Germany using his army and he still hadn't secured the needed port of Antwerp. 'He has only stepped on a hornets' nest', Sam complained to Madison.

The analysts were saying the German Army was on the verge of collapse and they were all starting to forget about the port of Antwerp, the German 15th Army; and the broad, powerful front with the ability to exploit opportunities. Eisenhower's flexibility was gone with one part to the front, under Patton, shut down and the other one, under Montgomery, halted.

At every level analysts were forecasting the imminent end of the war with the Combined Allied Intelligence Committee in London being the most optimistic. They believed that the German Army was incapable of recovery from the fighting in the month of August. Their report stated that, "Organized resistance under the control of the German High Command is unlikely to continue beyond December 1, 1944 and … may end even sooner." SHAEF's intelligence summary also stated, "…the August battles have done it and the enemy in the west has had it. Two and half months of bitter fighting have brought the end of the war in Europe in sight, almost within reach" They went on to say that, "The German Army is no longer a cohesive force but, rather, a number of fugitive battle groups, disorganized and even demoralized, short of equipment and arms." Even Major General John Kennedy of the British War Office, who was known for doom and gloom, stated on September 6 that, "If we go at the same pace as of late, we should be in Berlin by the 28th…."

When Sam and Madison heard the fact that, 'the Germans only have horses…..' brought into to some overly jubilant analysis they knew that there was a mass hysterical blindness going on in the Allied intelligence community. Every in-theatre military analyst knew that half of the mobility in the German Army was made up of horses, unlike the US Army and therefore its allies.

Only one other analyst was in agreement with 'Commodore' and that was a Colonel Oscar W. Koch, the intelligence chief for Patton's Third Army when he stated, "Barring internal upheaval in the homeland and the remote possibility of insurrection within the Wehrmacht… the German armies will continue to fight until destroyed or captured."

'Commodore' couldn't agree more with Colonel Koch and after the great attempt of July 20, a coup was not going to happen. On top of Colonel Koch's analysis 'Commodore' had their two models fall completely in place with each other on Wednesday September 6, 1944. This was the same day that British General Kennedy had stated that the Allies could be in Berlin by the 28th of September if they kept on the same path.

The path that 'Commodore' now saw spelled doom and a major setback for the Allies. Hitler was not going to let Antwerp, or any part of that port, remain in Allied hands and he would get the military to agree as it made sense to their survival. The two important models would come together and as the pieces of the puzzle started to fall in place a 'Crystal Ball' would emerge. This was all coming together with most of the supportable statistics that Sam needed, most. He did not have everything he needed although he was getting an incredible flow of equipment statistics from an underground operative in Holland near a bridge in a town by the name of Arnhem. The operative's name was "the French Dutchman" and that's all that Madison had on him other than the 'classified-U' qualifier as additional, reliable sourced, intelligence information coming through to Ultra outside of Enigma. It appeared that the man was overlooking the Arnhem Bridge and counting the German troops and equipment moving in both directions. It initially appeared that there was a great exodus of the German Army in Holland but that had slowed and now other units of panzer were showing up where they shouldn't be.

'Commodore' called a '**code Black**' on the same day. They signified a need to meet with the President as the **'code Black'** was time critical. Their reputation had proceeded them and they were given orders to be ready to be picked up at the 'Dome' at 0400 on the morning of September 7 for a flight to the U.S.. Stress was starting to show with Sam and the statistics that he was now seeing come together were presenting him with a frightening view of foreboding events, which weighed heavily on him.

The drive to Southampton was quick. They had been picked up in a staff car again but this time the security team wore no division patches. The staff car had a motorcycle in front and one at the rear and Madison had never remembered driving so fast in England, they were in Southampton in no time. It was maybe a half hour or so.

When she saw the Dixie Clipper tied up and being prepared in the early morning darkness she stopped and just stared. Sam just smiled at her and said, "You get your first class all the way."

The Clipper would take off in the dark and head west with the sun. They were the only passengers, along with some 'special cargo';

a '**code Black**' accepted by the Commander-in-Chief certainly got things done. Traveling on the Clipper as the sole passengers was highly unusual as the Clippers, at this point in the war, were engaged in clandestine transatlantic flights. They were always packed with important cargo and personnel on the crossing to England and they usually returned to the States carrying more than just two passengers. Their visit with the President had an extra element of security to it on the outbound leg 'home'.

They would fly on a different Clipper than the one Sam had first come in on. The Yankee Clipper had crashed on February 22, 1943 while in a descending turn from base to final approach, after catching the water with her left wingtip. Twenty-four of the 39 on board the full capacity flight were killed. Some mystery surrounded the wartime crash, although the mirror effect on depth perception was listed as the official cause. Sam had been made privy to the intelligence as part of a request for some statistical backup, but he wouldn't tell Madison. The thought of the secrecy around the crashed Clipper along with the fact that they were headed towards New York City reminded Sam of another flying boat. It was the model of the German Do X flying boat which hung in The Blue Ribbon restaurant off of Broadway on 44th Street. Sam thought briefly of how, on several occasions, he and Madison had enjoyed the German cuisine at this old family owned restaurant in the European tradition. It was a restaurant frequented by American actors in the 1920's as well as German/Americans. In August of 1931 the triumphant crew of the Dornier flying boat Do X had gone straight to the restaurant after their heralded landing in New York Harbor and presented the owner and his family with a scaled wooden model of the large six-engine Dornier, which hung from the ceiling at the back of the restaurant. Sam just shook his head briefly, with a slight ironic smile, at the thought of all this as the restaurant was now under surveillance for possible fifth columnists.

"Why are you smiling?" stated Madison not really looking for an answer.

"Oh, nothing," replied Sam thinking of how their world had changed in such a short time and the fact that there was such concern over fifth columnists that many German/Americans had been put in internment camps along with Italian/Americans, Hungarian/ Americans, Bulgarian/Americans, Czech/Americans and Romanian/ Americans as well as Japanese/Americans on the West Coast.

Returning his thoughts to the trip at hand he knew that they were scheduled to leave on the Dixie Clipper Boeing 314 tail number NC-18605, or the next number in line from the Yankee Clipper. Sam was not superstitious and he was looking forward to their 5 AM departure so that he could have some time alone with Madison surrounded by all things American and in the lap of luxury headed home, if only for a day.

The New York to Lisbon flight would typically be completed in less than a day, depending on the weather. It had actually been achieved in 18 hrs 30 minutes. But the Southampton to New York flight was normally a little faster not only due to the somewhat lessened distance but as well due to the priority of the flights. The weight of the Dixie Clipper had as well been reduced from an empty weight of 48,000 pounds with a further reduction down from its pre-war loaded weight of 84,000 pounds to enhance the flight times and increase the room onboard. Many of the Clippers had been stripped of their elegant interiors to make room for more cargo and personnel. They had been re-designated C-98's and they were making daily, somewhat clandestine, transatlantic trips with needed war materials. The Dixie Clipper retained most of its elegance for use with dignitaries and had ferried President Roosevelt and his staff most of the way to the Casablanca Conference, code named SYMBOL, in January 1943. They would be able to cruise at 9,000 feet in the un-pressurized cabin and their first and only refueling stop would be Botwood, Newfoundland before proceeding on to Manhasset Bay, New York to board a smaller plane to New Hackensack Airport near Hyde Park, New York. They would not be stopping in Foynes, Ireland as some flights had in the past.

Factoring in expected headwinds coming across the Atlantic, the trip would take most of a day and they would hope to be at the Hyde Park estate of the President by around 8PM the same day in the States or Thursday the 7th of September.

Speed was of the essence and they had made their point well enough in the '**code Black**' that the Commander-in-Chief wanted to see them immediately. In the **'code Black'** they had stated their concerns about a major drive into Holland by Montgomery with the intention of penetrating to the Ruhr. They saw this as a fatal mistake with the status of the German Army being underestimated and further to that they predicted a major counterattack that would set the Allies back on their heals, a counterattack as unexpected as the Kursk counter-offensive had been to the Russians before the **'code Black'** to Eisenhower. Operation COMET, or the use of British and Polish airborne to broaden and extend Montgomery's front, had been secretly expanded by Montgomery to do even more. The British were intentionally keeping this expanded operation from their American counterparts until Montgomery could ambush Eisenhower and convince him to give the green light. The British anticipated a green light based on the military's drive to get another airborne operation off the ground and the British concern over the V-1 Buzz-Bomb, called 'Diver' by British intelligence, attacks on London coming from Holland. They anticipated that they could use the destruction of 'Diver' as the political persuasive tool. But 'Commodore' had gotten wind of it through a brief, in passing, comment from Madison Bell's husband, Colonel Clive Mumfreys of British military intelligence, during his brief and unexpected return to their home in Aldershot at the end of August. The information in the **'code Black'** was even more provocative in that it implied a prolonged war and more political instability in the future of Europe if this setback were to occur and allow the Russians to expand their lines and their influence before the war came to an official end. They had the President concerned and they had a reputation for anticipating the future.

They were both seated comfortably in the main lounge as the four big Wright Cyclone engines popped and came to life one-by-one with a solid roar and then a strong cadence muffled by the soundproof cabin as the flying boat sat in the water away from its tie-up.

The pilot, Lieutenant Howard Cone, was a naval reserve Lieutenant who held a Master of Ocean Flying, or the highest commercial pilot rating available. He knew these big flying boats before the war and he knew them better than most. He got into a brief discussion about the four power plants with Madison, after they first came on board, and he told her how he truly enjoyed flying the reduced weight boat with that combined 6,000 H.P.. He talked directly to Madison about the engines because she had asked the pilot about the "..double row 14 cylinder radial air-cooled geared engines." He had been impressed and fell into a conversation immediately as though he were talking to a peer. He only stayed a few minutes while his co-pilot was pre-flighting the huge flying boat and Sam could tell that he would have stayed longer to discuss the attributes of this marvelous piece of machinery, with Madison, if he hadn't had to get to the flight deck.

Sam was left wide-eyed as Lieutenant Cone, dressed in green flight coveralls, left; and when he looked at Madison this way she simply said, "Some things you have yet to learn about this historian, I've had a growing fascination with engines as of late but didn't want to startle you."

Sam had just smiled back at her and shook his head. She never ceased to amaze and intrigue him.

◆   ◆   ◆

The dark pre-dawn take-off from the water, highlighted by a waning half moon, was nothing short of exhilarating. Madison was excited by the feeling of speed across the water. Even though it was still dark, outside the port window from her Main Lounge seat, she had a perfect view of the wake put up just behind her by the hull of the Clipper gaining momentum through the channel waters of Southampton. For a moment the war was forgotten and she and Sam had entered another world that reminded her of their days together before the war.

Facing her in the opposing upholstered lounge chair Sam watched her face as she smiled inwardly while looking out at the night's events lost momentarily in a better world. She felt his stare and turning smiled at him while reaching for his hand.

The interior of the Clipper was lavish with comfortably upholstered seating and thick carpeting. The carpeting in the lounge, where they were seated, was turquoise colored complemented by pale green walls. The next lounge over, had rust colored carpeting with beige walls. There were six compartments in all, not including the

Main Lounge and a deluxe suite. The lounge seating was convertible into privately curtained beds at night. As Madison and Sam were the only two passengers on this trip they could not have had more privacy. They were also told that the aft section of the aircraft had a 'honeymoon suite' or deluxe suite that was still furnished with the accouterments. This notification managed to elicit another lifted eyebrow from Sam and a mischievous smile from Madison.

As the big flying boat banked out towards Ireland and started to climb over the water Madison again turned back from the porthole and the stars and looked at Sam, this time with the beginnings of tears in her eyes.

"What are you thinking Baby?" Sam said squeezing her hand warmly to let her know he was there for her.

"The war and home. We're headed home and the Commodore will be so close but the war is still here."

"Maybe this is what we've been working towards these past couple of years with all the frustrations and the failures that we've experienced."

"The failures are what concerns me, our analyses were right on the money in the past and yet none were really acted upon with possibly the exception of Kursk."

"And it may be those 'Crystal Balls' that are getting us this first class ride to Hyde Park."

"I'm not doubting that, but I have the feeling that we're going to run smack up against politics once more. FDR wants to keep Churchill happy and taking their hero Montgomery down a notch is not going to help that cause."

"You're right, it would be easier if it were Patton we were trying to put the brakes on but look at it this way, our historical data is overwhelming," Sam added.

"Overwhelming to us Sam because we are historians and maybe, just maybe FDR's experiences in WWI will help him to see what we see so clearly; we still needed some more statistics on troop movement and equipment types to help make our arguments irrefutable."

"You're right there but we couldn't wait. The presence of the panzer and SS units that have been identified so far may take up the slack on the actual numbers. We are looking at elite units starting to move towards and into Holland."

"But it still reads as a German retreat in the order of a rout in too much of the analysis."

"Koch's analysis from the Third Army should help to back our cause and we have caught the Brits trying to keep an operation under raps until the last minute; I would venture to say that FDR is not aware of how Operation COMET has expanded. They've done such a good job of hiding it from American intelligence that it would not have made his briefings."

"Sam, if he doesn't listen it will be hell to pay and we'll still be in this thing in 1945 with mounting casualties on both sides." Turning back to the rectangular porthole she once again looked out at the stars as though in a trance or dream state and continued, "Did you know that C.S. Lewis's name is Clive, as in my Clive, but he chose to be called Jack for his dog Jackie?"

"What made you think of that?"

"Oh, I heard one of his BBC broadcasts a few days ago; I like the name Jack", she said still looking off in the distance past the stars outside the porthole, as if in a trance.

"I'll change mine for you."

"He talked about the Moral Law," not making note of his comment, "and said that the fact that we have a conscience in essence proves the existence of God, even in all this mess."

"Well, that is hopeful, now we just need to bring about a Global Conscience."

And as she came out of her daydream trance she turned from the porthole and looked back at Sam and just said, "I love you."

"Even if my name is not Jack."

She just smiled, leaned over, and put her arms around him.

◆   ◆   ◆

As the flying boat leveled off at 9,000 feet Lieutenant Cone came back into the Main Lounge with a smile on his face.

"You didn't think I was going to leave our conversation at the 6,000 H.P. available to this airframe." He said as he approached Madison. "How would you both like to see the flight deck of this flying wonder."

Madison's face lit up as she dried her eyes and looked at Sam with a smile.

"We'd love to", said Sam.

"Why are you not a Captain, lieutenant?," inquired Madison. "It would only seem appropriate if you're in charge of the Dixie Clipper."

"Ah, the Navy. I'm just a reservist who used to fly for Pan Am before the war and since some folks look at this as a plum job, while others are flying in and around combat, I remain a lieutenant which is fine as long as I get to fly the Clipper."

"It's a stately aircraft Lieutenant," commented Sam.

"Actually it is designated the President's plane; we flew him to Bathurst, Gambia on his way to Casablanca in '43."

"Well, now I do feel spoiled," smiled Madison.

The lieutenant showed them the spacious flight deck and even took Madison through one of the wing access hatches to view a Wright Cyclone in action. She was amazed that they could actually service these huge engines in flight. He wasn't finished there, before they headed back down the spiral staircase, behind the cockpit on the starboard side, and back to the Main Lounge Lieutenant Cone let Madison sit in the left-hand pilot's seat and feel the weight of the control yolk. He even had her put her feet on the rudder pedals, which were actually large pans that held the entire foot, and give them a slight wiggle to feel the power of the big flying boat. She was able to forget about the war again for a brief moment and escape into the feeling of freedom and safety that the power of those cyclone engines gave her. It was similar to the freedom and safety she experienced when she pushed the MG TA down Fleet Road and the feeling she had had when she had heard those Harley engines that July 4th when she had sent the 'Flash' to SHAEF.

Just as they walked back into the Main Lounge Madison stopped and turned just in time to catch Sam in her arms as he wrapped his arms around her.

"I didn't realize that you were such a daredevil but maybe I should've the way you throw that MG around turns."

"I wouldn't say I throw it, exactly, but both speed and powerful engines make me feel free and safe, almost as much as when I'm in your arms. I guess we're not going to take a sail in Whisper."

"Not this trip Baby, but we'll be back soon enough. They certainly won't need us for the post war analysis; that stuff is too political for us."

"And what we're experiencing now is not?"

"Well, true but an entirely different animal; I do think we have a shot of at least making the President acutely aware of the dangers of letting Montgomery move into Holland as a single deep penetration or, actually, 'thrust' to the Ruhr. If the panzer units that we're starting to see fully materialize and then get a hold of him on those narrow two lane dike roads he'll be mauled and shut down and then the 'complete' retaking of Antwerp might be ripe for the picking by what most think are phantom German divisions."

"Sam, we need to get him to act and if he doesn't act on what we're going to show him we need to get the back-up statistics as soon as we get back to England."

"I can be convincing, even with a consummate politician such as FDR; he does have some military background."

"Old naval knowledge is a bit different than understanding land warfare, especially as quickly as it can move today."

"Well, you have a point. We'll just keep it as elementary as possible and build the case of a mounting or escalating catastrophe. A stream of rolling events that cascade into each other to cause a major event at the end which is the polar opposite to the initial expected outcome."

"Oh that's simple and elementary alright."

"How about dominos with a fork at the end with both forks leading to a shared cluster. You push the first domino and it collides with the next one behind it like a stalled armor column on a single lane road getting nailed by German 88's in fixed positions. And it backs up the whole column then it all comes crashing down and a ripple effect knocks each domino down in turn past the starting point down two separate forks and into what had been the safe zone; well you get the point," Sam concluded with a hint of emotional concern in his voice.

"I'm usually the one who gets upset in these mock briefings and you're usually the calm calculated statistician with a dash of history professor thrown in."

"I agree but the catastrophic potential of underestimating German military strength and capability coupled with this, as we're getting from Clive, all or nothing single file dash for the German border of the bulk of our resources has me a little on edge. Just from a statistical standpoint, with both of the models in full unison, it has set all the bells off and under the calmness, that I am trying to maintain, is the fear of God," he said as the stress again started to show on his face.

"Just be your old convincing self."

"Oh, I will but one way or the other we'll need to head immediately back to England to collect whatever statistics we can add to this even if I have to go into Holland with American airborne troops because now they'll be the bulk of the airborne for this new expanded version of COMET."

"Well, put that one out of your mind; you are not doing anything like that in my lifetime. Promise me you will not bring that up to any ear who might think that it would be a good idea. I mean it"

"I won't." Madison still staring at him, "I promise you, I won't."

The only crew on board was the flight crew on the flight deck. To save weight there were no frills on this flight, no stewards and Lieutenant Cone had promised them that no one would come back into the Main Lounge unless called, or for emergencies, in order to give them their privacy knowing the priority of the flight and their level of clearance.

They followed the up-sloping contour of the big flying boat to the aft section to look at the 'honeymoon suite' and halfway there they stopped walking up the incline, looked at each other and smiled devilishly before turning and heading back to the large Main Lounge. Why not chance the possibility of being found in an embrace in the Main Lounge, it made it all that much more romantic and exciting.

They had been shown how to convert the lounge seating into bunk beds with privacy curtains and with the sun just barely detectable coming up over the horizon from their altitude they fell into each others arms, discretely disrobed and made love in one of the Clippers beds in the sky. They were making love close to two miles high above the earth and away from everything. It was like making love in heaven, and looking out to the port side of the flying boat they could see the first traces of orange-yellow and rays through the distant clouds that gave the effect of truly being in heaven together. The rays of light breaking through were magnificent and Sam smiled as he recalled a photographer he had known in college who called it 'the God effect'; it surely was.

◆   ◆   ◆

By two o'clock in the afternoon, Greenwich Mean Time, they were more than halfway across the Atlantic. It was now only 9AM in New York. They had traveled light but Madison had brought her emerald green dress suit with matching hat so that she would be dressed properly to meet the President.

They had changed and Madison was the epitome of beauty in that dress. Sam couldn't help but think how she would show up the best-dressed women at race day in Saratoga Springs and he made up his mind that he would take her there after the war, as she had never been. They would be traveling at least another 10 hours or so aboard the Clipper as they had run into headwinds crossing the Atlantic and Sam knew that at the end of that time she would look just as beautiful and fresh as she did at this moment. The crew had expected the headwinds and juggled their flight times so they would leave Southampton in pre-dawn darkness and arrive in New York just after sunset.

There were ham and cheese sandwiches and coffee in the galley and it was help yourself.

Madison and Sam worked over their material and tried to modify their presentation for a politician and not a tactician or acute military mind. They spent several hours with this and then tried to rest up in their lounge seats before the re-fueling in Botwood, Newfoundland. They wanted to get themselves on New York time as best they could so they would be fully alert when they gave the Commander-in-Chief their briefing. It would be made easier for them to put themselves close to New York time with the long and comfortable flight and having the ability to lay down in a bed. Sam had warned Madison; from his experience on the flight over, when they flew him to England, that it was a day or two to readjust but then he thought it might be easier for them heading west as they were moving with the sun.

The landing and the fueling in Newfoundland was done quickly and efficiently, sometime before dark as the sun was slowly starting to drop down in the western sky, and it was uneventful as they were off again, this time to Manhasset Bay, New York. They were both running a little on adrenalin not because of the time difference but because they would be home again soon after three years, even if it were not for a full day. The Commodore and their innocent memories were both getting closer.

The pre-dark landing in Newfoundland was just as impressive as the dark morning departure from Southampton but the nighttime landing just after sunset in Manhasset Bay was exhilarating. Due to some military aircraft in the area; from Grumman Aircraft Engineering Corporation and Republic Aviation, flying from dusk into night, any night approaches using Long Island Sound were tight. And on top of this, night landings were usually carried out with priority flights, and they also wanted to keep the profile of the large Clipper at minimum exposure. Due to German saboteurs having been landed on Long Island in June of 1942 it was assumed that there possibly were spies watching even though that one group, along with another one in Florida, had been rounded-up. With this in mind, along with the tight airspace, the priority landings of the Clipper were like a rollercoaster ride with a steep dive to the water and then a low bank and a straightening out of the big flying boat just before it touched the water with a sinking 'whomp'.

The boat settled quickly after landing and the momentary luminosity of her wake disappeared quickly as the wake lessened during the taxiing.

Madison had let out a gleeful, 'weeeee' like a child when the steep dive came and even though Lieutenant Cone had warned them Sam was left flush. He had simply said to Madison, "Traveling with you can be like one big amusement ride; I'll take the MG down Fleet Road any day."

Madison replied, "Ah, now I can really show you what that car can do."

"I've done it now", Sam had smiled.

◆   ◆   ◆

They came into the circular Art Deco rotunda of the Marine Air Terminal at New York Municipal Airport-LaGuardia Field, just after 7:30 in the evening, and were quickly whisked away by an Army staff car to the main runway of the field. As they were about to board a Cessna UC-78 small utility plane they were informed that one engine was down and they were quickly walked over to and put on an Army Lockheed UC-36A for the flight to New Hackensack Airport in Wappinger Falls, NY. This all caused a slight delay but the UC-36A was faster than the Cessna.

They flew in the twin engine Lockheed Electra or UC-36A, flown by a USAAF crew, to New Hackensack Airport just 20 miles down Route 9 from the President's estate at Hyde Park. They were only some 15 miles from the Commodore and the rendezvous that they did not make over three years earlier.

By the time they were seated in their third staff car in 24-hours, and headed for Hyde Park, it was 01:26 Greenwich Mean Time on the military watches that both Sam and Madison were used to wearing. They kept their watches on this time so that they would not confuse times the way they were used in their reports even though it was 8:26 in the evening local time. They would also leave their watches on Greenwich time so they would remain aware of the situational times in the European Theatre of Operations. They could not afford to remove themselves completely and they'd be back again within 48 hours.

"Sam, it's exactly 01:26 by my watch."

"I know, I was just thinking the same thing and realizing that we're only about fifteen miles from the Commodore."

"It's the closest we've been since that awful day when I thought I had lost you."

"But you haven't and you won't, I'm right here," he said as he took up her hand tenderly and looked through the semi-dark, of the back of the staff car, into her eyes.

There was a bright half moon out in the early evening and both Sam and Madison had picked out the 01/26 for the 26th day of June in the year 2001. It was also the time that they were to have met at the Commodore three years earlier; it was in many ways their meeting time as they had met again, after their resurrections, at King's Cross Station at 1:26 in the afternoon. They had both quickly drawn a correspondence between the time on their watches when they had realized that they were home again, near the Commodore, and how enduring was their love for each other that it would never die throughout time. They really didn't have to explain it, they did not have to say a thing, they knew each other's thoughts. They were close to where they had been happiest and they had both felt this and then pulled that important date out of the time as well as recognizing the time itself for what it truly meant to them.

Still looking into her eyes Sam said, "I'll never leave you, you know that."

"Promise me we'll meet again if anything happens."

"Oh God, baby I promise you. I'll never leave you alone wherever we may be. I'll always be there for you."

Madison in her beautiful green dress on this warm September evening just snuggled up against Sam in the back of that staff car headed for the estate of the President of The United States and not caring if she arrived rumpled or not, she had Sam.

September 1944 ---- Hyde Park, New York

Before long they were turning left off of Route 9 and onto a long dirt drive with young trees on either side of it, some looking as though they had been planted within the last ten years. At the end of the drive they pulled up to a large stucco home with a semi-circular colonnade at its center and two columns on either side supporting a small open veranda over the entrance to the home.

A young colonel greeted them and escorted them past the guard at the front door and into the main entrance hall with a staircase to their right. Their valises were taken by a sergeant and they were told that the President would meet them in the library down the hall to their left at the end of the house. Before heading down the hall Sam noticed the 18th century cartoons framed and hung on the walls in the main entrance hallway. They were early colonial humor directed at the British and as Sam pointed this out to Madison he started to laugh and then turning to her, still chuckling said, "History viewed from afar can be humorous I guess," then getting a more serious tone in his voice he finished, " but the Anglo-American relationship right now in 1944 is nothing to laugh about."

Madison, looking closely at the historical cartoons and characters, reached back and grabbed Sam's hand and squeezed it reassuringly. "Maybe we'll laugh about it someday when we're once again sailing on the Hudson in "Whisper".

From their right they heard a throat clearing and a voice that was oddly familiar to them, as that of a parent, state, "There is no fyna sailing than can be found on the glorious Hudson."

211

As they turned; the President, in a barely detectable chair with two wheels at his side, wheeled himself into the hallway with that famous cigarette holder between his teeth. Stopping and removing the cigarette holder with his left hand he looked up at Madison with a self-assured look of recognition on his face and said, as he extended his right hand, "Dr. Bell, the roomas of the undeniable presence that you bring to a room are wholly understated."

Sam was impressed, it was the first time since they had left the States that he could remember Madison being addressed quite correctly as Dr. Bell. And the President was right; standing there in that green dress holding the matching hat, which she had removed after they had stepped from the staff car, with her flowing blond hair highlighting her gray-green eyes bright with her self-assured intelligence, she was more than a presence.

Looking at her and still thinking this he heard in the background, "And you must be Dr. Harbour."

Coming back to reality Sam said, "Yes sir, they just happen to let me work with Dr. Bell," as he extended his hand to shake the President's.

"Ah, a man with hughma, I do like that," said the President. "What is 'Whispa' if I might ask?"

"She's a Wianno Senior sir. I used to have her tied up at Newburgh but now she's in storage for the duration."

"What a mavelous sailboat, I think I may have seen you in her before the war. Let us hope this all ends soon so we can get you both on the Hudson next summa. You are making me think of my days sailing at Campobello." Just as the President said this Sam heard the small padded feet of a dog come across the carpet in the hallway and up to the President's wheelchair with the sergeant behind him looking on. "Ah, my Fala. Scots are frugal people I am told but my political opponents say that little Scottie Fala here took an expensive boat ride from the Aluetians to get home." And they all chuckled over the Fala story of the President sending a destroyer back to the Aluetians to pick up the misplaced dog, which Sam and Madison had heard about while in England. "Shall we proceed to the library, and I must say, I am happy to be in the presence of such an august fella alumnus!" said the President as he wheeled around and led the way left to the ramp leading into the library.

Sam just raised his eyebrow at Madison in feigned sarcasm as she smiled back at him.

The library was warm in dark wood paneling with a red oriental rug in the center. The President wheeled himself around past a replica of the Winged Victory and over to a marble fireplace which had the remains of ambers in the hearth. Two overstuffed chairs faced the fireplace and the President gestured to Madison and Sam to take a seat as Fala jumped up onto his lap.

"The Scots are a curious people as well and I cannot keep Fala from these important conversations. The urgency of your message, as you can tell, was perceived as soon as it was in hand. I find myself concerned on the eve of victory in Europe and three days before I leave for Quebec to discuss the invasion of Japan at OCTAGON."

"Sir," hesitated Sam, "we see victory in Europe but much like The Winged Victory behind me she is headless with euphoric blindness."

"Touche young man, touché," smiled the President.

"Sir," led in Madison, "we are concerned with the northern sector of our front under direct control of recently promoted Field Marshall Montgomery. The Field Marshal is planning for a limited drive into Holland using British and Polish airborne troops, that SHAEF knows about, under Operation COMET; but, as we have come to find, he is privately planning, with British intelligence, for a much larger incursion that he intends to drop in Eisenhower's lap during a meeting on September 10."

"Please continue Dr. Bell. And excuse my manna's, would you like something to eat or drink? I know how exhilarating and how wearing a long flight on the Clippa can be."

"No sir," said Madison, "we're both fine between the coffee and the ham and cheese sandwiches."

"Fine fare; .... now Fala is curious about enemy troop concentrations as am I."

They remained in the library for close to two hours and in those two hours they explained to the President that the Germans were rebuilding in Holland with an eye towards retaking Antwerp.

They explained their two models and how both the German high Command and the Hitler models came into harmony on this one. They explained some of the troop movements that they were aware of, or the fragmented parts of elite panzer units moving into Holland. They went on to explain that Montgomery had left an entire German Army trapped around Antwerp but had not moved to capture them or encircle them completely, which the President had been informed about earlier. They further informed the President that the port might as well be completely in German hands because until the estuary was taken the port was unusable which defeated the purpose of transferring Patton's supplies to Montgomery. They concluded by pointing out that Montgomery's true plan was to use all airborne units in Europe, or what was now called the Allied First Airborne Army, with the bulk of it comprised of the American 101st and 82nd Divisions, to open up a corridor across the Rhine and into the Ruhr for his armor units of the British 2nd Army.

They explained to the President that this operation would be carried out on one two lane highway running approximately 64 miles and that the column did not have the force to put units out along the way to protect its flanks. The armor column would be vulnerable and the airborne units would be stretched. They continued by telling the President that the use of such forces would put the whole front, in front of Antwerp, in jeopardy from the southern boarder of Holland through the Ardennes and down to the northern boarder of France, if the attack were to fail. Montgomery was better suited to a defensive posture moving on a broader front with Patton leading the charge with the Third Army against the Saar. This they explained with the knowledge they had gained from their war gaming of the different scenarios after the Normandy breakout, comparing Patton and Montgomery. The key to this whole fiasco occurring would be the presence of German forces in this corridor, troops that most of the Allied intelligence did not think were present; but Sam's statistics were saying something else. On top of this, the Germans wanted Antwerp back in the worst way.

These German forces would throw the Allies off balance and while the Allies were regrouping the Germans would hit them below the belt by coming through the Ardennes with a little historical precedent backing such a move, and they'd run up north for Antwerp before the Allies knew what had hit them and in the process they would cut Allied lines in half and try for an envelopment of Allied forces.

Madison came in and backed up Sam's statistics and said that the Allies would have another Kursk on their hands, which she and Sam had predicted, but this time it would take place around a Belgium town which was the hub for the roads controlling the southern approaches to Antwerp with its seven roads in and out and that town was Bastogne. She talked about this as she thought back to Stalingrad and Paulus's 6th Army surrounded and freezing to death. She did not want to see this happen to American troops because of another crackpot. She also went as far as to indicate that the Prime Minister had promoted Montgomery to the rank of Field Marshall, a rank above Eisenhower, just six days earlier to appease the man who had to give up Ground Forces Command to Eisenhower as it had been agreed before D-Day. This appeasement worried her and the President admitted that it concerned him as well and that he would have a 'diplomatic' conversation with his old friend. Madison also knew that if Montgomery's operation went forward it would force the 'pinnacle' at a place called Bastogne.

The President understood Sam's statistics but not in the same context that Sam did as a statistician knowing that a certain statistical pattern could predict an inevitable situation. The President wanted to see more numbers on equipment and types but he was concerned and would address the issue with Eisenhower through a communiqué that he would send off that night; he would also address the issue with Churchill at OCTAGON in three days.

"Sir, the new Operation that the 'Field Marshall' is planning is called MARKET-GARDEN. MARKET represents the airborne segment and GARDEN the armor drive up through Holland and across the Rhine at a place called Arnhem. Much of our troop data is coming out of this town from a Dutch operative called "the French Dutchman" who is situated with a view of that city's bridge across the Rhine," concluded Madison.

"And how did you come by this information with regard to the operation my dear?," the President queried, already knowing the answer.

"My husband is a colonel in British operations and intelligence and as I have a high security clearance, and I am his wife, he felt he could tell me even if I am an American."

"Ah, but the American won out," stated the President with a conspiratorial grin.

"Yes sir, it did."

"Have you seen all of my hughma in the front hall?"

"Yes sir we have," smiled Sam.

"I must have a long conversation with my friend Winston, keeping some of those cartoons in mind", and then he chuckled and put his cigarette holder in his mouth as he tilted his head up, took a puff and contemplated the air above him for a moment as he thought about everything he had just heard.

Looking back at his guests he said, "The sergeant will show you to your rooms, you will be right down the hall from me. Now I do not sleep walk myself but I cannot vouch for Fala. You may be interested to know Dr. Bell that you will be staying in the room that Winston is most fond of; and you Dr. Harbour will be in the adjacent room. Do get a good night's sleep as I intend to give you a ride in my Phaeton before you leave tomorrow and I cannot vouch for my excellent driving skills." He smiled and again put his cigarette holder in his mouth and took a puff of his cigarette.

They said their goodnights and left the President still sitting in front of the fireplace smoking and looking up and contemplating. They knew he was concerned and felt that the man would probably not get to bed until early in the morning after this new revelation. A revelation that came from two of his young and highly touted analysts who seemed to have their hands on the pulse of German reaction and movement with regard to certain actions on the part of the Allies. Also, one of them had been one of the principles on the doctrine of 'unconditional surrender'.

The sergeant showed them to their rooms, which were adjacent and connected by a separate door. Madison's room was right off the main hallway and she loved the wallpaper, which was printed with large pink roses on lattice. She felt as though she were home again, especially knowing that the Hudson was just below them and that Newburgh was just a stone's throw down the river from where she was going to sleep. She was home and she wanted to stay, and stay with Sam; but they would have to get back to England for one last time before they could come back to the Hudson and the Commodore for good.

She and Sam said goodnight with a simple goodnight kiss and Sam closed the adjoining door out of propriety.

Sam quickly drifted off to sleep and found himself in a surreal dream conversation with the President:

"Sir, as you know, Great Britain was in no way able to back up their declaration of war in 1939. It was just a holding situation until we were dragged in and Churchill banked on that in his "Europe First" letter of 12/7/40".

"You are correct young man but you have a bull by the tail if you let that assertion influence you. A bull's tail is not the admired end."

"And so it is not taken strongly sir other than to determine where our English cousins may try to take us................"

He then calmed in his sleep and his thoughts drifted to the Hudson and the wind and the sun, and Madison.

Madison dreamed of sailing in 'Whisper' that night with Sam at the helm in full control. She did not have to worry anymore. She could just look back at the man she loved and listen to the water sing against the hull as they cut through the ripple of the Hudson towards Trophy Point. She felt safe for the first time since she last saw Sam in the States just before his staged death. They would finally have their lives together; just a little while longer and this war would be over and if the President took steps in support of their analysis it would be over sooner than expected. She thought of this all for a moment in her dreams then found herself again in 'Whisper' thinking of nothing but Sam and how lucky she was.

The next morning they were up just a couple of minutes after sunrise at 6:30. Sam had awoken first and sat on Madison's bed lightly stroked her hair until she purred lazily. He stroked her hair some more and then when he saw she was about to fall asleep again he bounced ever so slightly up and down on the bed and just chanted quietly in her direction, "horses, horses, crazy old horses," and she smiled, turned towards him, and put her arms around the waist of his pajama bottom. She was wearing silver and white stripped pajamas with thick strips that glistened just a little of the silk from which the pajamas were made. She had had them before the war and hadn't worn them since leaving the States. Now back in New York, even if briefly, she wore them again. She smiled with her eyes closed and remembered the last time that Sam had chanted that wake up call as he bounced the bed up and down. It seemed like another lifetime ago in Newburgh across the Hudson from where they were.

Once they were dressed they headed downstairs where they were ushered into the dinning room just past the adjacent music room or, as the sergeant called it when Sam asked, the 'Dresden Room'. The room contained porcelain pieces from Dresden as well as other items made in Germany.

As requested earlier, when asked by the sergeant, they breakfasted on buttermilk pancakes with real maple syrup and farm fresh bacon with a glass of orange juice, from Florida oranges, for each; and to top it off they had Columbian coffee, which it seems the President was fond of as well. They were really home and how nice it was. They were told that the President was in at his Hyde Park White House office, which was located in the Dutch Colonial building across from the horse barn and garden. The President had designed the structure himself and had it built in 1941 as the future repository of his Presidential records, which Sam found fascinating.

When told this by their constant sergeant Sam stated to Madison, "Just think, when this is all over we can come across the Hudson on occasion and do research on ourselves being here," and he concluded with an exaggerated grin.

"I don't think so," said Madison, " this meeting will never have taken place for many reasons and you know that."

"Well you are right but, at least we might eventually get a better idea of how this thing unfolded behind us."

"Speaking of the Hudson, we're right here and I need to see it."

Sam just smiled, came over to her side of the table, and took her hand as the sergeant guided them out and to the back of the house.

Looking down off the hill, at the Hudson, they could see her waters glisten and dance under the early morning light and they didn't say a word, they just grew closer and held each other as they stared down and out at the river. The sergeant stepped back, left them alone and smiled realizing for the first time how long they must have been away from home.

By 9AM, after Sam and Madison had visited the horse barn and strolled through the adjacent garden, the President was ready to take them for a ride in his dark blue 1936 Ford Phaeton. The car, the President and Fala were waiting for them engine running, in front of the house, as they exited the gardens. Their return Clipper flight was at high noon that Friday so they had a little time. The return flight would be high visibility as there would be some military officers onboard, they were told.

The car was magnificent and specially outfitted so that the President could drive it using his hands only. He even had an automatic cigarette lighter and dispenser rigged within easy reach on the left hand side of the steering column which he delighted in showing Madison, who sat up front with he and Fala. The President looked great even with the weight of the world on his shoulders. Sam could not help but to feel this as he watched him with a smile as he drove back and forth up the long driveway with his hat pulled down in a jaunty manner as if he were about to drive into a windstorm with his lit

cigarette balancing precariously at an up angle on the tip of his holder keeping the smoke out of his face.

He watched the President with a smile and he hoped to God that he would act on their analysis and confront Churchill, and make the appropriate decision. He also knew that he needed to get back as soon as possible and get some more statistics, certainly 'Commodore' in the 'Dome' had collected a lot more fodder for an upgraded analysis.

Madison was having fun with the President and looked beautiful in her simple powder blue blouse and white skirt down to her shapely ankles with a pleated slit in the back. She wore two-inch heel powder blue and white two-tone pumps and it all came together to show her shape in a way that Sam found intoxicating. He was actually surprised in a way that she didn't wear her blue jeans and Yankee cap but the fact that she could look great in both put a smile on his face as they drove down the long drive for the third time as the President enjoyed Madison's quick retorts to his quips.

◆   ◆   ◆

They were on board the Dixie Clipper and set to go by 11:30 that morning. The flight down from the New Hackensack airport had been too quick but they could see Newburgh and Trophy Point, and the Bear Mountain Bridge as the pilot used the Hudson to navigate down to LaGuardia Field. Madison had had tears streaming down her face and Sam had comforted her as they continued down the Hudson telling her it wouldn't be long before they were home to stay. She had just smiled up at him as he tamped away her tears with a linen handkerchief.

There were nine senior officers on board for this return flight and they had nice but somewhat perfunctory conversations with them not being able to reveal exactly who they were; the officers, as well, could talk of very little due to their different levels of 'war knowledge'. As far as the officers were concerned Madison and Sam worked for the State Department in public affairs. At least that's what Lieutenant Cone told them, who had a higher clearance than they with regard to basic knowledge of high level personnel, as he was the man ferrying all of these individuals.

The lieutenant again took Madison and Sam up to the cockpit and let Madison sit in the captain's position and make course corrections once they were over the Atlantic. Sam had said, with some humor in his voice, "Are you sure you want to do that lieutenant? She loved that diving maneuver of yours the other night and might be tempted to repeat it."

Lieutenant Cone smiled and laughed and added, "By the way she's eyeing the controls you may have a daredevil on your hands so be careful."

"Oh, I already know that lieutenant."

"Ah men, can't you let a girl scare herself a little," commented Madison as she held the plane's large steering yolk resting on the underside of her forearms with the delicate but firm touch of a practiced aviator while her legs extended her feet into the large rudder pedal pans. Sam and Lieutenant Cone just looked at each other and smiled.

September 9, 1944 ----- England

They landed in Southampton at 11AM on Saturday the 9th of September. The staff car was there to take them back to the 'Dome' where they found the MG TA waiting for them.

With a roar Madison drove out of the entrance to the Cambridge Military Hospital at a little after 12 noon and turned right, past the 1906 observatory and then double-clutched and downshifted into a sharp right turn then back up through the gears and then downshifting again into a left-hand turn towards Fleet Road and Fleet. As she hit Fleet Road in third gear she accelerated to a high RPM until she came to the large ancient oak on her left, shifted into fourth and flattened out at maximum speed. Sam was holding on and she was smiling as she ran the car at high speed with the wind in her hair, knocking the cobwebs of the long flight out of her head.

Sam was not thrilled but he was getting used to it, and this was really nothing compared to that night landing in Manhasset Bay. In his mind that experience was the closest that he would ever get to being a passenger on an elevator dropping uncontrolled for twenty floors.

They were in Fleet in no time and Madison downshifted beautifully at the Links and made the left hand turn onto Elvetham as she was starting to shift back up through the gears again. At the property boundary she was only down into second gear and she hit the right turn onto the pebbles of the short driveway at a perfect glide, faster than normal, and then in a subdued first gear drove to the back of the cottage.

"Gee, can we do that again?," proclaimed Sam with a smile and rumpled hair as the engine died.

Madison looking over at him smiled and then reached over and pulled him close and hugged him, and then kissed him. She was excited and couldn't be happier. After the pressure build-up of giving the presentation to the President, then having a good visit with the Commander-in-Chief, and seeing her home, and a long flight ended by a fast drive she was in prime form and Sam couldn't be happier seeing her like this.

"I'll do that all day long if I can get one of those kisses at the end," Sam said with a purposely demure smile on his face.

Madison leaned over giggling and kissed him again.

They retreated to their private island and, though tired from travel, they made love that day and night while they were filled with joy at the expectation of the war ending, and the two of them going home again. They were filled with dreams of sunny days on the Hudson and seeing young men on Trophy Point who would not have to go to war. It had been a long hard and tiring road from that sunny day when Madison, looking up at the men waving from Trophy Point, realized that war was imminent and a lot of young men would die; now they were almost through it. They were able to see the President and maybe they had stopped a major military blunder from occurring and if that were so the war would end even sooner, with a lot less death on both sides.

They slept one of the best night's sleep, in each other's arms, that they had slept since the war started. They looked forward to tomorrow as the first day at the beginning of the end and they would get the additional statistics to back up their brief to the President. They would hope to have it within a day or two and send it off in a 'Flash' to "Admiral Q". The President had two code names, "Victor" and "Admiral Q" and now knowing his sense of humor along with their brief discussion of sailing they would use "Admiral Q". It also never hurt to establish a human relationship when one wanted their intelligence accepted even if he was The President of The United States and this was something that Madison had learned from Sam early on.

The next morning, a Sunday work day, was glorious and at 8AM Madison kissed Sam good-bye with such joy and energy and love that Sam was left feeling that everything was already behind them and that they already had their lives finally together with each other. She knew she had plenty of time that morning to collect and correlate the new statistics as she backed up in the MG turning the large wheels to the right then looking forward she started to move towards the entrance to the driveway and Elvetham Road as Sam followed behind her smiling. He could see her glancing in the rearview mirror at him with the warmest smile on her face, one that he had not seen in over three years, as she pulled out of the drive. Just before accelerating into second gear she looked at Sam and blew him a kiss and mouthed the words "Three Letters, I love you" and then facing forward she stepped on the throttle and shifted up into the gear. Once she was well past the property boundary he, and the whole road, could hear her accelerate up into third gear as the sound of the MG started to fade down near the turn at the Links. Sam had this overbearing feeling that he couldn't last the day before he saw her again.

When she arrived at the 'Dome' there was a message from Clive waiting for her. He was coming into Fleet on the 12:05 train from London and wanted Madison to pick him up. This was rather strange as he usually came in to Aldershot and she never picked him up. There was always a staff car or Jeep ready to whisk him away. Something was up but whatever it was it couldn't be that important she would just have to compile and correlate and relate the statistics that she was working on with a little more speed. She wouldn't bother Sam about this and, at any rate, she wouldn't have enough time to run down Elvetham to see him quickly before picking up Clive.

Sunday, September 10, 1944 ---- Fleet Road

Clive was right on time and gave Madison a perfunctory kiss on the cheek saying, "Alow Maddi", looking a bit worn and a bit upset. She had seen him just the previous week and then only briefly, long enough though to know that he was working on Monty's brainchild MARKET-GARDEN. Even though they really were not close and hadn't seen too much of each other over the previous year she could feel his distress even though he was doing well to hide it. On her mind as well were the two 'fresh-off-the-presses' Spitfire recon photos she had just seen showing camouflaged German armor in and around Arnhem and the final objective of MARKET-GARDEN, which confirmed the warning they had given in their brief to the President; also on her mind was the need to let Sam know by day's end.

He did not say anything other than, "I'll drive," as they headed to the MG in the parking lot.

Pulling out of the Fleet Station parking lot and then heading out of town Clive did not say a word and Madison was getting nervous, she had never seen him like this before.

As they hit the straight on Fleet Road and accelerated Clive broke his silence against the roar of the wind coming into the car, "How could you?"

"How could I what?," yelled Madison against the air roaring into the car.

"How could you break my confidence and be so disloyal as to tell The President of The United States about Monty's plan. He's just going to present it today to Eisenhower and just this morning

I find that the Americans have been informed and how they were informed, and it turns out to be 'Commodore' and my wife."

"Have you forgotten that I am American and American intelligence, and do you realize in what jeopardy your general Montgomery is going to put the entire front?"

"He is a Field Marshall and it's a bold move that will end the war."

"It's a bold move that is going to get a lot of men and civilians killed so that your Field Marshall can briefly strut around like a male rooster."

"How dare you ridicule Monty in such a disgraceful way, typical Yank and I know about your affair with that other Yank as well, didn't you think I would," yelled Clive against the continual roar of wind.

"Sam was there before you were and you know that. I thought he was dead but he's not and I love him more than my own life."

"You bloody Yank, we'll see about that." And just as Clive made that statement the ancient grand old oak loomed off to the right of the road in the near distance and Clive started to head the MG towards it.

"My God, what are you doing?," screamed Madison.

"We'll see if he and your precious America are worth your life," shouted Clive.

"You're out of your mind," shrieked Madison as she leaned over right and tried to grab the wheel. As she did this, Clive jammed on the brakes and the MG turned 180 degrees and then slide sideways into that ancient oak jamming the small left side passenger door into Madison as the car came to a rest.

"Oh my God Maddi I was only trying to scare you. Oh God, Oh my God," he blurted out as he reached over to hold her head with his right hand, as his left arm was broken from holding the wheel firm when they hit the tree.

Just then a military ambulance from Aldershot came down the road from the base and quickly pulled up to the accident.

"Please do something," yelled Clive in shock as Madison stared into nothingness and muttered things that Clive could not hear in his state.

Two men came over with a stretcher and two others ran over from the cab of the ambulance. Together they lifted the back of the MG and moved it away from the tree to get to Madison.

They delicately lifted her onto the stretcher as she mumbled, "Sam..., Sam..., Sam....."

As they loaded her into the ambulance with Clive holding his arm and looking on in tears she uttered, "Sam please don't leave me, not now.........." and she just closed her eyes never to open them again.

◆   ◆   ◆

It was already Sunday, September 10th, just days before Operation MARKET-GARDEN, and Sam found himself worried about equipment statistics and the fact that there were odd types of equipment showing up with each other in different areas of Holland. He was trying to put this puzzle together when he heard the strong and distinct winding sound of an approaching American Jeep's engine and transmission which was now so familiar to him and was starting to remind him of home these days as more and more Jeeps appeared on the roads around Fleet and Aldershot. It sounded soothing to him until it was up to the property boundary where, at a relatively high rate of speed, it all of a sudden had its brakes applied with a screeching skid. Then he heard the Jeep at idle as someone jumped out.

Sam headed to the front door of the 'chimney sweep cottage' but before he could reach it there was a loud knocking accompanied by a familiar voice, "Dr. Harbour, Dr. Harbour please come quick............."

Before he could say anymore Sam had opened the door and there in the doorway was one of Madison's 'Commodore' team, who he had only met on one occasion and not knowing till later that he was one of the two members of the team, with tears in his eyes.

Sam knew immediately, "Where is she Al?"

"At the hospital", he said surprised that Sam had remembered his name, and as though he knew him personally, and then he closed the cottage door as Sam ran to the Jeep.

Al jumped in the back behind Sam and the sergeant, who Sam had seen before, wheeled the Jeep around in a middle of the road U-turn and sped off for Aldershot.

On the way Sam saw the ancient oak in the distance with something red up against it and before he had time to think he knew it was the MG. As they passed he could see the car had been up against the tree on the passenger side and the tree was left with a large section debarked and yellow-white where the car had impacted.

"Oh my God Baby........ ," muttered Sam to himself under the roar of the air coming into the Jeep.

In no time they were at the casualty entrance on the right side of the hospital and through the doors.

The faces inside were grim and they all knew who he was. A doctor greeted them and led Sam to a curtained section of the emergency room and before letting him in said, "I'm sorry old man, there was nothing we could do. Her internal injuries were too great and we lost her before she even arrived at the hospital. Let me know if there is an...................................". Sam did not hear the rest, he heard nothing more.

He stood there as the doctor closed the curtain behind him and just looked. Her face had been covered over and for a second he had hope that it wasn't Madison under those sheets, not his Madison, she was bullet proof. Nothing was supposed to happen to her not after that concocted death in an auto accident back in the States; even then he could not believe she was dead and he had turned out to be right. Oh no, it couldn't be her but then he could see her soft blonde hair, with that slight hint of brown, showing out from under the sheets and he knew of only one woman with such hair with subtle waves in it as to mesmerize the consciousness of any man.

He stepped over to the litter, which had been placed on top of a gurney, and pulled the sheets back. She looked asleep. Sam's tears rolled down his face and onto her's as he bent over and kissed her on the forehead, on each eye and then on the lips.

"Oh baby, you left me behind, I couldn't keep you safe." As he said these words to her softly he could hear his thoughts in her voice and the tears wouldn't stop.

He would never see the sparkle and excitement in those gray-green eyes again as he kissed her lightly on the lips once more as the tears flowed; they would never sail the beautiful Hudson together on a sunny day aboard 'Whisper' and they would never go to the Commodore again. He knew he could now not keep the promise he had made about not going into Holland with the airborne to get the needed statistics to back up their Antwerp counteroffensive 'Crystal Ball' if MARKET-GARDEN went forward. As Madison had said, not in her lifetime; now that she was gone he would go and try to do his best to end this thing.

He couldn't keep her safe anymore but he would make sure that she got home one way or the other.

September 15, 1944 --- Invasion-Holland

Operation MARKET-GARDEN was set to go on September 17th starting with a daytime airborne drop up the Dutch corridor with the 101st Airborne to go into the an area between Eindhoven and Weghel, Holland and the 82nd Airborne going in just north of this in an area between Grave and Nijmegen.

The 101st is to capture canal and river crossings over a sixteen mile stretch between Eindhoven and Weghel.

On September 15th Sam was picked up at the 'Dome' and taken to Newbury about 80 miles west of London. Behind the barbed wire encampment of the 101st Airborne Division Sam was informed that he would get a ride into Holland in one of the 101st's CG-4A Waco gliders going into Son, Holland. Almost half the Division would go in by glider this time and there was plenty of room for Sam. He was 'sealed in' in the encampment until take-off on September 17th. They were going in attached to the British 2nd Army and none of the troops were happy about that, and Sam knew why. Monty was not an American hero and British command did not have the highest regard for American forces nor was British command considered competent by American troops.

Sam was to go to Holland for what he knew was Monty's great folly with a force code named "Destiny" or the US Army. He needed the statistics to prove that the German Army was far from finished and was actually setting up for a counteroffensive or, actually, an offensive against Antwerp with the Belgium city of Bastogne, in the

230

Ardennes, as the first major hub on their run for the port city. Sam was already aware that days earlier Dutch resistance had warned of German armor units in the Arnhem drop area of the British 1st Airborne division but Montgomery was unwilling to make any changes to his plans based on this confirmed intelligence. Just before Sam had been picked up at the 'Dome' he was made aware of the fact that aerial reconnaissance of the British drop zones showed German tanks in and amongst the trees. He had expected Montgomery's reaction, which dismissed the tanks as probably broken down hulks with nothing to back his assumption.

They had given Sam a quick course in the use of a 30 caliber M-1 carbine with a folding stock and equipped him with airborne battle dress, jump boots, knife, helmet and ammo. His helmet had a white spade painted on it with a white dot to its right, at 3 o'clock, signifying the 1st Battalion of the 506th PIR 101st Airborne Division. He would not carry grenades, a sidearm or any other equipment which would weigh him down, equipment which he did not know how to use at any rate. He was attached to the 506th Regiment of the 101st Airborne Division and a seasoned lieutenant from the Normandy drop by the name of Bill Sanderson from Mahwah, N.J. of all places, not too far from the town in which Madison had been born. Sam felt at home with these men and many of them seemed to be from Pennsylvania and New Jersey, which made it feel even that much closer to home.

In the day and a half that he spent in camp with the men of the 101st, before departing, he found a bond among the men second to none, like nothing he had ever read about and surely like nothing he had ever experienced before; they were much more than a swell bunch of guys. They were truly a 'Band of Brothers', at least the 'old hands' who had fought together through Normandy and Carentan in the Cherbourg Peninsula, even more so than in Shakespeare's Henry V, Saint Crispen's Day Speech. He knew that there were no better men to enter battle with, for the first time, than these.

Sam saw his glider on the morning of September 17th at an airfield just outside the village of Ramsbury, England and it looked like an Army olive drab box with stars on its Hershey bar wings and wheels that seemed too small with skids to aid in landing.

Seated in the WACO glider on the starboard side, right up front, Sam looked down at the hands of his selectively issued army Waltham wristwatch just as the first jolt of the now played out 300 foot towline pulled the nose of the big WACO glider forward behind its C-47 tow plane or tug. It was 10:26 AM on September 17th. Sam just smiled to himself about the number 26 coming to him again and then he remembered a date well into the future and now this date had even more meaning. Could he see his Madison again? A tear ran into the corner of his eye at the possibility and then he was back again as the WACO went airborne and gained speed.

He was with 13 other men from the 101st and actually marveled at the simple ingenuity of the American WACO. It was built for quick mass production but felt stable in the air and looking at the pilot he did not see him correct or try to trim the aircraft too much. It seemed to fly nicely on its own behind the C-47. Told about the WACO before he boarded he was amazed that the nose came up, upon landing, in a very ingenious and pragmatic way when loaded with a Jeep pulling a howitzer or ammo trailer. A cable attached to the top of the hinged nose section ran along the top of the fuselage to the back of the aircraft, through a large pulley and down to the back of the artillery piece or trailer being pulled by the Jeep, when that was the cargo. The purpose of this was to prevent the cargo from killing the pilots if the glider hit too hard. If the glider did hit hard the heavy cargo would pull the cable on the pulley as it moved forward, breaking the retaining pins holding the cockpit in place and pulling the cockpit, with the two pilots, up and out of the way as it spit its cargo out. On a normal landing they would just drive the Jeep out, opening the nose in the same manner.

The flight was smooth and uneventful along the southern route they were flying over Belgium and into Holland. This was not the case for the Northern route of the 82nd and the British airborne, they later heard, as they encountered flak ships and barges around the mouth of the Schelde which Montgomery had not captured; so it started.

Sam had time to think as he listened to the sound of the C-47 up front and the whisper of the slipstream cradling the fuselage of the big WACO at something under 120 MPH. He thought of Madison and sailing with her on the Hudson and his thoughts were all in her voice, thank God for small gifts. He could never lose the sound of her voice or the warmth of her fragrance, or the beauty of her initial appearance wherever she turned up. Then he suddenly became frightened of losing these things, the only things he had of Madison. He started to sweat with this sudden realization and then, for one brief moment, the nose of the Waco went up in a draft and as he looked at the airspeed indicator in front of the pilot on the left, as he corrected the glider, Sam could see a warning label above it that read: "WHEN BEING TOWED BY A C-47 TYPE AIRPLANE EQUIPED WITH EXTERNAL GLIDER TOWING MECHANISM, THE ANGULAR DISPLACEMENT OF THIS GLIDER RELATIVE TO THE TOW LINE WILL AT NO TIME EXCEED **26** DEGREES UP, 20 DEGREES DOWN, OR 20DEGREES TO EITHER SIDE.

He couldn't believe what he was reading. Why 26 degrees and not 25 or 20. It was actually 26 and then he accepted it and he knew that he would not only not forget her and all of the little everyday things that made her who she was, but he would see her again. He looked down at his carbine in thought and noticed the manufacturer of the weapon and it was Singer. Singer Sewing Machine Company was now making guns and would soon be back to making sowing machines again. There was an ironic humor there that he knew Madison would have appreciated and he chuckled to himself briefly and then he remembered their Singer 'Victrola' and nights listening to Edith Piaf and Artie Shaw and he just smiled softly to himself. He then pulled out a stick of Beemans and offered a stick to Lieutenant Sanderson sitting next to him and then pulled out a scrap of paper and a short pencil, part of the kit he was carrying to record his statistics, and started to jot down a sonnet about Madison's voice; he wrote it straight through without hesitation:

Sweet voice and true humor doth make thee.
True it be, this voice is life to warm such tempered
Heart as not shown but lived in love's quiet refrain.
Such refrain be left behind when your voice announces
It's sweet arrival at my door, oh that morning come every
Day with such entry as my heart desire, quiet in its

Refrain until such gifted time.
Be it mine to embrace with quiet heart
Not meant to speak but feel life's wondrous joys
As it gives life meaning more than simple
Breath my heart supports in life's repose.
Its sweet song wakes the soul and stutters the breath;
I am truly alive at the call of that sweet song,
It is that life is about such wonder and sweet awakening

Sam smiled to himself and to Madison as he added the 14th line. Just as he tucked the sonnet away in his left breast pocket he felt the sudden release of the towline and then the pilot yelled, "Get ready."

The glider slowed and now Sam could only hear the quiet slipstream as the glider banked to the right. Sam looked out the cockpit window and he could see other gliders that had been released and then realized that his pilot was not only maneuvering for a landing site but he was also maneuvering to avoid other gliders.

With a sudden lurch left the glider straightened out then dove to gain speed. Sam looking at the airspeed indicator again, could see 65 MPH showing; a large drop from their cruising speed. As he was looking at the airspeed the nose came slightly up and the airspeed dropped dramatically making him look up and out the cockpit window just in time to see the glider hit the field and throw dirt up on the windscreen. It hit with such force that he was jammed down in his seat and his helmet came flying off as he hadn't pulled the chinstrap quite tight enough.

Before he knew it he had the door on the right side of the WACO open and was the first man out with Lieutenant Sanderson next. Sanderson stood next to the door, and Sam, and just said, "Hubba-Hubba, move those fat asses." Everyone was out and heading to a wood lot in less than a minute. Sam couldn't figure out why they'd given a new guy like him that job but maybe they did it so he would keep his mind off of what was happening before the landing so he would be out quick. It worked, he thought as he put his helmet back on, on the run. The last man off the glider had handed it to him with a relaxed smile that put Sam even more at ease.

September 19, 1944 --- Montgomery's XXX Corp

The 101st secured its southern section of the 64 mile long main highway running north through Holland across the Rhine by the second day and waited for the ground forces in the form of the British XXX Corp, who were late on that day.

The U.S. airborne units called it 'Hell's Highway' and the key element to success was speed. The British XXX Corp seemed to have no sense of urgency while airborne troops died taking the bridges that they would cross on this road, and then more died while holding the road open for the slow British advance.

The British armor literally stopped for tea and Sam watched in absolute horror as American airborne troops swore at them, and in a couple of cases openly. He even saw a non-com pull his 45 automatic out of his shoulder holster and start towards one of the British tanks swearing that there were airborne troops covering more than 60 miles of highway and "...you bastards are sitting on your collective asses and having tea. You're not going to leave those airborne units in Arnhem out do dry." He said this as he marched towards one of the tanks, with a stunned Britisher in a tank helmet up in the commander's cupula of one of the Shermans sipping his tea and dumbfounded. One of the enlisted men reacted quickly enough and tackled his sergeant, saying, "Sorry sarg but the bastard's not worth it." The young sergeant just smiled at the kid and muttered to him, "At least someone has brains today." And they both got up and walked away. The private looked back following his sergeant and just yelled, "If it was George Patton instead a ya'all he'd be halfway there by now instead of givin' away the whole shabang."

Sam was dumbfounded, he'd never experienced anything quite like it and the American airborne was not a happy group, as a whole, about the lack of progress by the British armor.

While still looking at the scene he felt a slap on his back, "FUBAR", said Sanderson as Sam turned to see who it was. "Montgomery is a dangerous man, a real doozy in the reverse, and our people know it. The kid is right. Patton would've done it right. Now those guys in the British 1st Airborne are going to die on the vine and there is nothing in this holy hell that we can do about it. Every one of these men knows it and they are on edge for their airborne brethren up north."

"I'm afraid Bill that this won't be the last time Montgomery gets in the way of ending this thing quickly."

"Yah, boy." Was all that Sanderson said in return as they watched the British fire up the engines on their tanks and slowly start to move out.

October 3, 1944 --- Near 'Hell's Highway', Holland

The 101st was meant to be on the line for 72 hours but Montgomery's plan had failed and by the 25th of the month the Germans were pulling back under heavy fighting to concentrate up around Arnhem and the German border. 'Hell's Highway' was earning its name in blood. On the 25th 2,398 British 1st Airborne survivors escaped the area around Arnhem by crossing the Rhine at night and returning to the new Allied lines; they had gone into Arnhem with 10,600 men; 6,414 were taken prisoner.

The 101st had actually, in the initial fighting, faced 1000 troops from the German 15th Army that had escaped Montgomery. By the 22nd of September 86,000 men, more than 600 artillery pieces, better than 6,000 vehicles, over 6,000 horses and a large quantity of war material belonging to the German 15th Army had escaped the Schelde and Montgomery only to be faced again, by Americans this time. Sam was informed of this in the field by the 30th of the month and he already knew this to be a fact by the unit markings he was recording along with the mix of statistical data he was collecting on equipment concentrations and types.

How could an entire Army escape to fight again? By all intents and purposes those men should have been POW's. They should have been taken out of the picture but they were not and this war would go on and their escape further backed the 'Crystal Ball' contention of 'Commodore' that the German Army would pull a winter counteroffensive through the Ardennes to run over Bastogne in a move on Antwerp.

Sam's numbers were finally coming together. He had suffered through artillery barrages and rocket propelled 150mm mortar rounds called 'Screaming Meemies' or Nebelwerfers, as they screamed as they came in one after another in groups after leaving their multiple tube launcher. Sam had seen one up close. It consisted of six tubes formed in a circle and mounted on a two-wheeled carriage. It looked harmless enough until you were on the receiving end. He experienced this along with firefights with the 101st. He had fired his weapon for the first time after the second firefight and really not like an experienced rifleman but just firing it by pointing it in the direction of incoming fire and pulling the trigger rapidly until he was through his fifteen round clip in no time. He had remembered Bill Sanderson looking over at him afterwards and just smiling this big 'ol grin and saying, "It ain't Kansas anymore, is it!"

Sam had just smiled back and muttered to himself, "Well I've heard that one before", thinking back to Goodge Street and Ike and Madison; it had then seemed like a lifetime ago. He remembered his thoughts had then quickly returned to the smell of cordite and the other sounds and smells around him that day and that he had understood why these men fought so hard, they fought for each other and formed what he had called in his analysis 'unit cohesion'. He could not have imagined the power of wanting to protect the guy next to you until he himself started to develop strong bonds with the guys next to him under fire.

Sam now knew the smell of war and it was something he would never forget; it was a smell all to its own of this earth but not of his world. He imagined that the smell of the slaughter in the Faliase Gap must have been overbearing with what he had recently experienced as the smell of burning rubber, burning wood and flesh and fuel, hot metal, and the smell of decay all combined into the smell of war. This was a smell that he would like to see put to an end, especially if he could help it.

After that fight Bill Sanderson had asked him how he had become so involved in history that he was actually making it and then for the first time, other than with Madison, he felt compelled to tell this man with whom he had risked life and limb. He started by saying: "It started in a little place called Kennett, Missouri. My

Father was from Kennett originally and he had an uncle fighting
for the British in the Boar War and as it would turn out there was
another Missourian fighting for the British. The two finally met and
found that not only did they have Missouri in common but one had
a niece and the other a nephew. The niece was not too far from
Kennett and that was my Mother. They were both young at the
time but became close friends and married when they came of age.
They were both special. He became mayor of Kennett when he was
only 18 and was promptly booted out when they found that he was
under age. One Fourth of July my Mother wanted fireworks for the
celebration. My Father had said no and as he walked out the front
door she emptied all six rounds from his Smith & Wesson police
38 into the ground of the backyard. She got her fireworks. I was
impressed with my parents and the love that came to them from two
men who had fought side-by-side for another country and they were
each something in their own right. My parents moved to New York
and their dynamic characters gave them happiness and success in
life with all who were around them. The whole experience of my
family and its origins got me interested." Bill had just smiled and
nodded his head as it made sense, and talk of love of family made
him think of the joys of home.

On his 17th day in the field, Tuesday October 3, Sam was out on
a recon with Sanderson; a non-com from Texas, that he had come to
know, by the name of Art Philips; "Doc" LeGrange and seven other
troopers. They were helping him to get some additional statistics
that he needed before he could feel satisfied and get pulled out to do
a follow-up report to SHAEF and the Commander-in-Chief.

They were just starting to move up over a dike with Sanderson
in the lead when a line of eerie pinkish tracers, highlighted by the
overcast, came in their direction from the north end of the dike. Sam
the statistician could hear the distinct tearing sound of the 1,200
round per minute, exceedingly high rate of fire, light weight, at '26'
lbs, 'Hitler's zipper' machinegun. Sanderson in the lead pushed
Philips back on Sam and yelled, "MG 42!,"and fell back down the
side of the dike with them. He looked at them and just said, "Let's
get outta Dodge boys," as he hand signaled the rest of the team. They
then headed south along the dike and ran into a five man German

patrol who they caught off guard laying fire into them quickly but before they could take the patrol out one of them had knelt down and managed to get a "Potato Masher" off throwing it in an arch towards Sam, Sanderson and his men. The "Potato Masher" was the Model 24 Stielhandgranate which looked oddly like a potato masher and Sam seeing it come in his direction, in slow motion, thought '..how odd, it really did look like a potato masher and maybe that is because the Germans like potatoes.' It was really irrational thinking and it accompanied the irrational act of Sam picking it up quickly just as it hit the ground and turning away from the men he was with to throw it away when the 6 ounce charge went off which in turn blew apart the Splitterring fragmentation sleeve which had been slid over the head of the grenade. The serrated sleeve was, in a flash, turned into multiple fragments half of which flew into Sam Harbour's chest, the other half flying harmlessly away from him and the men that he was with. He felt the flash more than he saw it, along with the impact of the fragments followed by the heat of the explosion and then the actual concussion. It all occurred, it seemed to him, in slow motion. How odd again he thought that there would be so much heat and then he was on his back trying to breath, as he heard the echo from the Thompson of Philips as he knocked down the last man of the enemy patrol, the one who had thrown the grenade.

Before he knew it the lieutenant started screaming to their rear, "Medic up! Medic up!" How strange Sam thought, that was probably "Doc" LeGrange; why is he calling him 'medic up.'? Then a surge of pain hit and he let out a half yell choked with blood as Sanderson jammed him with a morphine Syrette in the shoulder '*where Madison used to lay her head*' and dipped his finger in the blood all over his chest and wrote something on his forehead, and for a second Sam thought Sanderson was a kid playing a kid's game. He then pinned the Syrette to the material covering Sam's shoulder like it was a sheriff's badge; why was Sanderson playing like a kid? Then all of the sounds came back that he hadn't been hearing clearly for the past eternity and he realized what had happened. Sanderson had seen this before and when he knew that Sam was back he just said, "Shit Sam, why'd you go and do that?", just as "Doc" LeGrange arrived and, dropping his kit, knelt and tore open Sam's shirt.

Sam could hear Sanderson in the background giving orders to set up security for their position and Sam knew they had to get out of there but they weren't. Sanderson had set up the Browning 30 caliber machine gun in their rear to the north and sent two men south beyond the dead German patrol with the Browning Automatic Rifle that they had 'liberated' from Army stocks back in England in September. The BAR gave the recon patrol, just short of a rifle squad, extra fire power along with their 30 caliber machine gun.

"How's he doing Doc?," queried Sanderson as he came back.

"I've got my hands full."

"You saved our bacon Sam."

Sam just looked up; and half delirious, and with some difficulty he said, "You may my glories and my state depose, but not my griefs; still am I king of those. Oh God Madison where are you, where are you?............ it's cold," he then muttered half to himself as the voices grew distant and the light started to fade but he could now see Madison sitting in "Whisper" tied up at Newburgh with a smile on her face, highlighted by sunshine, waiting for him to untie her and get in.

"He's gone," sighed 'Doc' LeGrange to no one in particular.

"What was that he said?" asked Philips.

"It was from William Shakespeare's King Richard the Second," replied Sanderson looking quietly down at Sam.

Philips just looked at Sanderson in questioning amazement then bent down to check Sam's pockets for any important papers. He came up with a small piece of paper bloodied from his wounds. It was the sonnet he had written on the glider those many days ago now. It was the sonnet missing the last line, which had been torn away by a grenade fragment and imbedded in his chest near his heart. The line: *It is that life is about such wonder and sweet awakening.*

They wrapped Sam in a poncho and two men grabbed either end, and they walked him back to their lines.

That night Philips was talking to Sanderson about home and out of nowhere blurted, "Ya'll know Lieutenant I woan't furget him, I just woan't. He's what my Momma use ta call 'genel in Jewlie' 'cause he was easy goin' even when it was hot. Funna thang is he always wanted ta go ta Texas, now I can git back theair 'cause he can never see it. I'm tired a this here fuckin' war."

"You and me both Art."

◆   ◆   ◆

The 101st would stay on the line for a total of 72 days not 72 hours due to Montgomery's poor execution of a risky plan and they came up against combat troops from the German 15th Army; one of whom killed an analyst by the name of Sam Harbour, temporarily assigned to the 1st Battalion of the 506th PIR.

By the end of the day of September 25th the Operation was a failure as the British 1st. Airborne Division retreated from the furthest objective of the city of Arnhem and crossed the Rhine to Allied lines in the middle of the night.

Before the month was out Field Marshall Montgomery hailed the operation as 90% successful while Commodore and the rest of the Allies knew that it was a 100% failure that had set the Allied timetable, for an earlier end to the war, on its ear once again.

On October 14, 1944 Irwin Rommel, Hitler's ex-favorite, was forced to take poison as Hitler accused him of being involved in the July 20th plot on his life. He was given a state funeral and the German public was told that he had died of head wounds suffered in July.

On the 16th of December 1944 the German Army started a 'counteroffensive' with an offensive through the Ardennes comprised of the equivalent of 28 divisions and German armor. They met heavy resistance in the northern and southern shoulders of their attack but broke through in the center. The center was held by the combat hardened 28th Division and the green troops of the 106th Division who had only been on the Continent for 15 days. The American forces occupying the center of this "quiet sector" in the Schnee Eifel, from the 106th, were in the sector for 'orientation'. They had been in their positions for only five days and occupied a line, at 21 miles, that covered over four times the normal distance for a division on the front line. Their positions also jutted out into Germany in a salient extending seven miles. They had replaced the 2nd Division on the line and as this was a quiet sector there was no concern to having green troops spread so thin. But after three days of fighting the 422nd and 423rd Regiments of the 106th were surrounded while their sister regiment, the 424^{th,} to the south, was able to fight and withdraw. The surrounding of these two regiments opened a hole with the crossroads town by the name of Bastogne at its heart. The German Army had broken through for their move on Antwerp in the same manner that 'Commodore' had predicted and would create a deep bulge in the Allied lines, yet American forces were caught totally unawares. The intelligence analysis assessment of future enemy operations stemming from a failed Operation MARKET-GARDEN had never been passed down to the field.

On the 17th 113 American prisoners were herded into a field near Malmedy, Belgium and fired upon by members of the 1st SS Panzer Division Hitlerjugend who later walked the field and shot or clubbed to death men that were still alive, laughing as they went. Sixty-one men actually survived the initial massacre and tried to get up and run over an hour later and, of these, 19 never made it but there were survivors to tell the tale. Hitler's new favored commander SS-Sturmbannfuhrer Otto Skorzeny was seen in the area just before the mass execution. He had pulled up to the lead tank in his command car and talked to the officer in the commander's cupula who, after Skorzeny left, gave the order to kill the American prisoners. The SS, unlike the German Wehrmacht, were known for their brutality. The Wehrmacht technically encompassed all German military but the term was used by the Allies as a specific reference to the Heer or the German regular army which, unlike the SS, was respected as an honorable military force.

The 101st, who were getting ready to have their inter-division football game on Christmas day; called the Champagne Bowl, topped off with a turkey dinner and leave to Paris, were called at 4 AM on the morning of the breakthrough to move ASAP to Bastogne.

Lacking winter clothing and much of its weapons, which had been turned in to the armorers after Holland, and lacking ammo the Division was transported to the outskirts of Bastogne.

Hitler declared that Bastogne must be taken and Eisenhower declared it must be held at all costs.

They arrived just before the Germans, who had pushed a bulge into the American lines by 65 miles. Everyone was bugging out and instead of digging in the 101ˢᵗ decided to move out and hit the German forces head on. The Germans were caught off-guard and their advance was stopped.

By December 22 the 101ˢᵗ was surrounded. As one paratrooper put it, "The poor Kraut bastards have us surrounded, we're now the whole in their donut."

On the same day the German commander sent the American commander, General Anthony C. McAuliffe, an ultimatum that gave the 101ˢᵗ. 2 hours to decide if they would surrender and it ended:

"If this proposal should be rejected one German artillery Corps and six heavy AA Battalions are ready to annihilate the U.S.A. troops in and near Bastogne. The order for firing will be given immediately after this two hours term.

All the serious civilian losses caused by this artillery fire would not correspond with the wellknown American humanity."

McAuliffe, who at first thought they were surrendering when he heard of the German white flag coming through the American lines as he thought, 'we're giving them a good shallacking', simply threw the ultimatum down on a table in his command post and said, "Ah Nuts!"

The return message to the German commander read: *"To the German Commander, NUTS!, The American Commander."*

When the German officer carrying the message asked what 'Nuts' meant he was told, "In plain English, it means Go To Hell."

The 101ˢᵗ was fighting surrounding small unit guerilla engagements, which they were expertly trained at and which the German Army was not. They also had every crossroad zeroed with artillery and every time the Germans tried one of their single trust attacks, instead of attacking as a swarm from all points of the compass, they were repelled with the help of artillery. Tony McAufliffe; as acting commander of the 101ˢᵗ, while General Maxell Taylor was in Washington, was fortuitously enough an artillery general. He had the roads around Bastogne zeroed, with the help of 155mm artillery from the 9ᵗʰ and 10ᵗʰ Armored Divisions, and was counting his rounds, while also hitting different intersections at odd times to keep the German forces off balance. As a result, the Germans thought they were facing a bigger arsenal than they actually were as the randomly shifting fires created this illusion.

Re-supply had been impossible due to the fog and snow conditions, or what they called 'Hitler's weather'. American forces were low on ammunition with some men actually down to one round each.

Up north of the 101st, the 82nd Airborne was doing well fighting in the rear of the SS Panzer units of the northern penetration of the American lines by the German 15th Army, which had originally escaped Montgomery. They were causing chaos among these SS units until Lord Montgomery was given half of the ground command as a political gesture, anticipating the need for British reserves, and let it get to his head. He ordered elements of the 508th Parachute Infantry Regiment of the 82nd to withdraw because he did not understand airborne troops, who are trained to fight encircled and are not trained to withdraw. The order was initially refused until the Field Marshal became adamant. Elements of the 508th suffered heavy casualties in its forced withdrawal and the SS units experienced relief in their rear. The Field Marshal would later claim that most of the fighting and the blood lost that enabled the Allies to stop the Ardennes Offensive came from British troops, which was not even close to the truth. This comment would raise such a stir between the Allies that Eisenhower would talk of having Montgomery dismissed. Churchill would eventually correct this misinformation and apologize in the House of Commons for Montgomery's incorrect and insulting statements.

Montgomery had been given half of the ground command in the Bulge in case The United States needed his troops but he committed few British troops telling American General Bradley in his godlike and cautious manner, "I simply can't pass over to the offensive. There will be at least one more enemy blow on my flank. When the German has exhausted himself, then I'll attack." He never did. Montgomery said it would take him three months to flatten the 'Bulge' and push the Germans back to their start line; in the end it would take the American forces six weeks to flatten the 'Bulge' and the German Army would never rebound. Montgomery's publicly rude behavior towards American senior officers involved in the 'Bulge' not only helped to create more disunity between the Allies but on occasion caused chaos on the ground such as when he decreed that all transports drive on the left side of the wider roads instead of the right when there were only American troops in the sector. As Madison had once so simply stated to Sam, 'He is a viciously pompous little man who will get people killed.'

On Christmas Eve the Belgium transport Leopoldville carrying 2,223 American replacement troops, headed for the 'Bulge', and 237 Belgian, Congolese and British crew was torpedoed in the channel. The abandon ship was broadcast only in Flemish and the 237 crew and officers in charge of the ship fled taking all available lifeboats. Not one American soldier was found in a lifeboat and 802 were lost. All 237 of the crew survived and would be exonerated with honors by their countries.

On Christmas day 1944 Patton's 4th Armored Division broke through to the 'Battered Bastards of Bastogne' who "…did not need rescuing," as they saw it.

American forces suffered 80,987 casualties and of these over 19,000 were killed. German forces suffered 84,834 casualties killed, wounded or captured without a known count on the dead, the British suffered 1,400 casualties with just over 200 dead and 2,500 civilians were killed in what was to become known as The Battle of The Bulge. The German Army was pushed back and never saw Antwerp. Each side lost somewhere in the neighborhood of 800 tanks each and the Luftwaffe lost 1,000 planes, which finally broke the force.

It was the coldest winter on the Continent in 35 years and many hundreds of men froze. The coming spring would be a harvest of thousands of thawing bodies in the Ardennes.

From February 13th through February 15th the city of Dresden was area firebombed at night by the RAF and the rail yards were strategically hit in the daylight by the American Eighth Air Force. Churchill had demanded the raids against American opinion in order to appease Stalin. The British were now using the same doctrine that they had initially railed against in order to carry out their own scorched earth policy against Germany, as Madison had predicted. They were using now 'unconditional surrender' with a vengeance.

The Italian Campaign ended, after 20 months, on May 2, 1945 right to the end of the war and, just as Madison and Sam had predicted, the casualties were heavy. There were 114,000 American casualties and 10's of thousands of other Allied casualties along with 91,000 German and Italian military dead and 145,100 Italian civilians killed.

On the gray morning of April 9, 1945 Admiral Wilhelm Canaris, along with Dietrich Bonhoeffer, Major General Hans Oster, Judge Advocate General Carl Sack and Captain Ludwig Gehre were ordered to remove their cloths and were then lead naked to a courtyard gallows to the hooting and hollering of SS guards. They were jeered as they knelt under the scaffolding and prayed for the last time before being hung for attempting to rid Germany of Adolf Hitler and his following. Their bodies were left hung to rot. Admiral Canaris left behind a note, which had been smuggled out of his prison cell and which read: "*I die for my fatherland. I have a clear conscience. I only did my duty to my country when I tried to oppose the criminal folly of Hitler.*"

In April Lieutenant Sanderson of the 101st Airborne had 13 lines of a sonnet printed in the Stars and Stripes dedicated to Madison Bell from Sam Harbour, who had died in combat with the 101st in Holland. On April 12, FDR died in Warm Springs, Georgia just 26 days before the end of the war in Europe.

At the end of April the French 2nd Armored Division under General Jacques Philippe Leclerc, who some in the Allied forces saw as shifty eyed and pompous, was supposed to be on the right flank of the 506 PIR of the 101st Airborne Division heading south towards Berchtesgaden. The French division was often missing from that position and it was thought they were missing while looting German property. Nothing it seems had been learned from the failure of Versailles. This same French general summarily executed 12 POW's, who had been French members of the Waffen-SS, without a trial. He had just left their bodies by the side of the road where American forces found them and buried them.

In May, just days before the war ended, the younger brother of sergeant Philips, who was a corporal, found himself sitting up against the stone of the Great German Wine Door or arch near the town of Bad Durkheim in the Rhineland-Palatinate. It was the great door on the Wine Route.

He was sitting there with his battalion and of all things eating ice cream that had been mysteriously flown in to them. The ice cream had made him think of his brother's story of the man who saved his life and how he had lost the woman he had loved and the woman with whom he loved to share ice cream. He thought of this man wanting to see his home state of Texas and realizing that the man would never be able to do that the young corporal put down his ice cream and pulled out his bayonet, turned to the stone to the right side of the Deutschen Wein Tor and proceeded to carve.

It took him very little time and as he finished he felt a presence and turned to see a little girl of maybe five. She had wandered away from her mother briefly and in German asked if it was a Herz that he had carved; and not knowing what she had said he almost solemnly whispered, "It's Texas with Austin marked with a dot en' it hurts ta thaank a the reahson why I put it theair," more to himself than to the little girl as he touched his heart.

He then smiled and the little girl smiled and he gave her what was left of his melting ice cream. She had never tasted ice cream before and the smile that it put on her little face gave the 19-year-old corporal hope for a future even as he viewed the burned out and destroyed vineyards around him and the little stone house on the other side of the Door missing its roof.

The little girl's mother soon found her and smiled at the young corporal who smiled back. She had lost her husband at Stalingrad but the world was quiet once more and the spring was here and this young man had been kind to her daughter, it was a new start. As she was fluent in English she had also read a recent issue of Stars & Stripes to get a better understanding of these Americans and she had read a beautiful sonnet to a woman lost in the war by a man killed, maybe like her husband; there was hope and she would give that sonnet to her daughter. She would tell her daughter that when she had read that and the story with it she, for the first time since her father had died, felt hope for the future. The little girl would cherish that sonnet and keep it safely pressed in a book to give to her daughter because she also remembered the American with the ice cream.

The bodies of Madison Bell and Sam Harbour were finally re-interred, per Sam's instructions, in a private piece of ground overlooking the Hudson where they used to sail. It was a private piece of ground that would be kept so in perpetuity by a small trust set up hurriedly in the few days he had preceding September 15, 1944.

Fleet Train Station, England; 12:14 June 26, 2001

Without thinking I just said, "My God your voice is so beautiful, I've missed it." And then a sonnet came to mind and from where I had no idea but again I was helplessly compelled to repeat it to this woman who I had just met but whom I'd felt I'd known since the beginning of time and before:

"Sweet voice and true humor doth make thee.
True it be, this voice is life to warm such tempered
Heart as not shown but lived in love's quiet refrain.
Such refrain be left behind when your voice announces
It's sweet arrival at my door, oh that morning come every
Day with such entry as my heart desire, quiet in its
Refrain until such gifted time.
Be it mine to embrace with quiet heart
Not meant to speak but feel life's wondrous joys
As it gives life meaning more than simple
Breath my heart supports in life's repose.
Its sweet song wakes the soul and stutters the breath;
     I am truly alive at the call of that sweet song,
          It is that life is about such wonder and sweet awakening"

Startled Emma said, "Where did you hear that? That was the first writing in English that I learned to read, although at the time I didn't quite understand it."

"I don't really know." I said, "But I think I wrote it", and before I could stop myself, "I think I wrote it for you."

Startled with her gray-green eyes fully alive Emma blurted, "But you couldn't have, you couldn't. It was written by an American who died in 1944, during the war…but………. I've always felt that it was written for me. My grandfather died in the German Army at Stalingrad and this sonnet had given my grandmother hope again. My Mother passed it on to me and told me the story of a young American who had given her ice cream as a child at the Wein Tor and showed her an engraving of Texas and touched his heart. She never forgot that day and her mother later reading this sonnet even though she, as a child, didn't completely understand it. The only thing she did know at the time was that when her Mother read the sonnet it brought happy tears to her eyes. Why am I saying all of this?"

"I don't know but it all oddly makes sense."

"It is that life is about such wonder and sweet awakening," She repeated.

"The last line," I whispered knowingly.

"The last line was lost in the war, the sonnet only had 13 lines but you know the 14th."

"It's close to my heart," I said again without thinking.

Another train had just come and gone.

I pulled out a piece of Beemans to help me think.

"Can I have a piece, I like that gum; it's fun to be a child sometimes," reminisced Emma looking up at me with a warm but concerned smile on her face that was all too familiar and felt like home. I felt as though she had asked for a stick of Beemans in the past.

"How do you know this gum? It's even hard to get in the States. I have to special order it."

"I don't know, I just do and I also know that…………, that I have a strong feeling for you and I don't really know what is happening," and then a tear ran down her face, just one single tear.

I sat down next to her and gently pulled her over and into my arms and she tucked her head into my shoulder and under my neck and started to cry, "Oh Jack don't ever leave just hold me."

"I won't, I promise." I said and it all made sense. The reality of the day and who we where to each other in just a short period of time, as though we had known each other in another lifetime, was unquestionable.

We both felt we had been together many years before and in this town called Fleet. We couldn't explain why but we weren't going to question it as we didn't want to lose what had been given to us for some strange unknown reason.

We walked into the local pub called the Links and we sat at a table that felt comfortable to us both as though from a comforting dream one has and keeps tucked away until one day its memory comes forth and leaves you with an incredible warmth; except we both felt as though we had had the same dream. We walked out the front door of the pub, on the corner near the train station, and up Elvetham Road to the first set of three cottages on our right and Emma grabbed onto me tighter and we both, at that instant, knew that our lives were intertwined with purpose and intent and we were once again thankful. She just started to cry, as though a long separation had finally come to an end, and held onto me, burying her face in my shoulder without saying a word. She didn't have to.

We walked back up Elvetham on the right side of the road on this bumpy path made so by the roots of the grand old trees along its way, "Jack, I think I love you as I've loved no other man or could ever love another man."

I stopped and looked at her and said, "Oh God Emma I love you too, how did this all happen? " I felt myself saying with a familiarity only gained over time as though I were someone else.

"I don't know but I have never been happier and I've been sad for so very long."

"Maybe we're better off not knowing," I added as I looked at my watch which read 1:26. I felt a warm rush up the back of my neck and said without fully realizing why, "It's 1:26, thank God."

"And we're okay," she said with obvious relief, and with everything else that was unexplainable I knew what I felt and what she meant.

◆   ◆   ◆

Little pieces came back more in feelings than in solid memories as we walked. We felt as though time had separated us temporarily but that we had many things we had to do together and yet we didn't know what they would be. We felt as though we had been separated for an eternity that was actually a blink of an eye.

We walked back to the train station that afternoon and Emma wanted to take me to the hospital where she worked because she needed me to see it and I knew I needed to be there.

We walked to the parking lot and I walked straight to a vintage MG TA.

"I find it even more comforting that you walked to the right car without knowing," commented Emma with a warm smile.

"I just know that you like speed and this would be the car and I already know that you drive it well. I'm not into speed unless I'm behind the wheel but right now I feel more comfortable knowing that you're driving," I stated knowingly, and then I laughed briefly with relief.

We headed out and Emma shifted up through the gears better than I have ever seen anyone do in a standard sports car. As we drove she told me, above the roar of the wind, that she loved mechanics and powerful engines of all types particularly the "knucklehead" engine of an old American Harley-Davidson. I just raised my eyebrow at that and seeing this she just laughed affectionately.

We entered Fleet Road and headed to the town of Aldershot. Emma downshifted and slowed near the end of the road as we came up on the torn stump of what had been an ancient oak on our right and we were both quiet and solemn until we passed.

We passed an old brick observatory on our right after a left turn towards the town of Aldershot and then Emma turned left again into the hospital complex and there it was "The Dome", I blurted out.

Emma just smiled at me and tilted her head with a completely captivating, quizzically naive look that was both intoxicating and reassuring in a way strangely not new to me, and then parked the car. With that look I would give her anything she wanted and this, I knew, I had felt before. It all felt familiar again and with everything that we experienced together that was familiar our souls grew deeper together.

"I felt something, a special familiar embrace, like home, during the time I was working here but now with you here all these memories of having been here before but not having been here are flooding my mind. It's hard to explain but it is wonderful," she said as she turned on her toes with a big smile on her face, "and I know that I love you dearly," and then she threw her arms around my neck and hugged me. It was all almost overwhelming and beyond description. We knew at that moment that we would be returning to the States together without having to say a word about it.

Before leaving England we visited the Cotswolds and a town by the name of Cheltenham. We were taxied around town by an old WWII veteran of the D-Day landings, where he was wounded, and he told us of the secret goings on in the city during the war and of his father Jimmy meeting two American spies. The city was familiar and we just let our feelings take us there; it felt as though summer had returned after a long winter. I also had to take Emma to Cambridge to see King's Chapel and by the end we felt as though a great weight had been taken off of our shoulders and that we could head home together.

ome-------

In Flanders fields the poppies blow
Between the crosses, row on row,
That mark our place; and in the sky
The larks, still bravely singing, fly
Scarce heard amid the guns below.

We are the Dead. Short days ago
We lived, felt dawn, saw sunset glow,
Loved, and were loved, and now we lie
In Flanders fields.

Take up our quarrel with the foe:
To you from failing hands we throw
The torch; be yours to hold it high.
If ye break faith with us who die
We shall not sleep, though poppies grow
In Flanders fields

John McCrae
Canadian Field Surgeon 1915, the year J.C. Morgan was mortally
wounded.

Emma came home with me to Englewood, N.J. and she said she felt as though she was finally home after a lifetime's trip.

Emma had wanted to become a doctor as a result of what her grandmother had told her about the war and on Tuesday, September 11, 2001 she was in New York City early to meet a professional acquaintance at Beth Israel Hospital to get ready to continue her career in America. She had stayed with friends of ours in the city the night before and leaving from 78th and Broadway she took the wrong train and wound up on the Number 2 train just past 9AM. She was headed towards the World Trade Center without knowing it.

They didn't know why the train kept stopping and then eventually at Park Place the conductor told everyone to de-train, there was an emergency. As they were exiting a great rumbling started like a freight train and it kept escalating and growing closer and then clouds of white dust flooded down into the station from the street above pushing them back in but they couldn't get back to the train because of the one-way floor to ceiling turnstiles.

Several firemen rushed through the clouds of dust and pulled them all into a door that opened into the lower levels of an office building. Everyone was quite calm.

She spent the day walking up town after calling me on a pay phone while I sweated it out. I felt a fear of losing her that was real as though I had lost her once before.

She walked across the George Washington Bridge that night still covered in white dust and I met her at the Berger King on the New Jersey side as people milled around waiting for loved ones to cross. We saw each other through the crowd and she came into my arms and tucked her head under my chin and against my shoulder and cried lightly. We headed home.

For the next few days there were only F-15's in the sky above us and it was eerily strange but we had each other.

We went into the city three days later to see what they had done and I smelled something that I knew that I had smelled before and would never forget although I couldn't quite place where. It was the smell of burning rubber, electrical, wood and other toxic materials all combined into one. It was the smell of war and we just looked at each other sadly and left that day not fully understanding our feelings.

The next morning Emma talked about starting a magazine about truth and reality and calling it the "Pragmatist". I just told her that it was a good idea but too romantic as 'Political Correctness' in America, unlike in Germany, would never allow her to tell the truth.

Emma had insisted on buying the tickets and on Sunday, September 30 we saw Cal Ripken at Yankee Stadium playing his last game. He was given a standing ovation every time he stepped to the plate and couldn't get a hit as a result. The game had been rescheduled due to the attack on New York. We sat by the left field foul pole and ate cracker jacks and I snuck up to the concession stand and bought Emma a Yankee cap. When I returned with it she knew immediately and grabbed it from my hands almost longingly, as though I had hidden it from her, put it on and said, with a beautiful smile, "I've felt bare up until now."

I told her of Joe DiMaggio and Mickey Mantle although I only saw Mantle as a small child and I told her of Derek Jeter who we could both see together and remember to some future generation. She said she had heard of 'The Yankee Clipper' when she was a child and she had always wanted to see him not realizing he had stopped playing before she was born. The phrase Yankee Clipper caught me for a moment and I came back to reality just as Jeter swung and hit a ball into shallow right center behind the second baseman for a single and Emma, in surprise, muttered, "Texas Leaguer."

I just looked at her sideways in amazement and slowly said, " Yes, that's what they used to call it a long time ago......."

She just smiled with warm surprise on her lips and popped another caramelized piece of popcorn into her mouth with a twinkle in her gray-green eyes.

The game was called due to rain in the 11th inning and ended in a 1 to 1 tie, rare for the record books. Emma just said, "I guess we don't win."

"Well it doesn't count for anything at this point in the season but you always want to win especially when you take it past the 9th," I added. "That mindset fueled by the high end baseball knowledge of the average fan sitting in the stadium is also how the Yankees have been able to win '26' World Series................, it's a game where the statistics add up," I found myself adding without really thinking about it as we turned our heads and looked at each other calmly.

On Wednesday June 26, 2002, exactly one year after meeting in England, we found ourselves in Newburgh, NY. A friend had let us sail his sailboat out of its dock in town. It was a beautiful sunny morning and we sailed down the Hudson to West Point and towards the bend in the river near Noah Point. We found ourselves waving to the cadets way up on Trophy Point.

"Jack, who are they?," asked Emma.

"Cadets at the US Military Academy at West Point."

A tear came down Emma's cheek, "Oh Jack, they're not going to have to go to war are they? They seem so young and bright and happy, the thought is horrible."

"They're also capable. They're the best and the brightest and I couldn't feel safer knowing that. One way or the other they will be alright because of their capabilities and they know this." I had felt as though I had said this before and it was a little frightening. I let the mainsail down and let the boat drift with the headsail out and flapping lightly and harmlessly as I scooted over towards Emma and held her in my arms. This too I knew I had to do and we both felt better in each others arms and the unsettling feeling that we had both had about war was gone. Then for some unknown reason a thought came to my mind with information that I could not recall ever having read: The Purple Heart, awarded to American military personnel wounded or killed in action, was established by George Washington at Newburgh, N.Y. on August 7, 1782. It had originally been meant to be the only medal in the new Republic to symbolize valor but now it meant something else. The thought, not backed by any known knowledge to me, was startling and I decided not to mention it to Emma. These little events of unearned knowledge were starting to pop up irregularly out of nowhere.

We later turned the boat around and headed back towards Newburgh.

We tied up at 12:59 and as I helped Emma off the stern I noticed for the first time the name of the boat, "Whisper" and smiled to myself for what reason I don't know other than the fact that everything seemed right.

In less than a half hour we found ourselves in front of an Art Deco shop called the Commodore. I checked my watch and noticing that it was 1:26 I felt that warm rush up the back of my neck once again as Emma turned to me and put her arms around me. As we both looked at the building together she quietly said, "We're home, we're finally truly home," then she just smiled at me and moved a wisp of blonde hair away from her beautiful gray-green eyes as a slight summer breeze brushed lightly past us.

THE BEGINNING……….. again